"You went out to change, didn't you?" The sound of Eric's deep voice sent an immediate thrum of need blazing through JJ's bloodstream. *Damn*.

Eric dragged his hand across his chin. "So…I was wondering if you'd mind watching Garth sometime, so I can change, too. It's been a while."

What she'd give to see him change, or to be more specific, to be there when he exchanged his animal for that of a man, fully and gloriously aroused. A bolt of lust shot through her, so strong she nearly staggered.

"Tomorrow night should be fine." She hoped she sounded casual.

"Thank you." He grinned. "I hope I can repay you somehow."

Oh, she knew exactly how he could repay her. *Dang it*. Swallowing hard, she managed to smile back.

"Good night," she said firmly, unlocking her door and stepping inside, her entire body throbbing. Residue from the change, she told herself. Nothing to do with her tenant. Nothing to do with him at all.

HER GUARDIAN SHIFTER

KAREN WHIDDON

MILLS & BOON

First Published in Great Britain 2017
By Mills & Boon, an imprint of HarperCollins*Publishers*
1 London Bridge Street, London, SE1 9GF

© 2017 Karen Whiddon

ISBN: 978-0-263-93012-2

89-0717

Our policy is to use papers that are natural, renewable and recyclable products and made from wood grown in sustainable forests. The logging and manufacturing processes conform to the legal environmental regulations of the country of origin.

Printed and bound in Spain
by CPI, Barcelona

Karen Whiddon started weaving fanciful tales for her younger brothers at the age of eleven. Amid the gorgeous Catskill Mountains, then the majestic Rocky Mountains, she fueled her imagination with the natural beauty surrounding her. Karen now lives in north Texas, writes full-time and volunteers for a boxer dog rescue. She shares her life with her hero of a husband and four to five dogs, depending on if she is fostering. You can email Karen at kwhiddon1@aol.com. Fans can also check out her website, www.karenwhiddon.com.

To my dog rescue family.
Your love and support and kindheartedness
help make this world brighter.

Chapter 1

Damned if he did and damned if he didn't. Truer words had never been uttered. Hightailing it out of California with his infant son made Eric Mikkelson feel like some sort of criminal, even though he'd never broken a single law in his entire thirty-six years. Basically, he considered himself one of the good guys. Though his kind, the Vedjorn—bear shape-shifters—were by and large ostracized by the wolves, aka The Pack, since no one went around revealing what kind of shifter they were, his life hadn't been impacted as much as it could have been otherwise.

No, this journey had nothing to do with him, and everything to do with protecting his son. He wasn't sure why he felt as if he'd gone on the lam. After all, he'd been granted full legal custody of three-month-old Garth in a court of law. Without restrictions. So if he wanted to drive across the country to New York in the middle of winter, infant son in tow, there was absolutely no reason why he shouldn't or couldn't.

He had his reasons, of course. Even before Garth had been born, he'd asked for and received permission to take a sabbatical from his job as a college professor. As soon as his then-wife, Yolanda, had begun showing, so had her disdain for the *thing* she carried inside her.

The more she'd ranted and raved, the more worried he'd grown. She, too, was bear, and their kind were dwindling. A pregnancy would normally be a time for celebration. Not with her. Instead, she appeared to be coming unhinged.

In her third trimester, she'd finally come to him and asked for her freedom. She hadn't meant she only wanted out of the marriage. She wanted out of motherhood, as well. He'd negotiated with her carefully. Since he'd offered her a hefty settlement, she'd carried their son full term. Once Garth had been born, she'd refused even to look at the tiny, red-faced infant. She'd handed over the baby to Eric, checked herself out of the hospital and took off to have fun without being tied to anyone or anything.

The divorce had gone through without a hitch. Eric settled into his new life as a single father with bemused dedication and love. He'd been shocked to learn how much he loved his newborn son, and vowed to be the best parent he could.

He'd researched everything about babies. Heavily. Some things, such as the ingrained habits borne of years spent educating others, wouldn't be changed. He'd felt competent and prepared, until the first time Garth came down with a high fever that wouldn't break.

But he'd managed, and now, three months in, he would lay down his life for his son. Which was why, when his unstable ex-wife started showing up on his doorstep unannounced, insisting something was wrong with the baby and she needed to take him somewhere to have him fixed, he'd realized he needed to leave California for a while.

While he made his preparations, he'd received phone calls from colleagues and friends, informing him that Yolanda had been declaring to anyone who would listen that Eric had stolen her son from her and cheated her out of motherhood.

After he'd placated numerous people, the news got worse. Now it seemed that Yolanda not only wanted her son back, but she also wanted Eric dead. She'd gone twice to the Wolf Pack authorities, the Pack Protectors, and tried to convince them that Eric was a Berserker, a form of insanity unique to the Vedjorn. When a Berserker shifted from human to bear, he or she became a crazed killing machine. If Eric had truly been one, he'd be a danger to not only her son, but others. She also had hinted a few times that Garth might be a Berserker, as well. It was this last claim that worried Eric. He could defend himself against her attacks. His son could not.

The infrequent gene mutation among the bear shifters was the reason the others—especially wolves—avoided them. Since they were the largest group, the Wolf Pack had an entire division, called the Pack Protectors, devoted to ensuring humankind didn't learn about their existence. True Berserkers with their indiscriminate killing would endanger not only the bears, but all the others, as well. This could not be allowed. Anyone even seriously suspected of being a Berserker was brought in and contained, until the accusations could either be verified or denied. True Berserkers, though few and far between, were exterminated.

And Yolanda had named Eric a Berserker. Since this accusation was serious, one might have expected her to have some proof. Something to back her up, incidents of killing and maiming. Since she didn't, no one took her seriously. Including Eric.

Then, without warning, Yolanda had shown up on Eric's doorstep demanding to see *her* baby. She hadn't been even close to sober. He'd turned her away. She'd finally left, shouting about how their son needed healing. And how she was the only one who could provide it.

After that, she'd had an attorney friend contact him. Even though she'd willingly signed away all parenting rights, she'd now decided she'd changed her mind. Except she hadn't really. He knew all this was somehow related to her intense need to *heal* her son. From what, he wasn't sure. Maybe she truly did believe little Garth would grow up to be Berserker. But everyone understood those signs wouldn't start to exhibit themselves until Garth was able to shape-shift, which would be in his early teens. And if he truly ended up being Berserker, there was no cure.

With a bone-deep certainty, Eric knew his son wasn't Berserker. Unfortunately, Yolanda appeared equally convinced he was, despite having no evidence to support her.

She'd shown up twice more at his front door, cursing, screaming and crying. And threatening. He began to understand his son was in real danger from the woman who'd birthed him. When he caught her breaking the window on the back door in order to gain entry to his home so she could grab the baby, he'd realized it would be better to disappear. In fact, his Pack Protector friend Jason had strongly suggested it.

So early one morning Eric had quietly packed his SUV, locked his house and taken off cross-country with Garth securely strapped in his infant car seat in back. The rest of his belongings had already been picked up by a moving company and would be delivered a week later, including his painstakingly restored 1969 classic Camaro SS.

His destination was the tiny town of Forestwood, New York, where he'd rented the bottom floor of a house from a website he'd found on the internet, hoping it would look the same as the pictures that had been posted. He no longer would be teaching college. Instead he would open his own business doing something that until now he'd considered only a hobby. He planned to start an entirely new life, focusing on his son and keeping his head down.

Though her new tenant was supposed to pick up his keys today, Julia Jacobs eyed the blizzard raging outside and figured he'd call her to reschedule. According to the stern yet clearly excited weatherman on TV, officials were advising people to stay off the roads. Whiteout conditions and extreme cold didn't make for safe travel.

JJ didn't mind. She'd been anticipating the snow with the eagerness of a child. She'd dreamed it, after all. And snowfall brought her joy. In all kinds of ways. At the first sight of big, fat snowflakes drifting down from the leaden gray sky, she was filled with the excited anticipation of a kid on Christmas Eve.

Though she knew she was out of sync with the rest of the world, winter was her favorite season. The crisp bite of the cold air, her breath pluming as she exhaled. She loved the bundling up, the sweater and scarf and coat and hat and gloves and boots. Stepping out into the white wonderland and making the first set of footprints to mar the unblemished perfection. The way the world went absolutely still and quiet the morning after a snowfall, and how wonderful it felt to sit inside her warm house by the fire drinking cocoa and watching the snow fall. Snow always felt like a new beginning, a chance to start over.

She sighed, glad once again that she was alone, that she'd left Shawn and the hustle and bustle of New York

City behind. Even before his true abusive nature came out, her ex-boyfriend had ridiculed her love of all things winter, one of her many character traits that he'd found distasteful and disgusting. Of course, he'd been a summer person, while heat and blazing sunshine had only depressed her. That had just been the beginning and she'd finally broken free. This blizzard, already being ominously forecasted as the storm of the century, brought her nothing but joy.

She felt sorry for her new tenant, though. When he'd rented out the bottom floor of her house, his Norwegian accent had intrigued her. Of course, she'd Googled him after getting his name, noting he'd immigrated to California. She'd been impressed by his academic credentials. A college professor on sabbatical, he'd said. With an infant son.

The last might have given other landlords pause. After all, babies cried, and even though he'd be on another floor entirely, sound drifted in older houses like hers.

But JJ had never been a landlord before—heck, she was a brand-new homeowner—and she adored babies, so she'd immediately granted Mr. Eric Mikkelson the lease. He'd paid for two months up front, along with a perfectly reasonable security deposit. He didn't smoke or have pets, so she privately thought she might have actually managed to find the perfect tenant.

Even the few fuzzy photos of him she'd seen online jibed with his career. He looked the part, a stereotypical professor, round wire glasses and hair in a ponytail. She hadn't been able to tell if his hair was blond or gray, but supposed it didn't matter. He had a baby, which made up for a whole lot of other things, including any lingering intellectual snobbishness. Lord knew she'd had enough of that with Shawn and his Wall Street friends.

Again, she quickly put the thought from her mind. Enough time had passed that she ought to be able to relax, but she still jumped every time someone moved too fast or she heard a loud, unexpected noise. At least she'd re-taught herself not to keep her gaze trained on the ground anymore lest she be accused of flirting.

And the nightmares featuring Shawn had finally stopped. The horrible, awful dreams had her questioning her own sanity.

Heaving a sigh, she walked to the window to watch the beautiful snow fall, knowing this would instantly put her in a better frame of mind.

Meanwhile, meeting her new tenant would have to wait until after the storm. Which meant she was free to put-ter around the house, put a pot of butternut squash soup to simmer on the stove and go out and play in the snow.

Until she'd moved in with Shawn, she'd lived all her life in an apartment in New York City with her parents. If she and her friends had wanted to make a snowman, they'd gone to the park. Now, thanks to a distant great-aunt she'd barely known leaving her this house upstate in Forest-wood, New York, she could make a snowman in her own front yard. The prospect excited her, probably more than it should considering she'd just turned thirty-four. She'd have to wait to build it until after the snowfall stopped, but still wanted to go outside and check out the snow.

After bundling up—two pairs of socks inside her snow boots, scarf, and wearing a soft knit cap under her hood—she took a deep breath and stepped out into the swirling storm.

Wow. Stopping just outside the front door on her stoop, she stared. This was coming down fast and furious. She guesstimated already six to seven inches had fallen.

And so beautiful. Slowly she turned, squinting as she tried to see down the street to the other houses. Other houses! She'd lived her entire life surrounded by tall buildings, in the crowded city. She thought she could get used to this new life. Everything moved slower here. The pace suited her just fine.

One month and she'd unpacked nearly everything. Of course, she hadn't had much to unpack. Luckily, all her great-aunt's furniture had come with the house, since JJ had none of her own. When she'd moved in with Shawn, he'd convinced her to get rid of her own few eclectic pieces. After all, they'd clashed with his sleek, modern furniture. Bohemian, he'd called it, with the same disparaging intonation one would use with a curse word.

Shawn. She hated how her thoughts kept returning to him when they shouldn't. That part of her life was over. He no longer had any hold on her. He would never find her here. Even her mother had been sworn to secrecy, though she hadn't been told why. Pushing him and her former life out of her head, JJ returned her focus to the perfect snowstorm.

Unable to resist, she dropped to the ground and made a snow angel, even though fresh flakes would fill it in quickly. With her face lifted to the sky, she felt like a kid. The icy flakes stuck to her eyelashes and her lips, even her teeth, since she was grinning. The cold air hurt her skin, which meant she wouldn't be able to stay outside much longer, but she planned to enjoy what time she had.

The sound of a car door slamming made her sit up and blink away the snowflakes stuck to her lashes. What the… Someone had pulled up to the curb in front of her house. Driving some sort of compact SUV that she'd never in a million years have believed could make it more than a mile in this snow without snow tires and chains.

A tall, bare-headed man came around from the driver's side. As she stared, her first thought was of the mythological Norse god Thor. She forgot about the icy wind, the snowflakes swirling like dervishes. Because as he strode toward her, his long, wavy blond hair swirling around his shoulders, her entire body came alive. He moved with a confident, easy stride, as if the snow and ice didn't exist for him.

Damn. Realizing she was still on the ground, she clambered to her feet, dusting as much snow off her as she could before she looked up at him. And she meant up. This guy had to be way over six feet tall. Shawn had been six-two, and she'd bet this man would tower over him. Norse god, she thought again. Odd that she hadn't had a single dream of him. She'd bet she would from now on.

"Um, hi?" she squeaked.

"Ms. Jacobs?" he rumbled, his bright blue eyes sharp. Oh heck, his voice definitely suited him. Made her go weak in the knees. And that accent...

Belatedly she knew who this must be. "Eric Mikkelson?" She couldn't keep the disbelief from showing.

"Yes." He tilted his massive, unbelievably gorgeous head. "You weren't expecting me? I believe I confirmed I'd be here this afternoon to pick up the keys."

"I know, but..." She gestured helplessly at the storm raging around them. "You drove up here in this?"

"This?" Frowning, he didn't appear to understand what she meant. Before she could elaborate, he turned back toward his car. "I need to get my son. Do you mind if we continue this discussion inside?"

His son. Struck dumb by both his recklessness and his masculine beauty, she nodded. Then, because she loved babies as much as she loved snow, she followed him over to the car and tried to peer around him as he unbuckled his son's infant carrier.

She caught a glimpse of bright blue eyes peering out from a tiny, bundled up face. As she leaned in closer, her tenant, clearly not realizing she'd moved in so close, caught her with his elbow under the chin and sent her flying backward.

"Oof." Down she went, right on her behind. Luckily, all her layers plus the several inches of fluffy snow provided lots of padding. Nothing got hurt except her pride.

Her tenant glanced back over his shoulder at her, clearly unaware what had happened. "Are you all right?" he asked, his cautious tone telling her he'd begun to consider the possibility that she might be nuts.

For a split second she debated telling him what had happened. Pushing to her feet, she once again dusted off snow, the cold dampness beginning to seep through her layers to her skin. And then she caught sight of Eric's son, and completely forgot what she'd been about to say.

The instant the baby locked eyes with her, he grinned and wrinkled his cute little nose. All bundled up in his snowsuit, cap and mittens, he looked like a precious baby seal with bright blue eyes. As his daddy lifted him up, he cooed.

Like his father, his cuteness factor was off the charts.

"Come on," she said, conscious of the freezing temperature and icy wind. "I don't want him to get frostbite."

Eric Mikkelson stared and shook his head. "He has Norwegian blood," he said, as if that explained everything. "This snowstorm is nothing compared to the ones I grew up with in Norway. I dressed him warmly. He'll be fine."

Fine? She managed to refrain from shaking her head while she tromped her way through the deepening snow to her front door. When she turned back to look for him, for a second she couldn't see him, the baby or his car due to the blowing, swirling snow.

Chapter 2

An instant of panic disappeared the moment JJ caught sight of her new tenant striding up her walk, his son clutched securely to his massive chest.

Again with the striding? As if the snow wasn't even there. Maybe it had something to do with his height.

Then, before she had time to pretend she wasn't gaping, he reached her. Fumbling, her hands cold even in her lined ski gloves, she opened the door. "Come on inside."

As she began the laborious process of removing her many layers of warm clothes, she watched him shrug out of his coat and then get busy undressing the baby. In disbelief, she processed not only the fact that Eric wore just a black sweater under his parka, but that his infant son did, too.

Unable to tear her gaze away, even though she knew her stare might be rude, she exhaled.

Eric Mikkelson was a big man. Not just tall, not just broad, but an appealing combination of the two. Throw in some killer muscles, a narrow waist and lean hips, and he was the stuff of which feminine fantasies were made.

She frowned. Since when did she need to even start thinking about another man, never mind fantasizing about one? If her relationship with Shawn had taught her anything, it had shown her she clearly needed to live alone and figure out how she'd let herself become so…

Since leaving Shawn, she'd tried out several different adjectives and discarded them, because no one single word could adequately describe how much of herself she'd let Shawn destroy. Thankfully, she'd finally gotten the courage to flee.

No, she thought, eyeing the gorgeous masculine specimen in front of her, a man was the last thing she needed.

Still, she'd have to be dead not to appreciate this man's appeal. And of course, there was his baby.

The infant made a curious snuffling sound. She wondered exactly what species of shape-shifter Eric might be. His aura, like hers, revealed him to be a shifter, though not what kind. And while she hadn't met too many others, she knew there were many different types of animals besides her wolf. In fact, this little town had recently gained notoriety among shifters for revealing another rare species of shifter, the Drakkor, or dragon shifter. They'd welcomed several into life in their town, even though most of the residents of Forestwood were Pack, or wolf, like JJ.

She'd bet Eric Mikkelson wasn't wolf. Still eyeing him, she figured he might be a big cat, like a lion or panther. Though his movements and size reminded her more of a grizzly. She swallowed hard. The Vedjorn bear shifters were as rare as Drakkor, and for good reason. They were unstable and frequently dangerous. They kept to themselves and, unlike the other species of shifters, rarely if ever intermarried outside of their own kind. Not that anyone else wanted anything to do with them.

"Are you all right?"

Crud. She'd been standing staring at him, most likely with her mouth wide-open or a big, dopey smile on her face. Flustered, she nodded. "Yes, sorry. I'm fine. It's just that..." she began. Horrified, she realized she'd been about to breach the most sacred etiquette between shifters. Yikes. There was no way she could ask him what kind of animal he changed into.

"Yes?" he asked, his tone patient, a smile playing along the edge of his sensual mouth. Once again she'd gotten lost in thought. Obviously, her social skills had also vanished with her previous life.

"I'm sorry," she finally repeated, wincing as the second apology crept out. "It's just, I wasn't expecting you today and now that you're here, you aren't at all what I expected." As she wound to the end of her rambling, her entire face flamed.

"But I confirmed that I would pick up the keys today," he said, his expression puzzled.

"Yes, but..." She waved her fingers at her large picture window. "With the storm, I thought you'd reschedule."

Tilting his big, shaggy head, he considered her. Then he grinned, his blue eyes sparking with amusement. And just like that, he went from great looking to absolutely drop-dead sexy.

So help her, her knees went weak again and her breath caught in her chest. Damn.

"You're joking, right?" His good-natured question prompted her to agree.

"Of course I am," she managed to reply, attempting a wobbly smile. Thank goodness she at least didn't sound breathless. "What's a little blizzard to someone from Norway, right?" Even if that someone had been living in California for years, according to his application.

"Exactly." The warm glance he sent her invited her to share in his amusement. He swung his large head around to check out the central foyer, while expertly rocking his son's carrier. The stairs to her place were to the left. His front door was underneath the staircase.

"Would you mind showing me the way to my place? It's been a long day and I'd like to get settled in as quickly as possible."

"Of course." She matched his brisk tone. "Follow me."

When she'd arrived to claim the house she'd inherited, she'd been surprised to see it had been built as two separate living areas. Both the top floor and the bottom were self-contained dwellings, each with their own kitchen and bathrooms. She'd claimed the top floor. Years of living in the city had taught her she'd be safer there. And the bottom floor she'd rented out to him, her very first tenant ever.

Luckily, the top floor had its own separate entrance, so they'd both have plenty of privacy. And she would have some income to tide her over until she figured out exactly what she wanted to do.

"You'll have the entire bottom floor," she said, opening his front door and stepping aside. "Here it is. All yours."

Still bouncing the baby, he pushed past her and stopped, turning in a half circle to take it all in.

"Wow." His deep laugh reminded her of hot cocoa spiced with Kahlúa. "When you said it came furnished, I was relieved. I confess, I actually pictured Ikea or maybe an eclectic mix of garage sale and discount store. What I didn't envision was this. It's very…" Words seemed to fail him.

"Old lady-ish?" she suggested helpfully, unable to keep from smiling. "All of this stuff belonged to my great-aunt

Olivia." She didn't tell him the reason she'd kept the fussy, outdated furniture was because she not only didn't have any of her own, but currently didn't have the funds to replace it.

"I see," he said, eyeing a particularly delicate looking chair. "To be honest, I'm afraid I'll break that if I sit in it."

She had to admit he was probably right. "I'll switch it out with something else," she said, trying to sound businesslike. "Here are your keys."

When she went to hand them off, her fingers brushed his. Damn. A curious swooping pull swept through her, momentarily making her head spin.

"Are you all right?" he asked yet again, watching her closely, as if he expected her to fall over in a dead faint at any second.

"Yes." Biting back her second almost automatic apology, she forced a smile. Life with Shawn had compelled her to apologize for everything, even stuff that wasn't her fault. She'd been consciously trying to break the habit ever since she'd gotten free.

"I guess I'd better leave you to it," she continued brightly. "I'm just upstairs if you need anything."

He nodded. "I've got your number, as well. Thank you for everything." As she moved back out into their shared foyer, he firmly and quietly closed his door. A second later, she heard the sound of the dead bolt clicking into place. She couldn't help but wish she'd dream of him once she went to sleep.

Exhaustion had Eric wishing he could undress and crawl into bed, but little Garth would need a diaper change and some formula first. Shame about the landlord woman. Though she really was stunning with her fiery red hair, large green eyes and curvy body, she seemed a little daft in the head. The way she'd eyed his baby—as if she'd like to eat him up—had worried Eric. Had he escaped one crazy woman only to relocate with another?

Surely not. Most likely, he was overreacting out of fear. Still, just in case, until he knew her better, he'd make sure to keep his distance.

After he got Garth cleaned up, fed and burped, and put down for a nap, he finally rummaged in his backpack for the sandwich he'd bought at the last gas station. It had gotten crushed and didn't look the least bit appetizing, but was still cold. He wolfed it down in four bites, wishing he'd had the foresight to buy two. Tomorrow, he'd stock up on food, but for now he had enough of the two things that really mattered—formula and diapers. He had a portable crib in the back of his SUV and the rest of his things would be arriving as soon as the transport company got there.

The one thing he worried most about was his other car. The one he didn't want to take a chance on damaging by driving cross-country. And he sure as hell wouldn't be taking it out on icy roads recently coated with salt. He'd park it until the winter season had long passed. Late spring, at the earliest.

One of the reasons he'd chosen to rent this place over the others was that it came with a garage. According to the lease, his landlord got one side of the two-car, detached garage and he got the other. He didn't plan to use it for the SUV he'd driven across the country. No. He planned to store the 1969 Camaro SS he'd lovingly restored inside his slot in the garage. That car would be his advertisement for the business he planned to start.

Even in California, where customized hot rods were a dime a dozen, his car turned heads. He'd been asked several times where he'd had the work done. Plenty of people had wanted to hire him when he'd told them he'd done it himself. They'd been shocked to learn he worked as a college professor and that he'd restored the car as a hobby. He'd come to realize he might be able to do something he loved and actually earn a living at it. He'd started saving every penny he could, in the hope that one day he could actually start his own business. He'd just about had enough to get serious when Yolanda had gotten pregnant.

And then his life had gone to hell in a handbasket.

No sense in dwelling on the past. Tonight was the first night in his new home and tomorrow would be literally the first day of the rest of his new life. A life where he could keep Garth safe. A life where, hopefully, he could settle in, make friends, get his business established, and find peace and joy again.

The snow continued to fall all through the night. Eric knew because, restless, he got up several times to peer out the window to where the streetlight illuminated the now impassable street. The little house was snug—he'd give it that. No leaky windows, and the radiators put out plenty of heat. He felt cozy and oddly at peace, something he hadn't quite expected when he'd chucked his entire life and took off to start a new one on the opposite side of the country.

Now he suspected he knew what people who went into the Witness Protection Program felt like. Adrift, needing an anchor, but afraid to put down deep roots in case they needed to move on again. Hopefully, that wouldn't be the case here. No way would anyone—especially his ex—think to look for him this far from sunny California.

Finally, sometime around six, he got up, blinking at the brightness from the snow outside, and began puttering around his new living space. The old furniture reminded him of his maternal grandmother's house—fussy fabrics, lots of dark wood and elaborate ornamentation. He suspected there would have been a plethora of knickknacks covering every conceivable service, which Julia Jacobs had most likely cleared out once she'd arrived. The dark wood gleamed, evidently having recently been dusted and polished, and the space he'd rented looked clean.

Garth woke and Eric got busy changing his boy's diaper and warming formula so the little guy could have breakfast. Early on Eric had felt a sense of pride at the fact that he'd gotten quite adept at these basic parenting tasks, an accomplishment that had once both amazed and amused him. Now, taking care of his three-month-old was routine, second nature.

After Garth had been fed and burped, Eric sat on the couch and let his son play with a set of colorful plastic rattles. He'd brought only a few of the baby's toys with him; the others would arrive in the moving truck.

Eventually, Garth fell asleep again and Eric gently placed him back in his temporary crib. He stood for a moment watching his son sleep, his heart full. Finally, he felt like a weight had been lifted off his shoulders.

The knock on his door was decisive, yet quiet enough that it didn't wake the baby. When Eric opened it, he wasn't surprised to see his petite landlady standing there. If anything, she looked even more intriguing than she had the night before. He'd never been partial to redheads, but he'd never seen one as beautiful as her. Her emerald-green eyes and lush mouth contrasted with her spattering of freckles, giving her a sexy, girl-next-door vibe. Eyeing her, he felt a jolt of lust, which of course he instantly tamped down.

"Yes?" he asked politely, keeping his body between her and the inside of his place.

A shadow darkened her eyes, almost as if his intense need for privacy wounded her. "I just wanted to apologize," she said softly. "I know I acted a little strange yesterday and I'm sorry." Her slight laugh sounded a bit forced, though she kept her chin up and her shoulders back. "Anyway, welcome to Forestwood." She held out her hand. He noticed her fingernails were short and looked uneven, as if she maybe chewed on them.

The two of them shook. She had a nice, firm grip, which he appreciated.

"I made you a map of town, showing you where all the shops are. If you need anything else, please don't hesitate to let me know."

Once he'd accepted the folded map, she turned to go.

"Wait."

Stopping, she turned, one eyebrow lifted.

"Thank you," he told her. "As soon as the roads are cleared, I need to hit the grocery store. Any idea what time the plows will come through?"

"I watched the news and this storm was pretty bad. They may not. If the plows don't make it out this way today, they'll get our road done tomorrow."

His heart sank. "Tomorrow?" As he spoke, his stomach rumbled, reminding him he hadn't had breakfast or even coffee. "I have absolutely no food. I don't suppose you'd care to sell me a few things to tide me over until then."

"No food?" Tilting her head, she considered him. "Please tell me you have formula for the baby."

"Of course I do. And diapers. You can't travel cross-country with an infant without those. Little Garth is taken care of. I'm the one who needs provisions."

Amusement sparked in her green eyes. "I'm not going to sell you food," she said, disappointing him. "But you won't starve, not in my house. Come with me. I can feed you. I'm an excellent cook."

Even though his stomach still rumbled with hunger, he wasn't sure he wanted her to feed him. The idea of her cooking for him seemed way too intimate. Yet what alternative did he have? He could starve or he could eat.

Both embarrassed and wary and, damn it, hungry, he shook his head. "I don't know," he said. "I mean, I barely know you. You shouldn't have to…"

"It's food." Her smile tugged at him, invited him to smile back. "Not gold or diamonds or even splitting a bottle of red wine. A couple of simple, hearty meals. Let me make you something, starting with breakfast. You can pay me back after you've made it to the store. Now what'll it be? I've got eggs and bread, or oatmeal if you prefer."

His stomach growled at the thought. Still, he felt obligated to at least make an effort to decline. "I don't want to impose," he began.

"You're not." She turned to go. "Come on. And bring that adorable baby with you."

Heaven help him, he went. The small sandwich from the night before had long ago faded from memory and he needed to eat something. Anything. Even cold cereal. He figured he'd go with oatmeal, since she probably had instant, and it would be less trouble and less intimate than asking her to fry him up a couple eggs.

Since Garth was still asleep, it was a simple matter of picking up the portable crib and carrying it with him. Good thing the kid was a sound sleeper. Eric tromped all the way up the steep flight of stairs and his son never woke. Garth had always been like that.

His lovely landlord had left her door open for him. He didn't know why he was making such a big deal out of a simple kindness on her part, but he chalked it up to being gun-shy after what had happened with Yolanda. Still, he couldn't stand outside on the landing forever. At least, not if he wanted to eat.

Chapter 3

Taking a deep breath, Eric stepped inside and looked around. He didn't know what he'd expected, maybe a carbon copy of his, but her space looked completely different. Minimal furnishings, for one. Clearly, she'd chosen only what she wanted from the furniture her great-aunt had left behind. And then she'd added some other pieces, bright colors mostly. Lots of patterns, stripes and swirls and polka dots. Feminine stuff, but surprisingly comfortable looking.

Turning slowly, he wasn't sure what to make of it all. Instead of looking garish or confusing, the effect was cheerful and homey. In a bohemian sort of way. In fact, it reminded him of photos he'd seen of some of the dorms at the college where he used to work.

"In here," Julia called. He followed the sound of her voice and found her standing in front of the stove.

Her kitchen, too, appeared bright and clean. She'd made

an attempt to modernize it, though the aging appliances and chipped counters showed its age. He set the travel crib near the table and against the wall, hopefully out of the way.

"Welcome. So what'll it be?" she asked, her friendly tone and relaxed posture inviting him to loosen his guard.

"Oatmeal is fine," he told her. "I don't want you to go to any trouble. You have instant, right?"

She eyed him, her expression thoughtful. "I do. Are you sure that's what you want?"

It wasn't, but he nodded. "Oatmeal is great on a snowy morning."

"Coffee?" Handing him a cup, she pointed toward a half-full coffeepot. "Help yourself."

In California, he'd come to appreciate good coffee. He'd even purchased a specialty brewer, which was on its way here with his other personal belongings. But right now, he would have settled for instant. With no expectations other than it being hot, he filled his cup and took a sip.

It was good. More than good. Right up there with the gourmet coffee served at the corner java shop he used to stop at every morning on his way to campus. A second sip and he made a small sound of pleasure, causing her to swing around and grin at him.

He felt the power of that grin like a punch in his stomach. Slightly disoriented, he finally smiled back. He definitely hadn't expected this. Expected her.

"I take it you like my coffee?"

"I do." His third sip made him widen his smile into a grin. "It's delicious. I can't tell you how badly I needed this."

"I can imagine." She gestured at the table, a round wooden one that she'd painted turquoise. Around it were four wooden chairs, all painted different colors. "Sit. I'll have your breakfast ready in a minute."

Slightly less uncomfortable, he pulled out a chair. After bustling around for a second, she put a bowl in the microwave. When it chimed, she used pot holders to remove it, dropped in a handful of raisins and carried it over to him, along with a spoon and a paper napkin. "Here you go."

After one bite, he had to fight not to inhale the entire bowl. "This doesn't taste like instant oatmeal," he commented, before shoveling another spoonful into his mouth.

"Oh yeah?" She took a seat across from him, cradling her own mug of coffee. "It is, but I mashed a banana in with it before I micro-zapped it. It's one of my favorite breakfasts in the world. Then I added raisins and cinnamon. Do you like it?"

Since he'd nearly finished his bowl, he nodded. Two more bites and he was done. "Thank you," he said, meaning it. "I was really hungry." So hungry that everything tasted better around her.

"I could tell. I made two packets, since one is never enough."

He could have eaten two more, but he'd already imposed enough. Sipping his coffee, he nodded before glancing out her kitchen window at the snow still piled up outside. "Judging from your porch railings, I'd say we must have gotten at least ten inches."

"Yep. They said on the news it was more like a foot."

"I believe it." One more swallow and he'd emptied his cup. He wondered if she'd mind if he had another. "Do you really think it will be tomorrow until the plows come through? I need to get to a grocery store at least."

She seemed remarkably unconcerned. "It'll probably be today. That all depends where they decide to go first. But if you don't make it to the store, I'll make sure you don't starve. Oh, and if you do get out, I'll be happy to watch the baby while you shop. No need to have to deal with taking him out into weather like this."

Watch the baby? He glanced at Garth, still sleeping peacefully. After his initial frisson of alarm, he considered her. He really needed to stop being so suspicious. No way could every woman he met turn out to be as psychotic and unbalanced as Yolanda. He had to admit, if only to himself, maybe he'd gotten paranoid. But then, who would blame him?

The truth was eventually he would have to find someone who could babysit Garth from time to time. More, once he started scouting for locations to open up his custom car shop. He'd definitely need to get day care during regular business hours so he could work. The thought tied his stomach in knots. He didn't like being away from his son, not for more than a few minutes at a time. He didn't know how people did it, returning to work out of necessity when their child was only a few months old. Like them, he'd have no choice but to do the same. Not yet, though. Not yet.

One thing at a time, he reminded himself.

"I might take you up on that," he replied. Surely he could let her watch Garth for an hour while he stocked his fridge and pantry.

"Just let me know when."

Again he glanced out her window at the pristine white snow. "As soon as the plows clear the streets."

"Do you have personal items arriving?" she asked. "Baby furniture, your television, that sort of thing?"

"My moving truck is supposed to arrive in a few days," he said, eyeing his empty mug longingly. "Assuming the roads are good enough for them to get through."

"Good." She grabbed the coffeepot and brought it over. "More coffee? Don't worry, I can always make more."

Relieved, he nodded. After she'd refilled his cup, he took another deep drink and sighed. Just as good the second time. "I promise I'll repay you as soon as I can."

The snorting sound she made surprised him. Humor danced in her eyes, inviting him to share it with her. "Don't worry about it. It's coffee, not Patrón Silver."

And then she laughed, the low sound pleasing and harmonious. "Occasionally there's nothing better than a shot of really good tequila, you know?"

He actually did. After a second of hesitation, he nodded in agreement. "Thanks again for everything. I'm just not used to mooching off anyone."

When she pulled out the chair across from him, he saw she'd refilled her mug, too. Like him, she drank her coffee black. "Tell me about yourself, Eric Mikkelson. Why are you moving to the Catskills from sunny and hip California? Is it for a new job or do you have family here?"

Personal questions. Though instead of immediately putting him on the defensive once again, the friendly, casual way she phrased her questions actually relaxed him. She sounded *interested* rather than inquisitive. "No family. I moved here to go into a new line of work. I'm planning on opening my own business in town, once I find the perfect space."

"Awesome." To his surprise, she didn't ask him what kind of business. "But still. Why Forestwood? We're not exactly a metropolis. We're barely even on the map."

Since he knew from her aura that she, too, was a shifter, he felt comfortable enough to tell her the truth. "Because I read the article about the Drakkor. Any town that will lovingly shelter an individual without knowing or understanding what kind of being she might be is the kind of place where I feel I'll fit in."

At first, she didn't move. Didn't comment or respond,

just watched him, her big green eyes contemplative. "The Drakkor. After that article was published, we got a lot of tourists. Mostly, they just wanted to see a real, live dragon. But no one actually wanted to move here."

"For me, it isn't about seeing a Drakkor." The earnestness in his voice surprised him. "It's about finding friendly people. Neighbors who don't judge you because you're different. The sort of kindhearted community where I can raise my son." He stopped, slightly embarrassed to have revealed so much to a stranger.

Tilting her head, she considered him. Then a slow smile bloomed, transforming her from really attractive to stunningly beautiful. His heart actually skipped a beat.

"That's really pretty damn amazing," she said finally, her warm voice imbibing the compliment with more.

What was it about this woman? Though they'd just met the day before, he felt as if he'd known her for a long time. He wasn't sure what to think about that.

Instead of allowing himself to bask in the glow of her praise, he turned the discussion to her. "How about you?" he asked. "Were you born and raised here or did you make your way from somewhere else, too?"

Her smile faded. "I'd never been here before until a month ago. A great-aunt whom I didn't even know existed died. She left me this house and all the furniture, so I moved here."

"What about your job? Did you leave that, too, or are you able to work from home?"

Ducking her head, she shrugged. "I worked at a few different things. Dog walking, which is really in demand in the city, some waitressing and even some temporary secretarial work. None of it was difficult to leave."

"In the city?" He couldn't help but notice she didn't say

where precisely she'd lived before. Since he'd been open with her, he figured he'd ask. "What city?"

"New York. Manhattan to be exact." Again a shadow crossed her face. "Only a couple of hours' drive from here, but it might as well be across the country."

He knew what she meant. The difference between some areas of California was also like that.

When he finished his second cup of coffee, she poured him more without asking. Then she emptied the last of the pot into her own cup before she sat back down. "So far, I like it here a lot," she said. "Though I haven't been here very long. I guess we can learn the town together."

Together. What the... No, he was overreacting. No doubt she didn't mean anything by that. Again, he couldn't let what had happened with his ex-wife destroy his future. He would be vigilant and careful. And cautious. Yes, cautious. But his new landlord appeared kind and genuine. He would believe her to be so unless she proved otherwise.

"About watching Garth," he began. "What's your experience with infants?"

"Experience?" Shaking her head, she chuckled. "I just love babies. Always have. I'm not a professional nanny or anything, though I did once have a job working in a day care. Not in the baby room, though. But I'm reasonably sure I can manage taking care of him for an hour while you get groceries."

She was right. It wasn't as if he was asking her to be a full-time nanny. "Sorry." Glancing at his son, still peacefully sleeping, he sighed. "I've never left him with anyone before. I don't—"

"Really know me all that well," she finished for him. "I get it. Believe me, I was only trying to help. If you'd rather take him with you, I completely understand."

Her statement brought him a measure of relief. "I'll

think about it," he said. "Out of curiosity, have you found work here yet or are you still looking?"

She glanced down, which made his stomach twist, though he wasn't sure why.

"Oh." She flushed. "Right now, I'm still unemployed. My aunt left me a small inheritance as well as this house. I've only been here a month and haven't looked for anything yet."

Wishing he hadn't asked, he tried to lighten the mood. "Well then, we're two of a kind, since I don't have a job yet, either."

Her smile came back, a quick flash of self-deprecating humor. "I guess we are."

Startled, he realized he actually *liked* Julia Jacobs. At least what he knew about her so far. And he would need someone to watch Garth, at least part-time. For now, he'd keep his eyes open and not make any rash decisions.

"What kind of work do you do?" she asked.

Briefly, he considered and decided he didn't see any harm in telling her the truth. "I was a college professor, but I took a sabbatical when Garth was born. Now, I'm planning to open up a customized car shop. It used to be a hobby, but I'm thinking I can make a living doing it full-time."

"Customize cars? Like painting them?"

"That's part of it. Restoring older cars to their original condition, only better. Turning them into hot rods." Oversimplified, but adequate.

"Interesting." The little shrug that accompanied her comment told him she either knew zero about cars or didn't care to. "That's kind of the polar opposite from higher education, isn't it?"

"Maybe." He smiled. "I figure since I came to the complete other side of the country, I might as well make a major change to my life. It's something I've always wanted to do."

"Then good for you." She smiled back. "Not to be nosy, but what about Garth's mother? Where is she in all of this?"

He froze, aware his expression had completely shut down. But she couldn't know and her question had actually been perfectly reasonable, if a bit intrusive. "She and I are divorced. Turns out she didn't actually want a child. She signed over all parental rights to me."

If they'd been discussing any other subject, her disbelief and shock might have been comical. He could almost read her thoughts. Right now, she was dying to ask what kind of woman could abandon an innocent, tiny baby like Garth. From the grim set of her mouth and the way she'd narrowed her eyes, she must be wondering if Eric's ex was a monster. He didn't have the heart to tell her Yolanda actually was.

When he didn't comment further, she sighed. "I'm sorry. I didn't mean to pry."

Now he felt like an ass. After all, she'd opened her home to him and fed him. She'd been nothing but kind and friendly. "It's okay," he finally said. "It's just a sore subject."

"I can imagine." The grimness in her tone told him she agreed. "Anyway, if you need anything, please let me know."

He could take a hint. She'd fed him, chatted with him and now was ready for him to go. He stood, collected his son and let himself out the door.

Once back in his new, empty living quarters, Eric found he missed her. Or maybe he just missed having company. Someone to talk to. With the streets still impassable, he couldn't leave, couldn't drive around and check out the rest of the town the way he'd initially planned on his second day. Being stuck inside an unfamiliar house felt confining, to say the least. Plus he was impatient to begin scouting out a possible location to open his shop.

All in good time, he reminded himself. He needed to exercise a little patience.

He considered himself lucky that he had electricity and water. Since she'd never had them turned off, all he'd needed to do was change them into his name. And even though his television was on the moving truck, she'd left a smallish one in the living room, for which he was grateful.

Garth finally woke. Eric passed some time bathing and changing his son, giving him another bottle, and then just talking to him. Though at three months, little Garth couldn't do much other than wave his hands around and coo, being around him filled Eric with love.

Time passed slowly. He'd grown hungry again, but stubbornly remained in his part of the house, not wanting his landlord to feel compelled to feed him again. He didn't want to turn into a giant moocher, so decided to make do until he could get out and go to the store.

To his relief, he heard the unmistakable sound of the plow shortly after three. Rushing to the front window, he watched the big machine lumber down the street, plumes of snow shooting up to the side. Too late, he realized his vehicle would be buried, but since there was nothing he could do to avert this, he simply continued to watch. It wasn't like he hadn't dug out a car before, back when he'd lived in Norway.

Once the plow had passed, he shrugged into his parka and eyed Garth, now wide-awake and happily batting at the bright plastic toys Eric had strung across the front of his portable crib. He didn't want to leave his son alone, but couldn't just bring him outside while he cleared the snow from his car. Which meant he'd have to impose on his new landlord once again. Good thing she claimed to love babies.

Fifteen minutes, he told himself, picking up the carrier and trudging upstairs to Julia's place. He would ask her to keep an eye on the baby while he cleared his car. Then he'd retrieve Garth, bundle him up and put him in his car seat for a quick trip to the store.

Chapter 4

She answered the door on his second knock. To Eric's amusement, her gaze slid past him, right to the baby watching her with wide-eyed interest. "Well, hello there," she said, crouching down so she and Garth were at eye level. "I see you're finally awake, little sleepyhead."

Garth made a gurgling sound, jingling his plastic keys as he gazed up at her.

"You're so precious," Julia cooed. She glanced up at Eric. "Is everything all right?"

He cleared his throat. "I was wondering if you'd mind keeping an eye on him for a few minutes. The plow covered my SUV and I need to dig it out so I can head into town. I'll come back for him as soon as I'm done."

"No problem." She took the infant carrier and brought it inside. "Like I told you earlier, if you want, I can watch him while you go to the store."

Tempting, but again, he barely knew her and she'd already done more than enough for him. Leaving her in charge of Garth while he was a few feet away, outside, was entirely different than driving away without his son. "I appreciate that, but I'd rather bring him with me." He cast her a sideways look, trying to judge how she would take this news.

To his surprise, she smiled. "I understand. You don't know me yet and he's your entire world. Believe me, I wouldn't leave my baby for very long with someone I just met, either."

Relieved, he nodded. "I'm glad you understand. Fifteen minutes, okay? He's already been fed and has a clean diaper. I'm thinking this won't take much more than that."

"No rush." Her gaze had already strayed back to his son. "We'll be right here whenever you finish."

After the door closed behind her new tenant, JJ let out a sigh of relief. She liked looking at him, plain and simple. Even though another man in her life was the absolute last thing she needed right now. She hadn't worked through her recent past yet. Hell, she didn't even recognize the woman who'd fled New York City as if the hounds of hell were after her, with giant teeth. And of course, her dreams still haunted her.

This appalled her. She'd always been fierce, a fighter, but not a killer. She'd often questioned how she could have let herself become the woman Shawn had made her into, a woman afraid of her own shadow, too terrified to speak or even look at something the wrong way. She'd walked on eggshells, never knowing what might set him off.

Initially, she'd gone into the relationship a strong, female shifter. A she-wolf, proud of her heritage, confident in her humanness. Shawn might have been only human, but in the beginning he'd seemed kind and thoughtful and handsome. She'd also liked his size, instinctively feeling a large man like him would always protect her.

In fact, it had been the opposite. He'd used his size to intimidate and threaten and hurt. What she'd become after three years with Shawn…

Now, she knew personally how some abused animals felt. She understood the impulse that had them cringing at sudden movements or a raised hand. Objectively, she could see how several years of conditioning by a man she'd thought had loved her had made her this way. What confused and astounded her was how she'd let it happen. How she'd managed to come to believe it was all her fault. If she'd been prettier, smarter, quicker… A better girlfriend, a harder worker, more… As if he was the rational person and she was the one spiraling out of control.

She deserved everything she got. He'd actually said that to her, numerous times. Until finally, something had broken inside her and she'd known she'd had enough. That had been when she'd gotten the news of her great-aunt's death and learned she'd inherited a house in a town she'd never known existed. That had been when she'd realized she'd be all right, that she could leave.

She'd grabbed on with both hands and secretly planned her escape. When she'd fled, she'd taken care to make sure he was at work and had no idea. Even so, she'd been terrified he'd find out and catch her, and make her pay.

And she'd done it! Freed herself, and most likely saved Shawn's life. Because she'd always known, deep down inside herself, if he pushed her too far, she'd snap and shift to wolf. A cornered wolf would kill in self-defense. Even Pack law allowed this, but she didn't want to be a killer.

This had been her first major victory in nearly three years. Now she was here, a few hours north of the city, and Shawn had no idea how to find her. After taking a few deep breaths, she let the tension drain off of her.

Her throat tight, she rolled her shoulders. Focus on the positive. A house of her own in upstate New York. Enough money to tide her over until she figured out what she wanted to do, and now a paying tenant, which meant a nice revenue stream. Her way out, her ticket to another life.

When she'd first arrived, relieved to find the house completely furnished, she'd met with the attorney and signed the necessary paperwork. After, she'd slept for two days, not stirring from her bed except to guzzle water and use the bathroom. When she'd finally surfaced, she felt like a butterfly emerging from a cocoon. Full of possibilities and hope.

This was all still too new, only one short month along. She had the rest of winter to burrow in, claim her space and find her way. She needed to rebuild her life, piece by piece, not let herself get distracted by a man.

Or his too-adorable-for-words baby.

As if he knew her thoughts, the baby gurgled and flashed JJ a sweet smile. Her heart constricted.

"Hello there, Garth," she cooed, loving the way his bright blue eyes sparkled as he smiled up at her. Carefully, gently, she lifted him out of his portable crib, breathing in the sweet baby scent of him. Moving him to her shoulder, she murmured baby words and nonsense while swaying slightly. His tiny body nestled into her, relaxing in a way that let her know he trusted her to take care of him. She, who'd never even been able to keep a potted plant alive.

This would be her ideal job, taking care of this sweet baby while his daddy worked. Maybe once Eric got settled in and knew her better, he'd entrust her with his precious son for more than a few minutes.

Carrying the infant, she walked to the front window to

check on Eric. He was still shoveling her sidewalk. Heart in her throat, she continued to watch him, holding the baby and pointing out his daddy. Even in his bulky parka, Eric's movements were both strong and graceful, an intriguing combination. He left his parka unzipped and wore no hat, his long blond hair tied back in a sexy ponytail.

Baby Garth squirmed, making her realize he'd just dirtied his diaper. Since Eric had brought a diaper bag, she located the spares—disposables, thank goodness—without difficulty, along with baby wipes, and clumsily managed her first diaper change since she'd done babysitting as a teenager years ago.

Feeling pretty accomplished, she picked up the now clean and dry infant and went back to the window. Still holding his shovel, Eric had stopped shoveling snow. Instead, he stood on the freshly cleared sidewalk talking to her next-door neighbor. Rhonda and JJ had hit it off immediately and, according to Rhonda, were destined to become best friends. Like JJ, she was in her thirties and single, though unlike JJ, she was divorced and now actively searching for The One. The Right One, she often quipped, winking.

Judging from the way she was eyeing JJ's new tenant, Rhonda considered him a viable possibility. She'd even ventured outside in a ski jacket and snow boots, shovel in hand, as if about to start shoveling her own driveway and sidewalk. Since it had snowed a couple times in the last few weeks, and JJ had yet to see her actually use her snow shovel, she knew exactly what Rhonda was up to.

Of course, a guy as nice as Eric would in no way stand around and watch a woman shovel snow, so when Eric began clearing Rhonda's sidewalk, the satisfied look on Rhonda's face told JJ she'd expected no less.

To her surprise, JJ felt a tiny twinge of jealously. With

her long blond hair and perky upturned nose, Rhonda had the kind of looks and personality that attracted men like bees to a flower. From head to toe, she stood exactly five feet tall. Next to her, JJ felt like an ungainly giant. She and JJ were polar opposites, which was one of the reasons they got along so well, again according to Rhonda. JJ didn't mind; she actually found it a relief to let someone else do all the talking.

While she'd known Rhonda only a couple weeks, the two of them had been to dinner twice and had coffee together a few times. JJ genuinely liked the other woman.

Eric finished quickly and handed the shovel to Rhonda. With a quick smile, he went back to clearing the snow away from his car. His projected fifteen minutes had turned into thirty and he wasn't nearly done yet. JJ didn't mind. She not only enjoyed watching him, but spending time with tiny Garth brought her joy.

Her phone rang. Rhonda's number flashed up on the screen. Still holding the baby, JJ answered.

"Why didn't you call and tell me you had such a gorgeous male specimen living in your house?" Rhonda shrieked.

Since JJ had no real answer for that, she didn't say anything. As usual, her silence didn't bother Rhonda in the slightest. "So what's the story on him?" she asked. "I want details. All of them."

"I don't know very much," JJ finally admitted. "He's from California. Says he's going to open his own business. And his baby is adorable."

For once, she'd stunned her neighbor into silence. "Baby?" Rhonda finally said. She'd never made any secret of the fact that she didn't like children. "He has a baby?"

"Yes. A son named Garth. I think he's three or four

months old. I'm watching him while Eric digs his vehicle out from under the snow."

"Wow." Again the silence. But Rhonda being Rhonda, she didn't miss a beat. "Eric, huh? I didn't catch his name. He was kind enough to clear my driveway and sidewalk for me."

"So I saw," JJ drawled, continuing to bounce the baby. "Um, are you and he…?"

JJ pretended not to understand. "Listen, I've got to go." As if on cue, little Garth let out a loud cry. "I'll talk to you later, okay?" She ended the call without waiting for a response.

Garth squealed again, his bright blue eyes fixed on the doorway. She heard the clump of boots on the stairs, and eyed the baby thoughtfully. He seemed way too young to understand that the sound signaled his father's return, but judging from the way he waved his tiny hands, he clearly was excited about something.

When Eric came through the door, JJ smiled. Little Garth made a chortling sound when he saw his father, continuing to wave his chubby fists. Eric grinned, his bright blue eyes sparkling the same as his son's. "Hey there, little man," he said. Cheeks reddened by exertion and cold, he seemed to have been energized by the exercise. After he peeled off his gloves and shrugged out of his coat, he reached for his son. "Come to Daddy, baby boy."

Then and only then did she think to rush to the stove and put a kettle of water on. If she'd been paying more attention, she would have already done this and had a mug of hot cocoa waiting for him. As it was, he'd have to wait a minute or two for the kettle to whistle.

"Are you cold?" she asked, wincing at the unnecessary question. Of course he was cold. The wind-chill factor was in the teens.

Looking up from playing with his son, he shrugged. "It's a little chilly out there, but I find it exhilarating."

Stunned, she stared. He might be the only other person she'd ever met who'd described feeling that way in blowing snow.

The teakettle finally whistled, startling her out of her thoughts. She hurried to get it. "Hot cocoa?" she asked. Even though it was only instant, nothing beat hot chocolate after shoveling snow in the cold.

"Sounds great."

She made them each a cup, adding a little whipped cream on top. When she turned back, he'd placed his son in his portable crib, where Garth happily played with the bright plastic keys.

With her heart hammering for no good reason, JJ brought Eric his hot drink. Her mouth went dry as he wrapped his long fingers around the mug, and she let her gaze follow the line of his throat as he took a sip and swallowed.

She couldn't blame Rhonda for being excited. Eric looked like a movie star, or a comic book superhero come to life. Even better, the size of his aura indicated when he shape-shifted, it was into something large and magnificent. No doubt Rhonda had noticed that as well, since she, too, was a shifter.

On that, JJ agreed with her neighbor. Shifter to shifter, she couldn't help but appreciate everything about her new tenant.

Artwork, she told herself. She'd decided to try and simply appreciate his amazingly rugged good looks the way she would enjoy a great painting. Like art.

And if she got a tingly feeling every once in a while, so be it. Some things couldn't be helped. She was healing, learning to make her own way in the world, but she wasn't dead.

He caught her watching him and cocked his head. "I think I like it here," he said, taking another long drink of his cocoa. "California is nice, but they don't have real winters. Something about the cold makes me feel alive."

"Me, too." Another flash of delight made her insides quiver. She looked down to hide her excitement. "Most everyone thinks I'm crazy because I love cold and snow." Glancing at him through her lashes, she confessed, "No one likes winter as much as I do."

"Except maybe me." The easy smile he flashed made her catch her breath. "Thanks for the cocoa." Draining the last of it, he set the cup down on her counter. "Garth and I need to drive into town. You're welcome to come with us if you'd like. I could use someone familiar with the place to point me in the right direction."

Her heart gave an entirely unnecessary leap. "I'd love to go," she said, working to quash her enthusiasm so it didn't show. "But I've only lived here one month. I do know where the stores are and some of the restaurants, but I'm in no way a native." About to tell him asking Rhonda would be his best bet, she managed to bite back the comment.

"I forgot." Tilting his head, he eyed her. "You said you were from Manhattan."

"Right."

He continued to watch her, clearly waiting for her to elaborate.

"I needed a fresh start," she finally said, keeping her chin up. "Like you, I had some emotional stuff going on I needed to get away from."

To her relief, he nodded. "I know the feeling."

"It's not easy, that's for sure."

"What about your parents?" he asked. "Do they live close by?"

Normal conversation, she told herself. Asking casual questions, like regular people do. Not everything was suspect. Shawn wasn't his friend.

"My father died a year ago," she said, her words bringing back the pain of his crossing as if it had happened yesterday. "And right after his funeral, my mom closed up their apartment and hopped a plane to Australia. Turns out she'd always wanted to live there."

And her abandonment had felt like a second death, though JJ didn't begrudge her mom her happiness. The two of them talked on the phone about once a month.

"Wow. Adventurous," he said. "You have to admire that."

Out of habit, she caught herself looking around, as if someone else might be listening. Shawn had been human, and she'd grown used to hiding her true nature. Ironic that. In her wolf form, she could have taken Shawn down permanently. He might never have hit her if he'd known that.

Then again, he probably would have just swung harder. Some people never changed, no matter what the circumstances. And Pack law forbade her to reveal her true nature to anyone unless they were going to be mates. Since Shawn and she hadn't been engaged, she'd kept her mouth shut. Truth be told, she'd come to like having a part of herself untouched by him.

"It's okay," Eric said, correctly interpreting her movement. "It's just the two of us. No one else can hear."

"Sorry. I feel foolish, but you know how it is."

"I do." He reached for his son's portable bed, hefting it in one hand.

"What about Garth?" she asked, blurting out the question before she had time to think it through. "Is he full or a halfling?"

"Full." The shortness of his answer told her how dangerously close to the line her question skirted. "Thanks for the cocoa. Are you ready to go now? I'd like to get out there and back before it starts snowing again, just in case."

"Sure." After grabbing her winter coat, she shrugged it on. "I'll probably pick up a few things, too." Like wine. She couldn't believe she'd forgotten to get at least one bottle. Nothing better than a fire crackling in the fireplace, a glass of wine and an old movie in the DVR.

With Garth securely buckled into his infant car carrier, they started to town. Initially tense, JJ relaxed her death grip on the door handle when she realized Eric, despite having lived in California, truly appeared to know how to navigate his SUV on snowy roads.

The small local grocery store appeared to be empty.

"Is it even open?" Eric asked, pulling into a parking spot right near the front door.

She laughed. "The day before the storm hit, you couldn't even park in the lot. And yes, I'm going to say they're open, judging by that neon sign above the doorway."

"Great." Hurrying around to the back, he unbuckled Garth. "Hopefully, it won't take me long to get enough provisions to tide me over for a while."

She nodded. "I just need a few things, so I'll walk with you. Would you like me to hold Garth?"

"Sure." Without a second of hesitation, he handed over the baby. Garth cooed, apparently already recognizing her. In response, her heart squeezed. Ever since she'd realized how Shawn had been using her desire to have a baby as a trick to keep her on a leash, she'd pushed that ache deep down inside her. Being around this little one brought her longing right back to the surface. Maybe someday she'd be lucky enough to have a child of her own.

Chapter 5

By the time they'd reached the other side of the grocery store, Eric had a full basket. JJ had grabbed a bottle of red wine and some cheese and put both in the cart, feeling ridiculously domestic. When they reached the checkout, Eric grabbed those and put them on the belt first, followed by his own groceries.

"Let me pay for my things," JJ said, fumbling in her purse for her wallet while holding Garth.

"I got it." The easy smile Eric flashed had her insides going all tingly again. "A bottle of wine and a block of cheese are the least I can do for you after all the help you've been to me."

"Okay."

When they walked outside, it had started snowing again. Eric gave a good-natured groan, making her laugh.

"I like it," she said, twirling around in the parking lot. "Which would explain why I found you making a snow angel when I first arrived." After placing little Garth into his infant seat, he began loading groceries into the back of his SUV. At her laugh, he glanced over his shoulder at her, then returned his attention to the task at hand.

Too happy to care, she stuck her tongue out at his back. "This is why I couldn't live anywhere else but New York," she told him. "Well, this and autumn. I'm definitely a fan of the fall."

He closed the back door of his vehicle and walked the shopping cart to the front of the store. "No sense leaving it out here in the snow," he said. "Let's go home before the roads get too bad."

Home. How many times had she said that word back in the city, not really meaning it? Now, hearing him refer to her house that way made hope blossom in her chest. Not for him, not for them, but for her. She really could make this place her home. She really could start her life over.

Once at the house, she took baby Garth inside while Eric carried in his provisions. "Here you go." He handed her the bag with her wine and cheese. "Thanks for your help."

Though plainly, she needed to go, she lingered, searching for a valid reason to stay. Busy unpacking his groceries, he didn't issue an invitation. Finally, though, she thanked him again for the wine and made her way upstairs.

When the snowfall finally stopped an hour before midnight, her measuring stick on the back porch showed they'd gotten eighteen inches. She was giddy with happiness, deciding then and there that she'd go into the woods and become wolf as soon as darkness had fallen. Since moving here, she tried to shape-shift at least once a week. It was much easier to do so here than it had been in the city. Just walking alone into Central Park had been nerve-racking, though once she disappeared into the trees and changed into wolf, it had been fun. Though there had been wooded areas remote enough that a wolf could hunt unnoticed, always, always, always, she and all the others of her kind couldn't help but be aware of the perimeter. As wolf, of necessity they'd remained on alert, just in case they encountered a human, or worse, a gang of humans.

In Forestwood, all that had changed. Judging from the abundance of auras she'd seen, more than two-thirds of the town inhabitants were some kind of shape-shifter. The rest were human and seemed oblivious to the others living in their midst.

She'd never been so glad to see the first snowfall here. One of the things she loved best about snow was changing into her wolf self and going for a run in it. Her entire life, she'd never felt free. Especially, she thought ruefully, since she'd had to lie to Shawn about where she'd been when she disappeared for a few hours every couple weeks. But she couldn't tell him the truth, so she'd done what she must, because she'd had no choice.

Now she could finally experience a space without boundaries. The idea both fascinated and terrified her. Ever since arriving in the Catskills, she'd been itching to get out and do exactly that. Her inner wolf, the curious beast, had been pushing at the edge of her consciousness every other day now. She didn't mind, as this was the purest kind of freedom. Limitless and joyful.

Each day, she felt better and better. Her burden of insecurity had gradually lessened, day by day, the entire time she'd been here in her new home. With such tremendous possibilities open to her, how could she remain afraid to take the first, vital step?

Downstairs, her new tenant and his adorable baby were hopefully asleep. The full moon lit up the freshly fallen snow, silver and white ice crystals beckoning. She'd dressed warmly, aware she'd need to walk deep into the woods behind her house as a human, before shedding her layers and beginning the process that would result in setting her wolf form free.

Anticipation had her moving fast. Her inner wolf felt she'd waited too long to change, which wasn't a good thing for her mental health, though in actuality she hadn't. Still, each time she let her wolf self out to play, when she'd returned to her human form she'd felt better, more balanced and better able to face any unexpected challenges that might lie ahead.

Tonight, she'd think of none of that. Tonight, as wolf, she'd hunt.

After crossing the large field between her house and the forest, she stopped and turned to look back. Pride of ownership filled her, making her heart swell. Her home sat on a small rise, surrounded by a grove of trees that appeared to shelter the two-story, wooden building. Rather than stand out, the house seemed to blend with the landscape, as though it had always been there, standing the test of time.

Hers. Something permanent, a place she could hold on to. Where she could put down roots and change the path of her life. As she often did, she offered up a silent thank-you to the great-aunt she'd never known.

Turning back toward the dark forest, she began moving once again, lifting her feet higher as she trudged through the deepening snow. Here, near the edge of the trees, snowdrifts were deeper, making progress more difficult.

But she powered through, her heart rate quickening as the wolf inside her paced and pushed, ready to be set free.

Finally, she judged she'd gone far enough into the woods. She found a fallen tree and hung her empty backpack from one of the branches. Slowly, she began peeling back layers, already shivering from the cold, though she knew in a few minutes her thick wolf pelt would keep her more than warm.

Stuffing each article of clothing into her backpack, she eventually stood naked, the chill seeping up from her bare feet. She knew she had to act quickly before her poor toes got frostbite. Inhaling, she dropped to the ground and initiated the change.

The familiar sensation never got old. The changes that occurred to her human body—especially her skeleton—could occasionally be painful. More so when a long time had gone by since her last change.

Since she was rushing herself as she shifted, she expected this one to really hurt. Surprisingly, it didn't. Maybe the combination of adrenaline, anticipation and cold combined to deaden the pain somewhat.

Either way, as her bones lengthened, her hands and feet turning into paws, a savage sort of joy filled her.

Wolf-JJ was almost free. In a moment, she'd give herself over to the primitive nature of the beast.

Done. Immediately, myriad tantalizing scents beckoned. Her wolf nose, a thousand times more sensitive than her human one, picked up on the fact that a rabbit had recently crossed nearby, as had a skunk and a small herd of white-tailed deer.

Eager to explore, she bounded off through the snow.

Eric had heard Julia tromp down the stairs right around twelve, just as he was about to turn off the TV and head to bed. Curious, he waited for the sound of a car engine starting, but then caught sight of her moving slowly across a large, open field. Her bulky parka and layered clothing made movement a bit difficult as she headed toward the forest, no doubt to change into her beast, whatever kind that might be.

An instant of longing rocked him, his inner beast protesting with a roar that reverberated in his soul. He felt it had been forever since he'd shape-shifted, and his bear self was not at all happy about that. But what could he do? Taking care of an infant made it damn near impossible to go off by himself and change. While he'd gotten Jason, his Pack Protector friend, to watch Garth a time or two, he'd been able to shape-shift only twice in three months. Not good. At all. To go too long without letting his inner bear free was dangerous. He knew, as did all shifters, that doing so could lead to insanity or even death. Right now, Eric felt as if he could be pushing the limit. Maybe he'd see if his landlord would be willing to watch Garth for an hour or two tomorrow night so Eric could take his own solitary trip into the forest.

He resolved to ask her later. Right now, all he could do was watch until she disappeared from view, and push down his envy.

The hunt went well, JJ thought, as she hurriedly dressed after changing back to human. As usual, when in her wolf form, she had no sense of time passing, so she had no idea how long she'd explored the forest. She'd tracked and taken down a midsize rabbit, feasting until her belly was full. This would be her place, and though she knew there surely were other shifters in Forestwood, these few acres of woods were part of her property and would be where she went to let her wolf self run free.

Once again fully clothed, though everything retained a touch of a chill, she gave herself a few moments for the intense sexual arousal to recede. For whatever reason, this crazed need for bodily contact happened to everyone once they shifted back to human, no matter what kind of beast they became. Many people took advantage of this—she'd heard stories of wild and crazy orgies among groups who liked to shape-shift with others.

As for herself, she'd gotten used to tamping down the need. Even when she'd been with Shawn, she hadn't wanted to return home after having spent the night away and beg him to make love to her. Sex was another one of the things he used to control her.

So once the low thrum of desire had settled to a steady hum, she inhaled deeply and exhaled slowly, watching the plume her breath made in the frigid air. Centered, she felt normal again, so she wouldn't find herself at Eric's front door offering herself to him.

The thought sent a fresh wave of longing through her. Again she took deep breaths, focusing on the snow and the velvet ink of the sky, until she'd once again regained her equilibrium.

Then and only then did she turn to make her way back home. She followed her old footprints, glad they made the going much easier. The moon still provided illumination, though it no longer hung fat and sassy in the sky directly overhead.

A few hours then, she thought. Time well spent. Her entire body ached, a pleasant feeling. She let herself back into her silent house and went up the stairs, wincing as a few of them creaked.

She'd just about reached her landing when the downstairs door opened.

"Welcome back." The sound of Eric's deep voice sent an immediate thrum of need blazing through her bloodstream. Damn. So much for returning to normal.

Reluctant to face him, but glad of the several steps in between them, she turned, thankful for her bulky clothing.

"Thank you. You're up kind of late, aren't you?" Then, as a worrisome thought occurred to her, she raised her gloved hand to her throat. "Is Garth all right?"

"He's fine." Eric dragged his own hand across his chin. "You went out to change, didn't you?"

Slowly, she nodded, aware once again they were skirting dangerously close to the edge of what was considered acceptable conversation.

Shifting his weight from foot to foot, he nodded. It dawned on her he was clearly uncomfortable. "It's been a while for me and..."

"You can't just leave Garth."

"Right. So I was wondering if you'd mind watching him for a few hours so I can change, too."

What she'd give to see him change, or to be more specific, to be there when he exchanged his animal form for that of a man. At the thought, a bolt of lust shot through her, so strong she nearly staggered. "Tonight?" she managed to ask. "Because I don't know if I—"

"No, not tonight." One corner of his mouth tugged up in a tired smile. "I was thinking maybe tomorrow night, if that would be okay with you. If not, I'm open to whenever you can spare the time."

"Tomorrow should be fine." *Casual*, she thought. She hoped she sounded casual. Not at all like a woman who wanted to pounce on him because she couldn't help imagining being the one to greet him when he became human again, fully and gloriously aroused.

In fact, she'd better get back to her own personal, private space before she did something foolish, like reach for him.

"I really appreciate it, Julia." He frowned. "Is it okay if I use your first name?"

"My friends call me JJ," she told him. "I'd rather you use that."

"I will." Again the blinding smile. "I really appreciate all your help. Someday I hope I can repay you."

Oh, she knew exactly how he could repay her. Dang it. Swallowing hard, she managed to smile back.

"Good night," she said firmly, unlocking her door and stepping inside. Once she had it closed firmly behind her, she sagged against it, her entire body throbbing. Residue from the change, she told herself. Nothing to do with her tenant. Nothing to do with him at all. After the disastrous relationship with Shawn, she didn't need to be wanting another man, not now. Maybe not ever.

In the morning, a phone call woke Eric. It was the moving company notifying him they'd be arriving the next afternoon, weather permitting. Finally, he'd be getting the few personal items he'd kept, along with Garth's actual baby furniture. And his car. Most important, his beautiful car. Of course, the baby furniture was important, too, but if it had gotten damaged or lost, he could replace it. His car was irreplaceable.

Things were starting to look up. Eric found himself waiting with barely concealed anticipation for the sun to go down so he could go into the woods alone and change.

He'd have to be careful, though he'd actually chosen this town because they'd reportedly been tolerant, even kind, to the Drakkor woman they'd sheltered for years. She'd become a celebrity of sorts among paranormal creatures, dispensing wisdom and baked goods from her cottage on the shores of the lake. Another Drakkor and his shifter mate had also settled here. He planned to visit all three of them once he got settled, as long as they were open to visitors. Being bear, he felt a sense of kinship with other outcasts, other species of shifter who were rare and few and often reviled.

When his family had left their small village in Norway, they'd chosen a town in California where other Vedjorn lived. Since most bear shifters mated with their own kind, they'd wanted their son to have the chance to find a mate.

While he missed his parents tremendously, he was glad they hadn't survived to see what kind of a mate he'd chosen. If he had his druthers, he'd never hook up with another bear shifter. And since most of the other shifters were afraid of the bears, he doubted he'd ever find another woman to mate with again.

Which suited him just fine. Once had been enough. He had his son. As long as he could find a female who was open to recreational sex, he'd consider his life a happy one.

For now, though, the only thing he needed to worry about was letting his inner beast free to run and hunt.

Anticipation built in him as he waited for dusk. Somehow, his nervous pacing communicated to his son, rendering Garth unusually fussy. Even though he'd been changed and fed and burped, he started crying and wouldn't be soothed. This had never happened before. Jiggling him, rocking him, speaking in a soothing tone over and over—none of it worked. In desperation, Eric searched the internet for a solution, but found only variations of what he already knew to do.

Finally, little Garth cried himself to sleep.

Exhausted, Eric quietly transferred his son to his temporary crib. Then he sat down with his head in his hands and tried to think.

Teething? Again he hit the search engines and learned teething usually starts at six months, but can start as early as three.

A soft tap at his door startled him. After a quick glance

to make sure the sound hadn't made Garth wake, he hurried to answer.

"Is everything all right?" JJ murmured, as if she somehow knew the baby slept. She wore a flowing shirt and some sort of soft leggings that made her legs appear impossibly long.

"It is now," he said grimly, holding the door open and motioning her inside. "I couldn't get him to stop crying. He actually cried himself to sleep."

"Is he sick?" she asked, sounding worried. "From here, he looks feverish. Have you taken his temperature?"

That thought had never occurred to him. But then, Garth had only been sick once in his three months of life. Eric took comfort in the fact that his son was a full-blooded shape-shifter, and as such, only fire or silver could kill him. That could be both a curse and a blessing. He'd personally known a few people forced to live on in damaged bodies, enduring hell because they could not die. He wouldn't wish that on his worst enemy.

Chapter 6

Garth made a snuffling sound, drawing Eric's attention. His son might be all bear, but that didn't mean he couldn't suffer from illness. A fever could easily be rectified, however. Eric fumbled in the baby bag he'd packed, finally locating the thermometer. It was brand-new, still in the wrapping. He'd purchased the forehead kind, not wanting to deal with a rectal one.

Once he'd unwrapped it, he did a quick read of the instructions before swiping it over Garth's tiny brow.

"Ninety-nine point zero," he said. "Just a little over normal."

"Nothing to worry about, I don't think." JJ spoke with authority, despite claiming to know next to nothing about caring for babies.

"Maybe he's teething," she continued. "Is he drooling a lot?"

"Yeah." Eric hesitated, eyeing his sleeping son. "I don't

think I can leave him if he's sick." Inside, his beast roared in protest. "I'm thinking I probably should reschedule."

When he looked back up, Julia studied him, her head tilted. She appeared a bit shell-shocked, almost as if she'd heard his beast's roar. "It's up to you," she said. "I personally think he'll be fine. It's only for a few hours, anyway. But you're his father, so if you want to wait until another night, that's fine with me."

Again his beast made his presence known, rattling the proverbial bars of his invisible cage. Inside, Eric fought a minor battle. It had been too long since he'd let his bear out and the animal didn't take well to being confined for lengthy periods of time.

"I can see your problem," Julia said softly. "Your beast really needs to be free. Go change. Let your other self out to run and hunt. Make it short if you really feel you have to, but I'll be perfectly fine here with Garth."

Part of him wanted to leap for joy. The other, more rational part kept his feet planted firmly in place. "What would you do if he became sicker?"

"Take care of him," she said, turning away. "I seriously don't think there's anything wrong with him that a teething ring wouldn't fix. Do you have one of those?"

"A what?"

"A baby teething ring. You know, you put it in the fridge and once it's good and cold, you let the baby gum it." She frowned. "Though maybe those are for older babies. I doubt little Garth could hold it yet."

"I don't have one of those."

"That's okay. I've seen people use a cool, wet wash-cloth."

"You seem to have more experience with babies than you let on."

She smiled. "Just because I didn't work in the baby

room at the day care doesn't mean I didn't spend a lot of time in there. As I said, I love babies."

Again, his inner beast roared, fighting to break free. And once more, JJ cocked her head as though listening. He almost asked her what she heard, but restrained himself. "I'm going to go." He made a snap decision, knowing he'd have to shape-shift sooner or later, so he might as well do it and be done with it. A happy inner bear made life better all the way around.

"Good. I sense some discord between you and your beast."

Either she was unusually perceptive or he was giving far too much away.

"I'm fine," he lied. "Though I'll be better once I change and hunt." He studied his son. Garth made a snuffling sound and moved. Relief flooded Eric. Maybe she was right. Maybe his boy was just teething.

"I'm trusting you with my son." Even as he spoke, he couldn't believe what he was saying. He meant it, too, he realized. JJ, his landlord, was one of what his father used to call "good people."

"I promise I'll take good care of him," she said, smiling. "We'll be upstairs. I've got the perfect chair."

"Then let me carry up his diaper bag and portable crib."

Once everything had been set up, she smiled. "Now go. Run and hunt. I promise you'll feel much better once you've changed. Especially if it's been a while."

He nodded and then impulsively kissed her cheek. The instant he did it, he knew he'd made a huge mistake. Wide-eyed, she stared at him, while a rose color suffused her entire face.

Her scent—lavender—lingered on his lips after he moved away. "I'll see you in a little bit," he said, and hurried out the door before he did anything even more foolish.

* * *

Cheek still tingling, JJ watched from her window as Eric headed across the clearing toward the woods. With the full moon reflecting on the snow, she could see him outlined clearly, his parka dark against the glowing, magically pure whiteness.

Though she knew he hadn't meant anything with that casual kiss—on the cheek, no less—every fiber of her body had strained toward him, as if he were a lure she was unable to resist.

Luckily, she'd frozen in place instead of swaying toward him. Her blush had been the only sign of how his simple gesture affected her. Hopefully, he had no idea. Her secret attraction must remain just that—a secret.

Glancing at the still sleeping baby, she sighed. She'd need to be careful with these two. Both of them had the power to come dangerously close to stealing her heart.

Again her gaze drifted back to Eric, who was nearing the edge of the trees. Aching to be with him, she stood there until he vanished into the woods.

Her kind did best with others. They were called The Pack for a reason. But she'd always shape-shifted alone. Maybe it had been her natural reticence, but she hadn't been up for being around a group of people when she turned human again, battling a fierce arousal. She'd often wondered what it would be like, for curiosity's sake. She'd heard there were some groups for whom privacy was an option, who were not into random sex with strangers, but she'd always been afraid to take a chance. Though she'd often considered the idea, in the end she knew she did better alone.

Or so she'd told herself. Now, watching a gorgeous hunk of man on his way to shape-shift, she wanted nothing more than to do the same at his side.

Of course, assuming he was Pack. Why wouldn't he be, when 90 percent of the shifters she knew were wolves? There was no way to find out for sure, unless she accidentally came across him changing. Which was extremely unlikely to occur.

She sighed, unable to keep from imagining him as he transitioned from his animal form back to human. As always happened with their kind, he'd be fully aroused. Her body heated, the desire she'd experienced the night before back in full force.

And then she remembered he'd kissed her on the cheek. The cheek, not the lips. The kind of kiss a man gave to his mother or aunt or sister. Or friend.

That was what they were. Friends. She needed to constantly remind herself of that and she'd be fine.

She must have dozed, sitting in her armchair with a still slumbering Garth next to her. Eric's tread on her old wooden stairs woke her; no matter how quiet anyone tried to be, the third and seventh steps squeaked.

After pushing herself up and out of her chair, she pulled the door open before he reached it.

"Hey," he whispered. Even in the shadowy hallway, his blue eyes blazed. As he stepped into her living room, she could feel the satisfaction and coiled up energy rolling off him.

His inner beast had gone quiet. No longer restless, most likely sated by a run and a hunt. "How'd it go?" she asked, even though the question seemed unnecessary.

"It went well," he said. "Very well. I feel much better. How's Garth?"

"He slept the entire time you were gone. His color looks good. I checked his temperature one more time and it was the same. I'm sure he's fine."

Relief shone in her tenant's face. "I really appreciate this."

Mercilessly, she kept her gaze trained on his face, not daring to let it dip below his waist, though she badly wanted to see if his body revealed his certain arousal.

"I'd better go." He shifted his weight from one foot to the other. "See you tomorrow."

When he bent to retrieve the portable crib, she got a great view of his nicely shaped backside.

Giving herself a mental slap, she dragged her eyes toward the baby, where they needed to be.

"He's not moving," Eric said, panic edging his voice. "JJ, Garth isn't moving. I don't think he's breathing."

"What?" She reacted without conscious thought, reaching for the infant and lifting him up to pat him soundly on the back. He gasped, his eyes flying open.

And then he let out a cry, a screeching sort of wail, so wonderful she sagged in relief.

"Garth." Eric snatched him from her. "Baby boy?" Which only made him cry harder.

Trembling with relief, JJ reached into the crib and located the pacifier. She handed this to Eric, who held it to Garth's mouth. Latching on and suckling wildly, he instantly ceased crying.

"What the heck was that?" Eric asked, bewilderment and panic lacing his voice. "I swear, I put my finger under his nose and he wasn't breathing."

"I don't know." Privately, she wondered if Eric had imagined it. "He must have been deeply asleep." Tears stung the back of her eyes. "I'm so glad he's okay."

"Me, too." The fierce tone told her how much the man meant it.

Aware she needed to be careful, she took a deep breath.

"Earlier, you said he was full-blooded. If so, you know illness wouldn't kill him."

"I'm aware." The shortness of Eric's answer told her he was angry at himself for overreacting. "And while it's true such a thing might not kill him, death isn't always the worst thing that could happen to our kind. Think of a soul trapped in a nonfunctioning body. I've seen that before. A fever can cause brain damage."

Slowly, she nodded. "I haven't ever thought of it like that."

"It's because you're not a parent." He had no way of knowing how much those words stung.

All she could do was nod.

"What a night," he continued. "I'm going take him downstairs now and get the both of us ready for bed."

Good. Because maybe then she could sit down before her legs gave out from under her.

Apparently, he felt the same way. After jerking his head in a brusque nod, he grabbed the diaper bag and portable crib, then turned and left.

As soon as the door clicked shut behind him, JJ dropped into her chair, her entire body shaking. Had Eric imagined everything in a moment of overprotective panic, or had Garth really stopped breathing?

Truth be told, she didn't know. Personally, she tended to lean more toward imagination, because every time she'd checked on him, the baby had been fine.

But after this, she had a feeling Eric wouldn't trust her to watch his son ever again. Full-blooded or not.

Once he'd gotten Garth back home, Eric shook his head. What the hell was wrong with him? He'd never been the overprotective type of parent, stressing about his baby's every sniffle. But for one split second there he'd been filled with a visceral dread, convinced something terrible and unimaginably awful had happened to his son.

Then Garth had drawn a breath and cried. Clearly, he was fine. Relief mixed with chagrin. His son was okay. Teething a little maybe, but all right. And Eric's first reaction, that awful gut-churning response, had been to turn on the woman who'd been trying to help him.

He felt awful, though his one consolation was that maybe she hadn't noticed.

Of course she had. He would find her tomorrow and offer an apology. Once he'd made sure his son had a clean diaper, he put him down for the night and climbed into bed.

When his cell phone rang at 1:00 a.m., waking him from a deep sleep, Eric fumbled for the phone and finally answered.

"Yolanda has gone off the deep end," a familiar voice said. "That woman is stark raving crazy."

Blinking, Eric didn't speak at first while he tried to figure out why his friend Jason was calling. This was old news, restating the obvious.

"I thought I'd pass along a warning." Jason worked for the Pack Protectors and acted as a liaison between the wolves and bears. He'd been helping Eric with his case ever since Yolanda had started her crazy accusations.

It helped that the Wolf Pack had lately been trying to end the divide between the bears and everyone else. It was slow going, as the distrust was mutual, but Eric gave them kudos for even trying. He certainly could always hope.

Eric had been brought up by two people who refused to accept the status quo. In Norway, they'd settled away from the small enclaves of their own kind, living among humans and other shifters before immigrating to the United States when Eric had been ten and settling in California, choosing a town with numerous other shifters, including Vedjorn.

Growing up, Eric hadn't known there was any prejudice against bears. He and Jason—who had to be Pack, though of course they'd never discussed it—had been best friends since kindergarten. When Jason had gone into the military and from there the Pack Protectors, he'd never once lost contact with Eric. Even when his top-secret clearance revealed that his best friend was a Vedjorn bear shifter, Jason hadn't turned away. Instead, he'd asked to work on the task force dedicated to keeping the few remaining Vedjorn safe.

Yawning, Eric rubbed his eyes. Luckily, the ringing phone hadn't disturbed Garth, who still slept. Eric couldn't stop himself from once again checking to make sure his son was breathing. He was, of course.

"Thanks, man, but couldn't this have waited until morning? Is it really the kind of thing that warrants a phone call at 1:00 a.m.?"

Jason cursed. "I'm so sorry. I forgot you were on the East Coast. It's only ten here. I just got home from work. It's been a long day. Most of my afternoon and evening were spent dealing with your ex."

"She doesn't know where I am." Eric felt quite confident in that knowledge. "You're still the only one who knows, right? Everyone else—faculty, friends—all still think I went up to Seattle."

"Yeah, still true. But you know what? I really didn't get it before. Why you felt the need to put as much distance as possible between you and her." Jason's wry tone told Eric he did now. "Sure, she seemed a bit emotional. Dramatic, even. But not unstable."

"Is she still trying to brand me a Berserker?" Though he hated to even speak the word, Eric didn't have a choice. A true Berserker, though rare among their kind, was extremely dangerous. When Berserkers shifted into their bear selves, they could become uncontrollable killing machines.

The Wolf Pack Protectors had been working in conjunction with the Vedjorn Bear Council in making sure any true Berserkers were destroyed before they killed any humans and brought unwelcome notice to the entire shape-shifter population. In Eric's lifetime, he'd heard of only two, both back in Norway.

"Yes." Jason sounded tired. "I've shifted with you, remember. I know you're not. And I really don't understand her plan. What is she hoping to achieve?"

"If I knew, I'd tell you. Despite her claims otherwise, it's not like she truly wants our son—she handed him over without a backward glance and signed papers waiving all parental rights." Again, rehashing old news. The two men had speculated endlessly over Yolanda's motives. Since she wanted nothing to do with Garth, her reasons for stalking Eric remained a mystery.

"She flew into a rage at the office today when no one would tell her where she could find you. Something about having a score to settle. And needing to protect Garth."

"Again, that makes no sense." Before Eric could finish his statement, he heard an alarm that began shrieking in the background at Jason's place. "Are you all right?"

"Yeah. That's my burglar alarm. Perimeter alert. I need to check this out, so I'm going to let you go." He ended the call.

Setting down his phone, Eric shook his head. With her rants and raves about Berserkers and the possibility that a sweet, innocent baby could be one, Yolanda presented a very real danger. He understood she wanted to harm their child and destroy Eric himself, which was why he'd hightailed it out of Cali. Eventually, she would turn back to her partying friends and forget about them. Until then—and maybe forever—he'd keep a low profile. All that mattered was making sure Garth stayed safe.

The phone call had startled Eric, making him wonder if he'd be able to go back to sleep. But apparently shapeshifting and hunting earlier had exhausted him, because he drifted off as soon as he laid his head on his pillow. When he opened his eyes again, bright sunlight reflecting on the snow outside lit up his room.

Instinctively, he checked on Garth. His son still slumbered, the rise and fall of his chest steady. The sight filled Eric with so much joy his throat felt tight.

The possibilities of this new life, with this child...he could ask for nothing more.

Once his son woke up, cheerful as always, Eric changed him and fed him. Then he ate his own breakfast.

The chime of his cell phone broke into his thoughts. He grabbed it. Caller ID showed Jason's number.

"Jason," he said, bracing himself for more tales of craziness. "What's Yolanda done now?"

Silence on the other end. Then an unfamiliar male voice spoke. "This is Officer Frank DeLeon with the Pack Protectors. I regret to inform you that Jason is dead."

"Dead?" Eric swallowed hard, pain knifing through him. "I just talked to him around one this morning. His alarm went off in the middle of our call. What happened? Intruders?"

A pause. "We're reviewing the surveillance tapes now. It was pretty violent."

Then, while Eric was still trying to wrap his mind around that, the voice continued. "And there's more, unfortunately. We've also got a severely injured woman here. Judging from what we can tell from the crime scene, she and Jason were battling."

"A woman?" At first he didn't understand.

"Yes. She knew the drill, since she came armed with a

pistol and silver bullets. After she shot Jason, she turned the gun on herself."

"Who?" Eric cleared his throat, feeling as if he already knew the answer, but hoping he was wrong. "Who is the woman?"

"Mr. Mikkelson, we've tentatively identified her as your ex-wife, Yolanda. Your ex-wife and the person who was trying to make a case against you for allegedly being a true Berserker."

Chapter 7

Another pause. Had there been accusation in the Pack Protector's tone? When Officer DeLeon continued, Eric already knew exactly what he was going to say. "What I'll need from you, Mr. Mikkelson, is proof of your whereabouts since 1:00 a.m."

Stunned, shocked, Eric took a full twenty seconds to respond. "I'm in New York, sir. And yes, I can provide whatever proof you need."

It was only after he'd hung up that he allowed himself to give in to his grief. Jason was gone. Not only his best friend, but his contact inside the Pack Protectors. The guy who always had his back. And Yolanda had taken herself out along with him.

Unfortunately, the phone call had been all too real. Jason was dead. Yolanda was seriously injured and in intensive care. The doctor had told Eric he wasn't sure if she would pull through.

The taint of unspoken accusation had colored every sentence between Eric and Officer DeLeon. Even though it hadn't taken long for the Pack Protectors to verify that Eric was indeed in New York, on the opposite side of the country.

From what DeLeon had reluctantly revealed, it appeared Yolanda had gone to Jason's home to confront him. She'd purchased a pistol and some silver bullets, apparently with the intention of threatening him. Things had gone downhill from there. Everyone in Jason's division had been familiar with the woman and her crazy accusations. No one had seen her as a viable threat, least of all Jason.

Privately, Eric thought she'd purchased the one weapon that could kill a shifter in order to eliminate him, once she got Jason to reveal her ex-husband and son's location. He wondered if Jason had, before he died. Knowing his friend, Eric doubted it.

Poor Jason had been caught in the middle. A Pack Protector, he clearly hadn't taken Yolanda seriously enough. This broke Eric's heart.

Meanwhile, Yolanda continued to recover at the hospital. While a silver bullet could kill, she'd missed her heart and brain and any other vital organs. Now she had a fifty-fifty chance of survival.

One of their own had been killed and the Pack Protectors were in a frenzy to blame someone. At first it had seemed as if they were trying to figure out a way to accuse Eric, but in the end they'd had to acknowledge Yolanda had done this, and she'd acted alone.

However, Detective DeLeon's casual use of the word *Berserker* concerned Eric. He sounded as if he had no idea what a Berserker was. Yolanda definitely wasn't one, but the other man referred to her as a Berserker more than once. Luckily, as far as Eric and Garth were concerned, whatever caused bears to go wild was rarely passed down. Instead, it mostly appeared to be a random gene mutation.

Eric could not allow anything to happen to Garth, even if his birth mother was determined to be Berserker by people who knew no better. Eric had shifted with Yolanda and he knew beyond a shadow of a doubt that she wasn't.

DeLeon had said Yolanda would be charged with murder if she lived. Right now, no one seemed certain she would. If she did, Eric could only hope she remained in police custody. He couldn't help but pray that Jason, in his final moments, had not revealed Eric and Garth's location.

Though most of the snow had melted, except for odd little pockets of dirty whiteness in the shadows of buildings or a particularly large tree, the slate-gray sky and icy, gusting wind promised another storm would be on the way sooner or later. After all, it was January.

JJ, like most of Forestwood, bustled around trying to run errands and stock up on supplies before she was snowed in again.

Her mother called from Australia just as JJ finished putting up the groceries. It was summer there, and her mom always loved to tell her how much fun she had at the beach in the blazing hot sun. She didn't seem to ever grasp the fact that her daughter really preferred fall and winter.

"I heard you got a big snowstorm," Anita Jacobs said by way of greeting.

"We did." JJ waited for her mom to gloat.

Instead, Anita sighed. "I miss the snow."

This statement so boggled her mind that JJ couldn't think of a response. Her mother had always complained bitterly when the first snowflake fluttered to the ground.

"Listen," her mom continued. "I was wondering. Have you and Shawn kissed and made up yet?"

JJ couldn't suppress a shudder. Her mother had loved Shawn. Of course, JJ hadn't given her a reason not to. She'd been too embarrassed to admit the truth. "No, Mom. That's not going to happen."

"Because he wants to live in Manhattan and you're now living upstate?"

"If only it were that simple," JJ said.

"He called me, you know."

JJ felt a stab of fear, like a steel blade plunging into the middle of her chest. She cursed herself for not telling her mother the truth. "Please tell me you didn't let him know where I am."

"Of course not." Anita sounded offended. "You asked me not to and I promised. I am a woman of my word. But I need to tell you how worried that man is. He seemed frantic. Said he's been searching for you in all five boroughs."

Frantic? More like pissed.

"Mom, there's something you should know about Shawn," JJ began.

"No." Her mother snorted. "If he had an affair, I don't want to know the details."

As far as JJ knew, Shawn could have had twenty affairs. Cheating would have been infinitely preferable to the facts. "It wasn't that, Mom." Pushing away the wave of shame, JJ forced herself to continue. "Shawn was abusive." There. Finally, she'd given her mom the truth. Though *abusive* seemed too tame a word, it nicely summed up things.

"Abusive?" Anita sounded confused. "What do you mean? That man positively doted on you."

"In public." Hearing the defeat in her own voice, JJ winced. "Listen, it's a long story. I'll tell it to you sometime, maybe next time you visit. But for now, believe me when I say it's not safe for me if Shawn finds out where I am."

"Wow. I had no idea. I'm shocked. Truly stunned. I also don't understand why you didn't tell me."

A hundred reasons. Chief among them, JJ had been ashamed. Also, she figured the less people knew, the better. She couldn't live with herself if she put anyone else's life in danger because of her.

Instead of answering, JJ sighed. "I'm sorry, Mom. It's just been kind of crazy."

"I imagine it has been. I'm so sorry you had to endure that. I honestly would have tried to help you if I'd known. You know you're always welcome to come live with me in Australia."

Closing her eyes against the wave of pain her mother's words brought, JJ tried to formulate a response. "Thanks, Mom. But I'm fine here. I like this house and this town. And I have a new tenant renting the space downstairs. For the first time in a long time, I think everything is going to be all right." Maybe if she said it enough, she'd believe it.

"Really?" JJ could hear the surprise in Anita's voice. "That's wonderful. Just remember, though. You always have a choice."

"We all have free will, Mom." This last came out sharper than JJ had intended. "Sorry." She took a deep breath and tried to take her tone down a notch. "I'm still adjusting to getting away and starting a new life."

Silence. Then her mother sighed. "I'm happy for you, sweetheart. Truly happy. Again, I find it painful that you never said anything to me. I could have helped you. Just because I moved away doesn't mean I abandoned you."

Hadn't she? JJ no longer had any idea what to think. To be fair, she'd told her mom as little as possible about that aspect of her life. It wasn't exactly something she wanted anyone else to know about. They hadn't really discussed it since her mother left.

This time, JJ didn't answer. After a few seconds of silence, Anita spoke. "Do you need me to come see you? Maybe visit for a couple of weeks, just until you get settled? I still know a few people in that town."

Did she really mean that? Ever since the day her mom had packed up and moved to Australia, leaving alone a daughter still grieving over the loss of her father, JJ had struggled with the question of whether or not her mother really loved her.

She still didn't understand how a mom could move to the other side of the world from her young daughter who might need her. JJ got that they had both been in pain, shell-shocked and reeling over their mutual loss, but who simply took off without a backward glance, leaving behind the only family member you had left?

She still felt resentment, even after all these months. Another unwelcome emotion.

"Honey? Did you hear me? I can book a flight and be there in a few days if you want."

"That's okay," JJ finally said. "I'm still trying to find my footing. I told you I got a tenant to live in the downstairs unit. So I have his rent for income until I find a job. And I've made friends with the woman next door. So it's not like I'm all alone."

"Well, all right." Did her mom actually sound disappointed? "But promise me you'll let me know if you need me, okay?"

This was a new one. Her mother had never really appeared to care if JJ was in trouble. "Okay."

With that assurance, her mother hung up.

Odd. It was almost as if she was hoping JJ would actually need her. Shaking her head, JJ couldn't help but wonder if Anita had gotten bored with her life down under and was hoping for a little excitement to stir things up.

The next morning, JJ woke early. She showered and dried her hair, dressing warmly before heading into her kitchen to make a pot of coffee.

Even though it was below freezing, JJ bundled up and carried her coffee outside to the front porch to drink it. She needed to get out of the house. It felt like the walls were closing in around her.

Since snow had piled up on the outdoor chairs, JJ stood. Next door, the front door opened and Rhonda came outside and waved. "Come over here," she ordered, cupping her mouth with her hands to make sure the sound carried. "I just made a coffee cake. And I have plenty of java. We're overdue for a chat."

Thankful for the welcome distraction, JJ said she'd be right over. After draining the last of her coffee, she headed next door, glad of the still-shoveled sidewalk. Once inside Rhonda's cheery yellow kitchen, she shrugged out of her parka, hanging it on the wooden coatrack near the back door. Accepting a cup of steaming coffee, she chose one of the bar stools and sat at the bar instead of the kitchen table.

Smiling, Rhonda cut two large slices of coffee cake and brought them over, along with her own mug of coffee.

"It's so good to see you. But you don't look like you've been sleeping well," Rhonda drawled, her blue eyes sparkling with humor. "Is there a reason? Such as a certain handsome hunk of tenant keeping you up at night?"

Heaven help her, but JJ blushed. "I wish," she said, meaning it. "But no. I just had a bad night last night."

Taking a large bite prevented her from acting on the urge to over-confide. As if aware of this, her neighbor watched, sipping her coffee, while JJ chewed.

"Why?" Rhonda finally asked. Her coffee cake still sat untouched.

"I have no idea." JJ pointed toward her own half-demolished slice. "This is really good. Aren't you going to eat yours?"

"Maybe." Using her fork, Rhonda cut a teeny, tiny bite. "Mmm. It is good."

JJ shook her head, eyeing her neighbor in disbelief. "Unless you scarfed down three pieces before I got here, please tell me that's not all you're going to eat."

"Hey!" Rhonda's heavily penciled-in eyebrows rose. "Maybe I'm just trying to look good. Bikini season is right around the corner, you know."

This made JJ laugh. "It's January," she snorted. "I'd say you've got several months before you need to even think about bikini season. Unless you're going to Australia to visit my mom."

"Nope." Rhonda shook her head. Her expression got serious. "Listen, can I ask you something?"

"Sure."

"Are you and Thor involved?"

It took JJ a few seconds. "Thor? Oh, you mean Eric. My tenant. No, we're not. Why?" She asked the question even though she already knew what the answer would be.

"Because he's superhot." Rhonda sighed. "And also seems nice, which is rare in a guy who looks like him. But I didn't want to poach on your territory, so if you want dibs, let me know. Before I go making a fool of myself."

Dibs. Dismayed and alarmed at the rush of jealousy that flooded through her at the other woman's comment, JJ looked down at her half-eaten cake. To give herself time to decide how to respond, she took a long drink of her rapidly cooling coffee.

Finally, she decided to just go with the truth. "I don't know, Rhonda. He hasn't been here all that long." She met her friend's bright blue eyes. "But as far as who he might want to date in the future, I'm thinking it should be up to him, not us."

"True." Rhonda grabbed JJ's cup and refilled it. "But you're drop-dead gorgeous and you get to live with him. You have the home field advantage. I'd have to put in some pretty intense effort to even get him to notice me."

JJ laughed. "Have you looked in the mirror lately, my friend? He might just be partial to petite, well-endowed blondes. He came here from California, after all."

"Did he?" Rhonda purred. "Then maybe I might have a chance."

Though it took an effort, JJ managed a casual shrug. "You might. As long as you can stand being around his baby."

Rhonda flashed her a horrified look. "I completely forgot about his kid. I know you mentioned it, but I must have blocked that from my mind." While she sulked, she shoveled a larger bite of her coffee cake into her mouth and washed it down with a gulp of coffee.

"Well, that's not going to work," Rhonda finally said. "Unless you'd be willing to watch the baby when he and I go out."

"Not a chance," JJ replied cheerfully. "You have to take one if you want the other. They're kind of a package deal."

"I'm not going to marry him," Rhonda protested. "Just have a little fun."

For whatever reason, JJ couldn't see Eric and Rhonda together. At all. Did that mean she wanted him for herself? She wasn't sure. "Good luck," she said.

Tilting her head, Rhonda searched her face. "You sound like you really mean it."

Again the twinge, which she disregarded more forcibly this time. "I just got out of a long-term relationship," she said. "And it wasn't a good one. I promise you, right now I'm not in the market for another."

She wondered why saying the words felt like a lie.

Staring out his front window at the slate-gray sky, Eric wondered if he'd made a mistake coming to Forestwood. Did the sun ever shine here? Coming from sunny California, he'd read up and thought he was prepared for a New York winter. Apparently not. He had to admit, once or twice the idea of returning to Cali had crossed his mind, but he'd made a plan and committed himself to it. He had to give this town and this new life a chance. Plus, of course, his son was a lot safer this far from Yolanda.

At least there hadn't been any more snowstorms. Yet. The entire town appeared to be collectively holding its breath. He hadn't seen JJ since the incident when he'd thought Garth had stopped breathing. Two days. He found he missed talking with her. While he wasn't sure if that was because he knew absolutely no one else here, he didn't feel the urge to go next door and hang out with Rhonda.

No, it was JJ he wanted.

As if they were friends. Though they barely knew each other, he considered her a friend. As long as he pushed back his attraction—which he had to, since he had to focus on new beginnings and raising Garth—he believed he and JJ could become friends. Nothing more. Which he surprisingly regretted.

Right now, he couldn't help but wonder if she missed his company as much as he missed hers. He decided he'd go up to her place later that day and see if she wanted to talk.

Later that afternoon, when a sharp knock sounded on his front door, his heart stuttered as he jumped to his feet. Maybe JJ had come to visit. But when he yanked open the door, instead of a petite redhead, a dour-faced middle-aged man stood on his doorstep. The long overcoat he wore, along with his short, military-style haircut, proclaimed him law enforcement.

"Frank DeLeon," the man said, holding out his hand. "Pack Protector."

Chapter 8

Stunned, Eric shook the other man's hand.

"I hope you don't mind me dropping in on you like this."

Actually, Eric minded. He minded a lot. If this guy could find him, then so could Yolanda. Not just that, but he couldn't help but worry about his son's safety. As long as the Protectors were floating around the slightest possibility that Yolanda might be Berserker, Garth would be in danger.

"What do you want?" He didn't bother to keep the hostility from his tone. "Surely you're not here because of Yolanda."

"May I come in?"

Reluctantly, Eric stepped aside. In the long run, it would be better to make this man his friend. "Sure. Take a seat. Can I get you something to drink?"

"No, thanks. I'm good." Rather than sitting, DeLeon stood, awkwardly twisting a sheet of paper in his hand.

"Listen, Yolanda took off from the hospital. We think she got into a car that exploded, though it's been extremely difficult to ID the body."

Eric stared. "What? A car explosion? I don't understand. How was she even well enough to leave the hospital? I thought she was in critical condition from her self-inflicted gunshot wound."

"She had help. Security footage showed another woman came and helped her. The hospital garage showed the two of them getting into a red Fiat. After that, we don't know where she went. Two hours later, the Fiat exploded on a construction lot three blocks west of the hospital. Only one body was recovered, so we aren't sure if it was Yolanda or the woman who helped her. Forensics is working on this as we speak."

Something in his tone didn't ring true. Or, Eric thought to himself, it was possible he was just being paranoid.

"Thanks for letting me know." Eric wasn't sure what else to say. "You came all the way out here just to tell me this?"

"No," DeLeon admitted, watching him closely. "There's more. A lot more. But I must say, you don't seem very grief stricken."

"I'm not. Shocked, yes. Sad, because she wasted her life and she was the mother of my son. But beyond that, there's nothing. Whatever we had between us died a long time ago."

"I see." But DeLeon's tone said he didn't.

Crossing his arms, Eric nodded. "Go ahead. You said there's more."

"In the course of this investigation, we've learned your ex was hanging around with a group of—and this is putting it mildly—deranged individuals."

"I'm not surprised," Eric said. "She always did like to party."

Now DeLeon dropped into the chair. Dragging his hand through his close-cropped hair, he sighed. "It's more than that, I'm afraid. These individuals have founded some sort of cult. The Bear Council as well as the Pack Protectors are extremely concerned with their activities. It seems they want to breed Berserkers. We're not sure why—their own little army, maybe? For whatever reason, this is why Yolanda was so focused on getting your son. She has convinced herself that the baby carries the necessary gene mutation to become Berserker."

As he tried to process DeLeon's words, Eric waited for the other man to laugh and admit he was joking. When he didn't, Eric swallowed hard. "That's crazy. Surely you're not serious."

"Unfortunately, I am." DeLeon grimaced. "Even worse, your ex-wife was one of the founders. There are reports— unsubstantiated as of yet—of her changing into a bear in front of some humans. Why, we aren't certain."

Immediately, Eric understood the rest of what the other man hadn't said. This was not only an extremely serious violation of shifter law, but dangerous. Doing something like this could bring everything crashing down, exposing millions of shape-shifters' lives, and sending humanity into chaos and war once they learned of the existence of others who previously had been only the stuff of legend and folktales.

"I see you understand the seriousness of this situation," DeLeon continued.

"I do. I don't see how it could get any worse."

DeLeon eyed him for a second. "It can and does. Even if the body we found was Yolanda's, there are many unknown people who belonged to her group. Your son's life is still in danger."

Dread shuddered up Eric's spine. "That's why I chose to move so far away. In fact, Jason was the only Protector who knew where to find me. I'm assuming since you came all the way here, there are others who know my location, as well."

"Yes. I'm sorry. And we still don't know what Jason revealed to Yolanda before she killed him. Even if he kept your secret, his cell phone disappeared after he was murdered. We used the GPS to track it, and it was found in a Dumpster near where the car exploded. We aren't sure what may or may not have been on it. End result? We're afraid some members of the group might be coming after your baby."

Over his dead body. As the words sunk in, Eric's bear roared to life inside him, furious in defense of his cub. For a split second or two, he allowed his beast to rage unchecked, while he tried to throttle the anger boiling up inside him.

Watching, DeLeon recoiled, as if Eric's inner struggle had become visible. "Are you all right, man?"

It took another couple seconds before Eric could push a single word past the hard lump of fury in his throat. "Actually, I'm not. No way in hell any of them are getting near my son."

"I concur, I concur." DeLeon hurriedly raised his hand. "I just wanted to make you aware of the situation. The Pack Protectors have graciously offered to extend to you our Witness Protection Program, even though you're not exactly a witness."

The words didn't register at first. "What do you mean?"

His expression earnest, DeLeon leaned forward. "You and your son can have our protection. We'll set you up a new identity somewhere far away. Those crazies won't have any way to find you."

"This *is* my new location." Eric shook his head firmly. "I just traveled all the way across the country, from one coast to another. I don't plan on going anywhere else. What kind of life would that be for Garth if I'm constantly on the run?"

"I understand." DeLeon's steady gaze was probably meant to be reassuring. "But we can't protect you here. If you come with us, we can. If you stay in Forestwood, you'll be on your own."

"Why?" Eric crossed his arms. "Why can't your people assign someone to watch over me here, just like they would if I went somewhere else? That doesn't even make sense."

Now DeLeon looked away. "I agree," he said quietly. "And I'm working very hard to convince my superiors. Right now, you have a fifty-fifty chance of them finding you. Please consider allowing us to use our vast network to help you and your son disappear."

Still stunned, upset and worried, Eric nodded. "I'll think about it," he said. The new life he'd so been looking forward to might not work out the way he'd hoped.

After her conversation with Rhonda, JJ kept expecting her neighbor to show up at Eric's. But Rhonda stayed home, at least for now. As for Eric, JJ hadn't seen him since he'd thought Garth had stopped breathing. She'd noticed a strange car parked in front of the house and assumed he'd had company, though she'd never seen the car leave or even who it belonged to. She wished she could ask him, but since it seemed he might be purposely avoiding her, she couldn't.

The strange thing was, she missed him far more than she should have missed a man she barely knew.

To be fair, she and Eric hadn't sought each other out. Not since the incident with little Garth. Though it had been only a couple days, it seemed longer. The few times she'd gone into town, she'd felt uncomfortable in her own stairway, rehearsing what she'd say if she ran into him.

Meanwhile, she set about enjoying the outdoors—and the winter weather—as much as she could.

Though the forecasters kept insisting they'd see another snowstorm soon, nothing happened. The already existing snow stuck around in the below-freezing temperatures, declining to melt. Of course, since it was January, it seemed the sun had taken a leave of absence, hiding behind a thick veil of gray clouds.

She, like probably everyone else in the area, had gotten to the point of completely disregarding the weather report, which seemed constantly to be all doom and gloom and unwarranted agitation. She was simply adopting a "wait and see" attitude. So when the next blizzard finally hit, she didn't see it coming.

Caught by surprise, she found her first warning was the howl of the wind. It woke her from a sound sleep and had her sitting up in her bed, disoriented. The wind whipped around the corners in a rage, testing the windows, seeking admission. She shivered, snuggling under the covers in search of sleep, even as the house stood stalwart, denying entrance.

In the morning she woke to the same sound. Exhilarated and thrilled, she hurried to the window and peered outside, seeing only wild swirls of wind-driven snow. Visibility was next to nothing, which meant whiteout conditions. When she turned on the TV, the weather forecaster was talking excitedly, calling this winter one for the record books. A travel advisory had been issued, and everyone was urged to hunker down until the storm passed.

Glad she'd stocked up at the grocery store the other day, JJ wondered if Eric had enough provisions. Because he was new to the East Coast, she couldn't help but worry, though she told herself it was none of her business.

Some might have felt trapped, housebound by the weather. Not JJ. She spent the day puttering around her little house, cleaning and baking, which filled her space with mouthwatering scents. She figured she'd take a few baked goods downstairs to Eric, as a sort of peace offering. Even in the city, none of Shawn's friends had been able to pass up her brownies.

The warm, cozy feeling she always got when snowed in relaxed her. After she'd cleaned the place and put some homemade stew in the Crock-Pot for dinner, she caught herself again wondering what Eric was up to. The brownies were wrapped up and ready to go. Briefly, JJ considered making a quick jog downstairs to deliver them, and inviting him to dinner while she was at it, but she wasn't sure how it would make her feel if he declined, so she didn't. She'd take him the baked goods when she could think of facing him without her heart thundering in her chest. Right now, humming as she puttered around, she just wanted to enjoy her space on this glorious snowy day.

She'd built a fire in her fireplace, opened her bottle of wine and gotten settled on the couch with a blanket, and a bowl of fresh-popped popcorn to tide her over until later. Now she was trying to decide on which of her favorite DVDs to watch, since cable TV had gone out. As she sorted through them, someone knocked on her door.

Someone. Right. Her heart kicked into a rapid beat. Because who else could it be but Eric? Even Rhonda wouldn't have attempted to slog through that mess outside to come over. Everyone else had been trapped in their homes by the storm.

And now her heart was racing again. Wishing she'd worn something other than the faded, yet oh-so-comfy sweatpants and old red sweatshirt—she could almost hear her mother lecturing her on how redheads didn't look good in red—she answered the door.

"Hey," Eric said, smiling. "The cable is out. There's no TV."

"Yeah." She managed to smile back, though she directed it at baby Garth, even though he appeared to be deeply asleep in his portable crib. "My neighbor told me that basically happens every time there's a really bad storm. Rain or snow."

"Really?" Peering past her, he eyed her setup on the couch. "What are you watching?"

"I don't know yet." She opened the door wider. "I'm going through my DVD collection now. You're welcome to join me if you'd like."

Part of her hoped he would. The other, more rational part figured he wouldn't.

Relief shone in his bright blue eyes. "I'd like that. I was feeling a bit trapped. I guess I've lived in sunny Cali for so long I'd forgotten what a beating it is when you're snowed in."

A beating? She'd never looked at it that way, but then she'd been told her entire life that she was unusual in her love of winter. Opening the door even wider, she gestured. "Come on in. I just made some popcorn. And we have wine."

Placing little Garth on the floor near but not too close to the fireplace, Eric grinned and held up a paper sack. Inside, she saw a six-pack. "I brought beer."

At her stunned look, he shrugged. "Just in case you were as bored as I am."

Which, she thought ruefully, put everything back into perspective.

"It smells amazing in here," he said. "Though I can't place that combination of scents."

Trying for nonchalance, she grinned anyway. "I made brownies and French bread and beef stew." She grabbed the plate of brownies she'd fixed for him. "I was going to take these down to you later."

Grinning back, he accepted. "Thank you. Chocolate is one of my weaknesses."

Funny how the room seemed to shrink with him in it.

"Did you have a lot of college coeds throwing themselves at you when you were a professor?" she asked, wincing as she realized she'd spoken her thoughts out loud.

One brow arched, he tilted his head. "That's kind of a strange question. Is it because of the Thor thing?"

Her shock must have shown on her face, because he laughed. "Your neighbor Rhonda called me that the other day. And I had a couple of friends who teased me relentlessly about looking like Thor. I honestly didn't see the resemblance. Until one of them took a photo of me when we were surfing and compared it to a movie poster of that guy that plays Thor."

Surfing? Her mouth watered at the image of him tanned and shirtless, riding a surfboard up into a giant wave.

"You mean Chris Hemsworth?" she asked, collecting her thoughts enough, hopefully, to sound coherent.

His grin widened. "Yeah, that's the guy. Don't tell me you think so, too."

"Of course not," she scoffed. "You're much shorter than him."

He laughed. "Touché."

Flustered but hoping she didn't show it, she gestured to the stack of DVDs she'd placed on her coffee table.

"Take a look through those and see if there's anything you'd like to see."

"I don't care. You pick." He pulled a beer out of his sack. "Is it okay if I put the rest of these in your fridge?"

"Sure."

Once he'd done that, he returned and took a seat on the couch. After a second's hesitation, she dropped down next to him, wineglass in hand. Careful to keep as much space between them as possible, she grabbed the DVDs. "Romantic comedy or action adventure?"

He took a drink of beer and laughed again. "What do you think? Of course, I'll watch whatever you want."

"Bruce Willis it is then."

Once she'd popped the DVD in, she put the popcorn in between them. "Help yourself."

"Thanks." He sniffed. "Did you already eat the stew? It smells amazing."

"Not yet. That's what's in the Crock-Pot. It's still cooking." About to ask him if he wanted to stay for dinner, she held off. She was curious to see if he'd mention what had happened the last time she'd seen him, and if he actually had been avoiding her.

"I love beef stew," he said. A hint if there ever was one.

She only ducked her head, pretending to be focused on the popcorn. "Maybe I can dish up a bowl to take home with you later."

"That would be great." If he minded or even noticed she hadn't invited him to eat dinner with her, he didn't comment. "Sorry I haven't been around much," he continued. "I've been trying to get situated. In addition, I've been dealing with the moving company, trying to find out why my stuff isn't here yet." He sighed. "The weather has been bad all through the middle of the country, too. The trip that they originally estimated would take a week is taking much longer."

Inserting the DVD in the player, she waited until it cued up and then hit the pause button. "Wow. That stinks. What all are you having brought here? If you need me to move some furniture out to make room for yours, let me know."

"I will." Taking another swig of his beer, he grinned at her. "Mainly, I'm worried about Garth's crib and my Camaro."

Perplexed, she eyed him over the rim of her wineglass. "You shipped a car?"

"Not just any car." His grin widened, captivating her. "A fully restored 1969 Camaro SS. My other baby."

"Oh." She wasn't sure what to say. She knew next to nothing about cars, though of course she was familiar with a Camaro. A new one, that is. She'd never understood what the big deal was with old cars.

At her expression, he laughed. "It's okay, I get it. I'll show you the car when she arrives, though. She's gorgeous. I plan to use her as an advertisement for my new business."

Relieved and slightly amused that he referred to the vehicle as a female, she nodded. "So you're opening up some kind of body shop, right?"

"A car customization shop." The happiness in his voice made her smile. "I've always wanted to do that. I've been saving for a few years. Now that I've sold everything I owned, I have enough cash for the startup."

"Isn't that kind of...specialized?"

He nodded. "It is."

"Forestwood is a really small town," she said cautiously. "Do you think there will be enough work here to keep you busy?"

He laughed before taking another drink of his beer. "Definitely. What you don't understand is that people will travel all over the country to find a good shop. All I need are the first few jobs. Once those are done, word will get out. People will flock to me."

Smiling back, she nodded. She liked his confidence. In fact, she liked a lot about him. "So you haven't been avoiding me?" Might as well clear things up.

"Avoiding you?" He couldn't be faking that level of astonishment. "Why would I do that?"

"Because of what you thought happened last time I watched your son." There. Best to have that finally out in the open. There was nothing she disliked more than playing games. Especially after living with the master game player, Shawn.

"Oh." Eric went quiet for a moment, as if considering her question. When he turned to fully face her, the serious expression he wore had her stomach tying up in a quick knot. "I panicked, JJ. Garth is everything to me. I wasn't blaming you or accusing you of doing anything."

"I didn't notice his lack of breathing," she stated. "If he really had stopped and I didn't see that, how could you not blame me?"

He frowned. "JJ, I'm not sure *I* would have noticed. Heck, I don't even know if he really stopped breathing or if it was just my overactive imagination kicking in. It's not like I expected you to do nothing but sit and stare at him."

She had to smile at that.

"Like right now," he continued. Gesturing toward his still-sleeping infant, he shook his head. "I'm here with him and you. I have no way to know if he is breathing unless I stick my finger under his nose, which would probably wake him up."

The humor in his tone coaxed a chuckle from her.

"Truce?" he asked, raising his beer can toward her wineglass.

"Okay." The clink of the glass and the metal made her smile again. "Are you ready to watch the movie?"

When he nodded, she hit the pause button again to unfreeze the DVD.

Überconscious of him next to her, she drank her wine faster than she usually did. When her glass was empty, she glanced sideways at him. He seemed to be totally engrossed in the film, one she'd watched a bazillion times. She could even recite the lines.

Getting up, she poured herself a second glass of wine and returned to the couch. He didn't even look away from the TV.

Reaching for popcorn at the exact same moment he did, JJ felt their fingers brush. She froze, resisting the urge to yank her hand away. What she really wanted to do was to hand-feed him, one kernel at a time.

Blinking, she looked down and took a deep breath. Where had that come from? She needed to get control of her crazy libido. Sleeping with her tenant would not be the smartest business move.

But oh, it would be fun. Possibly amazing, even. But a complication she definitely did not need.

As a distraction, she took another deep sip of wine.

"I'm sorry," he said, his voice a sensual rumble.

Forcing herself to look at him, she tilted her head. "For what?"

"Hogging the popcorn. Here." He pushed the bowl toward her. "There's still plenty left."

Eyes wide, she stared at him, unable to move. And then, just when she thought she'd be okay, she leaned in to get the popcorn and somehow winded up with her mouth pressed against his. Who moved first—did he kiss her or she him? Dizzy, she wondered if it even mattered.

She tasted the salty butter of the popcorn on his lips and then, when their tongues met, the yeasty flavor of his beer.

Kissing him was everything she'd ever imagined. And she had thought about it plenty.

When he deepened the kiss, she opened her mouth in welcome.

And then he broke away, pushing himself up off the sofa. "I'm so sorry," he muttered, dragging his hand through his unruly mane of hair. He wouldn't meet her gaze. She tried to speak and failed.

"That should never have happened," he said. "I can promise you, it won't happen again."

Chapter 9

Though JJ nodded in agreement, disappointment flooded her. She hadn't kissed anyone except Shawn in over three years. According to Shawn, no other man would ever find her desirable or want her, besides him. While she knew this was one of the numerous mental games he played on her, years of constant reaffirmation had made her wonder if it was the truth.

Which was no doubt why she took Eric's rejection way harder than she should. "It's okay," she managed to reply, her throat tight. He still kept his gaze averted, which hurt.

Pushing herself up, she walked to her kitchen and re-filled her wineglass. Then, staring at the half-empty bottle, she tried like hell not to cry.

"JJ." He'd followed her.

Fiercely wiping at her stinging eyes, she took a swig of her drink before turning to face him.

"Are you all right?" Gaze gentle, he crossed the space

between them and cupped her chin with his big hand. She suppressed a shiver at his touch.

"I'm fine." Lifting her chin, she tried for carefree, but ended up only sounding sad. Aware she had to come up with something to say that would fix that, she took a deep breath. "We need to stay friends, okay? Nothing more. No more kissing."

Surprise flashed across his handsome face. "I agree. I went through a horrible divorce."

"And I an awful breakup." Crud. She hadn't meant to reveal so much.

"You did?" He met her gaze, his own warm. "So that was the emotional 'stuff' you had to get away from. At least, I assume he wasn't here, in Forestwood?"

"No." She felt like she shouldn't talk about it, as if by doing so she could somehow draw the darkness of Shawn's energy into her home, her safe haven.

When she didn't elaborate, Eric sighed. "Friends, okay? I'm sorry for what happened. I like you and I really don't want to lose your friendship."

"Same here," she told him, telling herself that she spoke the truth. If some small part of her wanted more, then she'd have to deal with that, until it went away for good. And she had no doubt it would. Right now, she was bruised and wounded.

They watched the rest of the movie in a silence she hoped was companionable—at least to him—but as far as she was concerned felt really awkward. She'd get over this. She had to. Because Eric had made an excellent point. She liked him and wanted to be his friend. That, in her humble opinion, was much more rare and valuable than a fleeting romance.

After the movie finished, he stood and stretched. Though she tried, she couldn't manage to keep her gaze on his face. Instead, she watched him with a kind of mindless hunger. The kind that made her feel hot and bothered and completely out of sorts. She served him a big bowl of stew —enough for two meals—and broke off some French bread for him to enjoy with it.

Juggling everything, he carried the food downstairs and then came back for Garth. They said their good-nights and he picked up his still-slumbering infant and left.

After he'd gone, she caught herself staring at the door, imagining him going downstairs and enjoying the meal she'd prepared. She felt an instant of regret, wishing she'd invited him to eat with her, but knew she'd probably done the right thing. Especially since she couldn't help but imagine him later, climbing between the sheets of her aunt's antique queen-size bed, probably naked. Her blood heated at the thought.

More foolish daydreaming. She figured this was her way of trying to distract herself from worrying that her ex would somehow find her and cause trouble. Shaking her head at herself, she rinsed the empty popcorn bowl, turned out the lights and went to bed. Hopefully, the plows would come through early so Eric wouldn't feel trapped in his home.

The strident sound of her fire alarm jolted her out of a sound sleep and extremely pleasurable dream. Sitting up, she breathed in, immediately swallowing a lungful of smoke.

Not. A. Malfunction. Coughing, heart pounding, she picked up her phone and dialed 911, even as she moved toward the doorway. She wondered if they'd even be able to get to her house with all the snow. On the way out, she snagged her parka off the coatrack near the door.

Clattering down the stairs, she pounded on Eric's doorway. "Fire," she yelled, and pounded again.

He yanked the door open, clearly half-asleep. "What's going on?"

"Fire. Grab the baby and come on. There's a fire in my unit. We've got to get out."

He didn't waste time questioning her. Turning, he ran for his son. She stepped inside, found the baby's coat, as well as Eric's. When he reappeared, holding his sound-asleep infant, she urged him outside.

Eric saw her eyeing his son. "This kid can sleep through anything," he said wryly.

Once they were outside, she could see flames shooting from her upstairs windows. The sight chilled her even more than the brisk wind, making her want to weep.

They struggled to move through the deep snow, trying to get some distance from the house. On the front lawn, she helped Eric make sure Garth's coat was zipped and they put a knit cap on his little head before pulling up the hood and turning him to keep his face out of the wind. This startled him awake. Of course, he immediately wanted his bottle, which Eric didn't have, though he'd had the foresight to grab a pacifier, which seemed to satisfy him.

"This is awful," she said. "I called 911 but I don't know if they'll be able to make it, since the road isn't plowed." Amazing how things could change in the matter of a few hours. Before she'd gone to sleep, she'd wondered if she'd feel shy around Eric after the hot kisses they'd shared, but this crisis shoved all that out the window. Talk about perspective.

He eyed her and then squinted out toward the street. "It looks like the plow might have come through earlier. Maybe when we were watching the movie. There are really high snowdrifts on the other side."

Trying to hide her agitation, she tromped through the snow to see. "Thank goodness," she told him when she returned. "I hope they hurry." She pointed to the flames. "It appears to be getting more intense. I don't want the entire house to burn down."

As she finished speaking, she heard the sirens. "I hope they can put the fire out in time." She felt like chewing her nails, a habit she'd cured herself of shortly after moving here. Her thick gloves helped with that, too.

"They will. It'll be fine. Let's move a little farther away, just to be safe. Even though the fire is upstairs, you never know if it'll burn through the floor or something. Let's go. Just to be safe," he repeated.

He had a point. Huddled together, they all moved closer to Rhonda's house, hoping the structure would provide some shelter from the bitterly cold wind. From there, JJ could see flames were now shooting from the attic area above her unit. It looked like her entire floor and above might be a total loss.

The fire engine pulled up, lights flashing. The siren gave one final whoop before the driver cut it off. A police car came around the corner, fishtailing as it took the slippery turn too fast. The officer at the wheel parked right behind the fire truck.

"I'm surprised they didn't send an ambulance," Eric remarked. "At home when the fire department comes, they always send a paramedic, too."

"We only have one," JJ told him. "They aren't going to tie it up unless they know for sure it's needed." Though she stood perfectly still, her insides jumped and jangled. How could this have happened, just when she'd begun to feel settled and happy? "They have to put this fire out," she whispered. "I can't lose my home."

Instead of answering, Eric squeezed her shoulder.

Over the next hour, everything seemed to happen in slow motion, while she watched as if from a distance. It felt like someone else's nightmare. Using a huge hose, they doused her pretty little house with water, firemen in yellow suits heading inside. She winced when she heard the sound of an ax hitting wood. And she prayed silently, head bowed, as hard as she'd prayed the last time Shawn had come home drunk and mean. There had been no divine interference then and she didn't really expect it now.

As she swayed from exhaustion, barely containing her panic, Eric put his arm around her. He'd shifted little Garth to against his chest and under his coat. "It's all going to be all right," he said. "I promise."

"Is it?" Turning on him, unable to control her shivering, which wasn't from the cold, she gave in and let herself collapse against his strong chest right next to his son.

"I'm wondering if you should wake Rhonda," he said. "Get inside and warm up."

She started to shake her head, but he continued. "I'll go with you. I'm worried about little Garth. Even though he's bundled up, he's shivering."

Stunned, JJ raised her head to check on the baby. Wide-awake, he watched her from Eric's chest. His bright blue eyes, so similar to Eric's, were wide-open. He should have been snug as a bug in his little hooded parka, but his cheeks were rosy from the cold.

Instantly contrite, she nodded. "Oh, my gosh. I'm so sorry, I didn't even think. You and Garth need to go inside. I can't. I've got to see what happens with my house. I'll go with you and then come back. Follow me."

The sidewalks weren't shoveled, either. Crossing the remaining distance between her house and Rhonda's was slow going and surprisingly treacherous. Several times she paused, looking back over her shoulder to make sure Eric and Garth were behind her. She was glad he allowed her to go first, though normally he would have been the one to forge the path, since he was taller and larger. But she figured he was glad to use this to distract her. As if anything could. Once she'd delivered him to Rhonda, she planned to go right back to her own house.

Finally, they reached the wooden steps leading up to Rhonda's porch. The house remained silent and dark. It seemed really odd that Rhonda hadn't come outside to check out the commotion.

JJ climbed onto the first step and nearly wiped out. Only a quick grab for the railing kept her from landing on her behind. "Careful," she told Eric. "It's black ice."

When they all were finally up on the porch, JJ pressed Rhonda's doorbell and waited. She heard the chimes echo inside. Nothing. After a few seconds, she rang it again. Still nothing.

"This isn't like her," she told Eric. "It's weird."

"Try knocking."

So she knocked, though with gloves on the sound was muted. Again, no response.

"Maybe she's not home," Eric said, hunched against the cold.

"Maybe not. I thought it was strange when she didn't come out once the fire truck got here." But JJ still couldn't shake a nagging worry. "I'm going to call her just to make sure."

"It's two o'clock in the morning," Eric reminded her. "If she's out of town, you'll wake her and probably scare the hell out of her."

He was right. She nodded, sliding her phone back into her rear pocket. She'd have to wait until a decent hour to check on her friend. Even though she knew if Rhonda had been planning to go out of town, she would have asked JJ to keep an eye on her place.

Meanwhile, the water spray the firefighters had sent

had frozen, making huge rivers of ice on the side of her house. As far as she could tell, the fire appeared to be out. A heavy lump of worry settled in her stomach.

Again moving together, they trudged back through the snow.

"I'm worried about the baby," she said. "I'm going to ask one of the firemen if you and Garth can sit in the cab of their truck. It's bound to be warmer."

"Wait." He grabbed her arm as she turned to go do exactly that. "What about you? You must be cold, too."

"I'll be fine," she said, gently pulling herself free. The dull chill that had settled in her bones had little to do with the temperature. "Until they tell me the fire is completely out, I'm not letting my house out of my sight. This is all I have in the world, my safe haven. I can't lose it. I simply can't."

Eric felt strange taking refuge in the warmth of the fire engine cab while JJ braved it out in the cold. He supposed he could go get his SUV and start that, but he really didn't want to leave the scene just yet. Plus he had his son to think of, and even though leaving a woman alone outside might not be gentlemanly or chivalrous, he was doing what was best for his baby.

Or so he repeatedly told himself, while he fidgeted inside the warm truck.

Finally, he couldn't take it any longer. Garth had fallen asleep, so Eric left him there, going to stand outside where he could see everything, but close to the door just in case.

JJ caught sight of him and hurried over.

"What's the word?" he asked.

"They don't think there was any structural damage." JJ sounded both relieved and anxious. "Lots of smoke and water damage, though." Her voice wavered and she looked down.

He realized she was fighting to keep from crying. Balling up his hands into fists to keep from touching her, he nodded. "What about the downstairs unit? My place."

The dullness in her gaze as she looked at him told him she was operating on the last reserve of her waning strength. "I didn't think to ask," she finally admitted. "Since the fire didn't spread beyond the second floor…" Heaving a sigh, she blinked. "Let me go back and find the guy who said he was in charge." She hurried off.

When she returned a few minutes later, he saw the answer in her eyes. "Looks like we're both going to have to find a new place to stay for a little while." Panic flashed across her expression before she covered her face with her gloved hands. "I don't know what I'm going to do. I'm so sorry. I know you didn't plan on this."

"None of us did." Acting instinctively, he reached for her and pulled her close in a hug. "I'm sure Rhonda will let you stay with her," he said, hoping to reassure her. She smelled like smoke and water, completely different from her usual lavender scent.

"Maybe. I don't actually know her all that well." JJ looked up at him, frowning. "I wonder if she'd consider allowing you and Garth there, too. Even though she doesn't like babies, this is kind of an emergency."

"Kind of?" he teased, realizing he'd do just about anything to wipe the worry and stress out of her gaze. "Don't worry. Everything will work out."

Though her nod came slowly, at least she agreed. "Thank goodness your furniture hasn't arrived yet. I'd feel terrible if it had gotten damaged in the fire."

"It wasn't your fault," he said, then reconsidered. "Was it? Do they have any idea what caused the fire?"

"They're thinking an electrical short. Nothing that I did. Even though I had built a fire in the fireplace, that wasn't where the other fire originated." Shoulders slumped, she stepped away, out of his arms. He let her go.

Someone called to her and she hurried off without a backward glance.

Though standing around doing nothing went against his nature, there wasn't any way Eric could get closer to the hub of activity without endangering his son. So he stayed put, watching from a distance, and wishing he could offer more assurances and comfort to JJ. While he didn't know much about her personal circumstances, she didn't appear to have a good support system or many resources she could fall back on, being new in town. Of course, he was in a similar situation himself.

Wow. Just wow. When he'd planned on starting over, beginning a new life, he hadn't imagined anything like this. But he'd be okay, even if he had to tap into some of his savings to pay for another place to live.

It appeared that the fire department was wrapping things up. Eric checked on Garth, who, amazingly, continued to sleep. When one of the sooty firefighters came by, Eric questioned him. "How bad is the damage?" he asked.

The man shrugged, dragging his arm across his sooty face. "Lots of smoke and water damage. We had to cut a couple holes in the walls to check for flames. Maybe one or two in the roof, as well. Some of the windows were broken."

Eric nodded. "Is it safe to go inside?"

"Actually, we'd prefer you didn't."

"I have a three-month-old son." Gesturing at the truck cab, Eric frowned. "We lived in the downstairs unit. I just need to get his formula and diapers. Who do I need to talk to in order to get permission to do that?" Getting permission was only a formality. If they refused, Eric would simply wait until they left to go inside and grab his things.

"Talk to the chief." The firefighter pointed at another man, who was heading their way. "Good luck."

The chief listened while Eric repeated his request. "Fine," he said. "You can go. But only to grab what you absolutely need and get out. And you'll need to do it quickly. The soot and dirty water might make you sick. Don't eat or drink anything. Oh, and you'll need a flashlight. We had to cut the utilities for safety. Too much chance of gas leaks or electric shorts that could have endangered my men or you. Do not attempt to turn them back on yourself."

Eric nodded. "When can we get a copy of the fire report?"

"It'll be ready in a few days. Just stop by the fire marshal's office."

"And after that?"

"You'll need to contact your insurance agent." The man peered at Eric. "You did have insurance, right?"

Since he could only assume so, Eric nodded. "Right. I mean, who doesn't have insurance?"

"Exactly. Once the insurance company comes out and takes a look, they'll hire a company to come in and do cleanup. I think they'll also make any and all repairs needed."

The firefighter caught sight of Garth. "Hey, is that your kid?"

"Yes. I put him in there to keep him out of the cold."

The man eyed him. "Good thinking. Listen, do you and your wife have someplace to go?"

"Oh, she's…" Eric swallowed. "I'm sure we'll figure something out," he said instead.

"Glad to hear it. If not, you can always contact the Red Cross or the Salvation Army. Now if you don't mind grabbing your baby, we've got to get back to the firehouse."

After retrieving Garth, Eric and JJ stood side by side

and watched the fire engine pull away, the police car right behind it. A few of the neighbors—though not many, since the icy night wind still blew—had come out on their front porches to watch. One by one, they went inside. Aside from the lingering scent of charred wood and smoke, the neighborhood returned to the way it had been.

Chapter 10

"From this direction, the house still looks the same," JJ mused, her voice wobbly again. Eric put his arm around her, offering support. Though initially she stiffened, a second later she relaxed and leaned against him.

"They said we can go inside and get out what we need," he told her, repeating what the chief had said.

"Good." She shook her head. "I don't mind helping you, since we can't go to the top floor. I doubt anything of mine is going to be usable, anyway."

Keeping his son's carrier close again, Eric started for the front door. Garth had opened his eyes and appeared to be looking around, but hadn't started crying yet. They needed to get formula and diapers, as well as multiple changes of clothing.

When he realized JJ wasn't following, he stopped. "Aren't you coming?"

Still standing in the same place, she cut her gaze from

him to the house. Finally, she swallowed hard. "I guess so. It's silly, but I'm afraid to see what's happened to the inside."

"Come on." He held out his free hand. "You might as well. You've got to face it eventually."

She searched his face and finally nodded. "You're right," she said, sliding her gloved fingers around his. He liked the way it felt, much more than he should have.

"Do you have a flashlight?" he asked as they climbed up on the porch. "They had to cut the power."

"I keep one in my kitchen, for when the electricity goes out. But that's upstairs."

Inside, the dank smoke smell was even worse. Eric repeated what the firefighter had said.

"So we have to get what you need and get out?" she asked. "And then what? Where can we go?"

"We'll figure that out," he assured her. "Right now, let's grab what we can. Once we're in my car, if you can point me to a motel, we'll get a room so we can all get some rest."

She opened her mouth and then closed it. "Okay," she finally said. "As long as we're here, I want to check out the damage upstairs. I'll meet you back here in ten minutes."

"I'm not sure it's safe," he told her.

"I'm just going to open my front door and peek inside. I might as well see how bad it is."

He hated letting her go upstairs alone, but there was no way he was taking Garth up there. "Are you sure you really need to? I can buy you some clothes or makeup or whatever else you need."

"It's okay," she said quietly. "I'll be careful. See you in the foyer in ten minutes." She paused. "Do you have a flashlight or do you need to borrow mine?"

"I've got one." He'd found one inside the drawer of a

small curio cabinet near the door. All it had needed was new batteries and it worked perfectly.

Watching her as she climbed the stairs, he finally shook his head, picked up Garth's carrier and headed into his own space to gather what he needed. Inside his place, there was a lot of water damage and he thought maybe some smoke damage, too, though it was hard to tell, using the small beam of his flashlight.

One half-full box of diapers and a carton of formula, plus clothes for both himself and the baby. Unfortunately, he couldn't carry all this and Garth, too, so Eric moved as much as he could to just outside his front door. He'd get it in the car once he could ask JJ to keep an eye on Garth.

When he returned to the foyer, she was already waiting. She agreed to watch Garth in the SUV, so once he'd loaded the baby into his infant carrier and her duffel bag into the back, he went inside for his things.

She directed him to a small motel a few miles away. When they pulled up shortly after 4:00 a.m., he parked and turned to her. "I'm going to get us a room, okay?"

"I'll need my own," she told him, clearly exhausted. "I can pay."

"What if we have to stay here for a few days?" he asked. "Or even longer. I'm not trying to be nosy, but I don't know your financial situation."

"It's…fluid," she said, flashing him a quick, embarrassed smile. "Cash poor, right now. I've got a bit in savings, but I'll need some of it to meet the deductible on my policy. I'm going to call my insurance company in the morning," she continued, lifting her chin bravely. "After I get some rest, I'll figure out where exactly I'm going to live until everything is repaired. Hopefully, Rhonda will allow me to bunk on her couch or in her guest bedroom for a few weeks."

He nodded. "Sounds like a plan."

"But what about you? What will you do if this turns out to be some long, drawn-out thing?"

"I've been checking out some buildings online for my business. I'd planned to meet with a Realtor soon, so I'll do that. Maybe I can find one with a small apartment above the garage. That's not ideal for the long term, because I have to keep a clear separation between home and work, but maybe it'll do for now. At least until the house is repaired."

"Whew." A ghost of a smile flitted across her lips. "I was worried you'd say you and Garth were going back to California."

Surprised—and a bit touched that she even cared—he grimaced. "There's nothing back there for me."

After he'd paid the deposit and received a room key, he reconsidered. Maybe he *should* get her a separate room. But tonight, they were both so tired that all they wanted to do was sleep—if Garth would let them. Eric decided for tonight they'd share. If she wanted to change things up in the morning, he'd deal with it then. Most likely, she'd get ahold of her friend next door and go stay there.

Once they were inside the small room, she dropped her duffel on a bed and vanished into the bathroom. He changed Garth, thankful that he'd bathed him before he'd gone to bed, and warmed up some formula using the little hotplate he'd thought to bring along.

Once his son had been fed and burped, Eric carried him around the room, swaying softly and singing an old Norwegian lullaby he remembered his grandmother singing to his younger brother. They'd been born in the United States, but after their father's disappearance, their mother had taken both her sons to Norway and left them with her own mother, who'd raised them. Despite their young age—

Eric had been three and Lars just eighteen months—they hadn't seen or heard from their mom again until they were teenagers. Then, both parents had shown up at their doorway and moved them all to California. It had been difficult for them to readjust to a family they'd never known, but they'd managed. Now, Eric could see why his parents had done what they did. What he couldn't understand was why, a day after Lars had turned eighteen, both Mom and Dad had vanished again. This time, they'd never come back.

Another reason Eric would never leave his son.

Once little Garth had fallen asleep, Eric set him in his portable crib—thank God for that thing—and stripped down to his boxers before climbing in between the sheets. He planned to only rest his eyes until JJ returned. He figured they'd talk a little and then they'd both catch some much-needed sleep.

After washing her face and hands, JJ grimaced at her image in the bathroom mirror. She felt grimy all over and her hair stank of smoke. Yawning, she knew she should take a quick shower, but she wasn't sure how much longer her wobbly legs would hold her upright. It'd have to wait until she got some sleep.

A sound from the other room... She strained to hear. When she realized what it was, she smiled. It sounded like Eric was singing some sort of lullaby to his son. When he stopped a moment later, she figured the baby had most likely fallen asleep.

Speaking of sleep. All she had left to do was brush her teeth and she could do the same.

When she'd finished, she opened the door slowly and quietly, not wanting to wake Garth. To her surprise, she saw Eric had climbed into one of the beds and dozed off.

This lessened the awkwardness somehow. Tiptoeing

to the other bed, she turned out the light and pulled back the covers. About to get in between her sheets, still fully clothed, she hesitated. Her clothes smelled like smoke and soot. What about Eric? Had he stripped before getting into his bed? Peering over there, she judged by the little pile of clothes on the floor that he had.

Holding her breath and hoping he didn't wake, she hurriedly stripped down to her bra and panties. Then, at the last moment, she removed her bra. Much better. Once she'd gotten decently covered, she breathed a sigh of relief. And then found herself imagining his buff body naked against the sheets.

Ah, good thing she was so exhausted. Too tired to do more than briefly picture waking up next to him, she closed her eyes and willed herself to fall asleep.

An infant's cries startled her awake. She sat bolt upright, blinking. Sunlight sneaking from the sides of the curtains brought some light into the room. Enough to see Eric, wearing nothing but a pair of plaid boxer shorts, swinging his muscular legs over the side of his bed as he hurried to attend to his son.

She couldn't stop staring. She slid back under her sheets and watched through her eyelashes, hoping he'd think she still slept.

Muscles she hadn't even realized he possessed rippled along his back as he bent over to pick up the baby. The whole broad-shoulders-narrow-waist thing worked for him, too. Her entire body tingled.

More than that—watching the tenderness with which he treated his son, she wanted to melt. In her experience, men like him were rare. Shawn had cared about only his job and his status and himself. Oh, he'd known how badly she wanted her own family, and he'd dangled this possibility like a carrot in front of a starving rabbit. But after a while she'd come to realize he'd never meant a word of it. He'd made no secret of the way he despised children. The idea of him ever becoming a father was frightening.

The same way marrying him would have been.

Eric coughed, drawing her attention back to him. "Are you going to get up or just lie there and pretend to be sleeping?" he asked, his voice teasing.

She blushed—all over. "I was waiting for you to finish up first," she said, which wasn't entirely untrue. "I didn't want to hog the bathroom if you needed to use it."

"Oh, go ahead. I was up earlier and it's going to be a little while before I get done taking care of Garth."

Sitting up, she blinked and tugged the covers back to her chin. She'd completely forgotten she'd stripped down to her panties and nothing else.

Keeping the sheet wrapped tightly around her, she reached down and fumbled around on the floor until she'd located her bra and clothing. When she looked up, she saw Eric watching her with an amused expression.

"It's about to get even funnier," she told him, as she yanked the covers up and over her, making as big a tent as she could so she could dress.

"There." Triumphant, she threw back the covers and got up—only to realize she had her shirt on inside out and backward. At least she was covered. She marched off to the bathroom, knowing a hot shower would do wonders toward making her feel human again.

Later, she made some phone calls and watched the baby while Eric showered. He'd given his son a sponge bath earlier, which made little Garth all giggles. JJ had melted watching this, and had to resist the urge to ask if she could help.

Her insurance agent had already heard about the fire. He promised to put a rush on processing a claim, adding that he'd make sure and have someone out there quickly to take a look.

When Eric emerged from the bathroom, his hair still damp, he suggested they make a stop at the pancake house for breakfast and then check out her place. Though part of her dreaded seeing the damage in the stark light of day, she knew she needed to, so she agreed.

Breakfast was lovely, the three of them in a back booth, while JJ struggled to remind herself this wasn't her family, even if the waitress persisted in thinking they were. But this scene reminded her of what she'd wanted for so long. Shawn hadn't succeeded in killing that dream for her and she still had hope that someday she'd have a husband and child of her own. For now, she had too much reality to deal with.

The instant they pulled up in front of her house, her heart caught in her throat. Last night, after the firefighters and police had left, she'd seen the place only in darkness. Now, in the unforgiving light of day, she saw the soot staining the formerly white wood, the busted-out windows and the long, spiky icicles that had formed where the water had drained. Her pretty little house looked awful. Damaged and deserted, like something after a war.

"Oh," she said. Only it came out like something else entirely, a low, guttural sound as if from an animal in pain.

Eric looked at her. "It'll be okay, I promise. Once your insurance company gets started, they'll have this place looking as good as new."

Blinking back tears, she nodded. "My agent says the company will send a claims adjuster out here sometime this week. They also need to review the fire report. They told me I'd need to find another place to live for at least thirty days." Her voice broke and she took a deep breath, determined to steady it. "He also said it could even be longer."

Eric squeezed her shoulder. "I'm sorry. Hopefully, it won't be. Come on, let's go take a look. We just need to be very careful. At least now that it's not dark, we can find our way around, even without electricity."

"I'm worried about the pipes freezing," she said, as she pushed open the car door and stepped outside. She waited, shivering in the chilly air despite her warm jacket, while Eric unbuckled Garth's carrier. He'd dressed his son warmly, from a little knit cap to matching mittens and boots.

As she watched, the baby caught sight of her and grinned. Her heart stuttered in her chest. "He's so adorable," she said, unable to help herself.

"Thanks." Eric looked at her, his expression curious. "Are you okay with going inside?"

"Are you?" she countered. "I don't want to endanger Garth."

"I talked to the fire captain again this morning. The building is structurally safe and, since the utilities are still turned off, there's no danger from a gas leak or anything. He said it would be fine to go inside."

She shot Eric a cross look. "Why didn't you mention this to me until now?"

He shrugged, glancing at her. "Sorry. I figured you probably called, also. I heard you on the phone earlier."

"With my insurance company." She sighed. "I don't mean to be snippy. I apologize. This is very stressful. I didn't mean to take it out on you. I'm glad you called. Thank you."

"You're welcome." He hefted his son's carrier. "Come on. Let's go inside."

Once they entered, she stood in the foyer, undecided where to go first. "Let's check out your place before we see mine. That way I'll have some warning what to expect."

Since his would be in better shape than hers, she figured she could build up to the worst.

She waited just inside his living room with baby Garth while Eric went from room to room, assessing the damage. She imagined he was really grateful his personal belongings and furniture had been delayed. All this stuff had belonged to an old lady and wouldn't be even close to his taste.

Or hers, for that matter. But JJ had fled the city and her bad relationship with limited funds, and she'd been grateful for the gift of the house being fully furnished. She'd intended to use everything for as long as she could and gradually replace one item at a time.

Now, hopefully, the insurance would pay out enough for her to replace all the damaged furniture at once.

"Hey, there." Eric reappeared, carrying a large, black trash bag. "I grabbed some more clothes for both me and Garth. I think once I wash them, I can get the smoke smell out."

"Great." She couldn't help but glance apprehensively at the stairs.

Following her gaze with his own, he set his bag down near the door and picked up Garth. "Are you ready to go up?"

After taking a deep breath, she nodded. "As ready as I'm ever going to be, I guess."

"After you." He made a sweeping gesture with his free hand.

As she stared at him, there in the dim light of the sooty foyer, he looked dangerous for a moment. And unbelievably sexy.

Of course, she was only looking for a distraction. Something to take her mind off the mess her home would be in the cold light of day.

Chapter 11

As JJ opened her front door, the first thing that hit her was the smell. Smoke and soot and…ice. Shocked, she saw that her window had been broken and the cold outside air chilled the room.

"My pipes," she said, unable to take the steps that would carry her to the sink to open the cupboard doors.

Eric's hand came down on her shoulder, solid and reassuring. "It should be okay. They turned off the water when they cut the utilities."

Some of the tightness in her chest eased, though she fought the urge to lean into his touch. Slowly, she turned to look at her things. They were ruined. Every single item. Soot stained, water damaged… She didn't see how any amount of cleaning would be able to restore them. Her poor aunt would be turning over in her grave if she saw.

JJ felt as if she were wandering through the landscape of a bad dream. She went into her bedroom and stood, staring at the one piece of antique furniture she'd truly loved—the massive, four-poster bed.

Inching closer, she held her breath. While the comforter—and most likely the mattress—appeared unredeemable, she didn't see any real damage to the wood itself.

"I think the bed frame itself is all right," she breathed.

"I agree. And more stuff is probably salvageable than you think. They have restoration companies that specialize in this type of thing."

Numb, she headed toward her closet.

"Here. I got another trash bag so you could grab some more clothes."

Accepting it, she murmured a thank-you. She braced herself and slid the closet door open. To her surprise, all her clothing appeared untouched.

"Yeah, that's what I thought," Eric said, at her comment. "But smell it."

When she did, the acrid odor made her sneeze. "I wonder if any amount of washing will get that smell out."

"I don't know. All we can do is try."

Once she'd finished, she carried her bag down to the foyer. Her home, once cheery and slightly fussy, now looked grim and sad.

"At least no one was hurt," Eric said, almost as if he read her mind.

"True." She tried hard to push away the bleak feeling that had settled over her. "I'm sure as soon as the adjuster approves my claim and repairs are made, this place will look good as new."

She wasn't sure she really believed it.

Needing something to distract her, JJ glanced at the house next door. "I'm going to check in on Rhonda again," she said. "She must be out of town. There's no way she wouldn't have been out here already."

Sure enough, the ringing doorbell went unanswered, even though she could hear the chimes echoing inside the house.

"Are you going to call her?" Eric asked, when she got back to his SUV.

"Yep." She already had her phone out. Punching the icon for Rhonda, she listened while the phone rang and rang. As it flipped over to voice mail, she left a quick and terse message, asking her friend to call her back.

"No luck?"

"Nope." JJ slid her phone back into her purse.

"That stinks." He grimaced. "Now there's even more bad news. The radio weather report says we're going to get another snowstorm. Come on, now. Are they serious? Does it ever end?"

Shaking her head, JJ shrugged. "I'm so sorry. This time, I'm with you. Normally, I love the snow. It always feels like a second chance. A new beginning. But there's too much going on. Right now I really could use a break, until my house is livable again."

"I like that," Eric said. "I never thought about snow that way before. A second chance. A new beginning. Which we all need."

"True. Just not right now. After my house is repaired and I can enjoy watching the snow fall from my living room, with a fire roaring in the fireplace, yes." She blinked, surprised to realize she was on the verge of tears.

"There's a lot of snow," he continued. "I take it this weather is worse than normal? The way the TV forecasters are acting, it's like the Armageddon of snow this winter."

"They're always like that. The weather people, I mean. Some years are worse than others. I imagine coming from sunny California, this must seem awful."

"No," he said thoughtfully, after a moment. "Not awful.

Just different. It's been a long time since I lived in Norway, as a child. I remember the winters were long and snowy there, too."

Just then, a taxi pulled up, stopping at Rhonda's. Her neighbor emerged, gaping at JJ's house. She flung a few bills at the cab driver and ordered him to leave her luggage on the street by the mountain of snow on the curb. Rushing over, she enveloped JJ in a big hug.

"Oh, my gosh, what happened?"

Once she'd pulled herself free, JJ explained. "They still don't know how it started. As soon as my insurance adjuster gets out here, I can get started on making repairs."

"Of all the times for me to go to the city! I can't believe I wasn't here." Rhonda's gaze drifted from the house to JJ and past, settling on Eric. "Were both of you impacted?"

Slowly, Eric nodded. "Since the fire was upstairs, JJ's place got the worst of it. But mine still has smoke and water damage."

"Surely you're not staying there?" Hand to her throat, Rhonda looked from one to the other.

This time JJ answered. "No. The firefighters cut the utilities, so there's no electricity or heat. We're staying at the Innbrook Motel on Sixth Street."

"Well, go pack up and check out. You both can stay at my house. I have plenty of room."

Waving his chubby fists, Garth made a warbling sound, drawing her attention. A brief frown clouded her bright blue eyes, but a second later it cleared and she smiled again. "And the baby, too, of course."

Though this was what she'd hoped for in the beginning, now JJ hesitated. Something about the way Rhonda looked at Eric, as though she could eat him up for lunch, bothered her.

Telling herself to stop being ridiculous, JJ took a deep

breath. "Are you sure? It might be a few weeks or more, depending on how much work needs to be done."

"I'm positive." Beaming brightly, Rhonda turned on her heel and went to collect her bags. "Give me an hour to get everything ready and the beds made up. I can't tell you how happy I am to have company."

They both stared after her as she disappeared inside her house.

Eric had a bad feeling. For no good reason, but still… It sat on his shoulders like a heavy weight. Though he hadn't always, he was beginning to learn to trust his gut instincts. "I'm not sure about this," he said, turning to face JJ. "You go ahead and stay with your neighbor. As for me, I think I'd rather just remain in the motel."

"Seriously?" One corner of JJ's mouth quirked in amusement. "You're frightened of a tiny blonde woman?"

He had to chuckle at her choice of words. But then again, maybe she wasn't far off. "I wouldn't say frightened. Just…uncomfortable."

"Whatever." Plainly, she didn't believe him. "Now we just have to kill an hour. Maybe I should go back to the hotel and pack up my things."

He glanced at his watch, considering. "Come with me and look at commercial buildings for rent," he suggested, smiling at her startled expression. "It's something to take your mind off all this. I need to find somewhere to store my furniture. It should be here any day. And to be honest, I could use a second set of eyes."

"Don't you have a Realtor?"

"I do." He couldn't help but grimace. "His name is Greg Stenorio. I'm supposed to meet him in ten minutes. He's kind of pushy."

"I hate that."

"I do, too, but I have to deal with him. I'm meeting him downtown, so I need to get going. You're welcome to come."

She eyed little Garth, wide-awake and playing with his colored keys. "I guess I could. I can keep an eye on the baby while you look around the various places."

More pleased than he wanted to admit—or reveal—he nodded. "After we're done, I'll buy you lunch."

"You have a deal." Her smile stole his breath. "And while we eat, we can talk about why you really don't want to stay with me at Rhonda's."

He couldn't help but grin. "You're almost as pushy as my Realtor. The two of you should get along great."

In fact, once the real estate agent got a good look at JJ, with her lush curves, long mane of red hair and emerald eyes, he barely spared a glance for Eric. Normally, Eric would have found this amusing, but the quick, panicked looks JJ kept sending his way signaled that she was uncomfortable with the unwanted attention.

Greg wanted to use his car, but Eric didn't want to transfer the car seat, so insisted they go in his SUV. Greg wanted to ride in the back seat with JJ and the baby, despite her repeated declinations. Eric settled the issue by reminding the other man he was the client and would need help with directions.

Luckily, the Realtor took the hint.

They had three places lined up to look at, but the instant they pulled up in front of the first, Eric knew this was the one. In an older, yet restored part of town, the building had already been used as a body shop. It had been shut down when the owner died in a freak car accident, according to Greg. Even the signs remained.

"You could even keep the name if you wanted," he

pointed out. "I'm sure there's some legal stuff you'd have to do, but it would save you a fortune on signs."

Eric didn't bother to tell the other man he'd use his own name, one he'd imagined back when he was a kid and had dreamed of building custom cars. Before he'd become a college professor, of all things, and relegated that dream to "someday."

After Garth's birth, he'd decided to make "someday" now.

"I want to make an offer on this one," he said, after they'd toured the inside. Both Greg and JJ looked at him in surprise.

"Let's at least take a look at the other two," the agent advised. "You never know."

"He's right," JJ interjected, coming up with Garth to stand next to him. "After you see the others, if you still want this one, then you'll know for sure."

He already did, but their logic seemed inescapable.

After viewing the other two places—one still operating as an oil change business and the other some sort of warehouse, Eric knew his first instinct had been correct.

"And I'll need to work out a lease agreement with them so I can store some belongings before closing," he added, after hammering out the terms of his offer with the Realtor.

Greg, who'd been staring at JJ, returned his attention to Eric and nodded. "I'll get right on it," he said. "I should have an answer by the end of the week."

"Perfect."

"Listen, JJ?" Greg touched her lower back, causing her to start. Almost flinch, Eric thought, concerned.

"Would you like to have dinner with me sometime?" the agent asked, the confidence in his tone letting her know he expected her answer to be yes.

"I'm sorry, but I'm not interested." Though she gave

Greg a polite smile, Eric couldn't help but notice the flash of panic in her green eyes.

The Realtor opened his mouth, apparently intending to press his point, but Eric's hand on his shoulder stopped him. "She's with me," he said, surprising himself. And JJ, too, if her startled look was any indication.

"What?" The Realtor's face grew mottled. "Why didn't you say so?"

"Why would I have to?" Eric asked. "She and I met you together. She's made it clear she's not interested. And I'll be honest, your behavior is making me wonder if I need to find someone else to handle this real estate transaction."

Jaw tight, Greg shook his head. "My apologies." His stiff, formal tone let them both know he wasn't happy.

Eric didn't really care. He'd hired the guy to help him find a shop. Once that was accomplished, Greg could collect his commission and move on.

"Let's head to my office and write up the offer," Greg suggested, a patently false smile on his face. "It shouldn't take very long and then you two can be on your way. I'll call you when I hear something from the seller."

Once this was done, Eric and Greg shook hands. Noting the way the other man's gaze kept flicking toward JJ, Eric made a point of putting his arm around her and drawing her close. She held herself stiffly, though she managed to send him a grateful smile.

Once they were back in his SUV, Eric took a deep breath. "Are you all right?"

She nodded.

"What was wrong back there, when Greg asked you out?"

She wouldn't look at him.

"Come on, JJ. It's me. I saw how you flinched, how something about his invitation panicked you. What's going on?"

Her sigh seemed to come from deep inside her. "I told you I was involved with someone before I came here," she finally said. "It was a bad situation. I left the city to get away from him. Your real estate agent reminded me an awful lot of Shawn."

"Shawn." Eric let the name roll out of his mouth, disliking it. "Were you—are you—afraid of him?"

She still wouldn't meet his gaze. Her silent nod made his chest feel tight. He ached to hold her, but now he understood her unusual reticence. He wanted to tell her he'd never hurt her, wanted to promise her he'd protect her from any man who tried, but he hadn't earned the right to say those words, so he didn't.

"It's going to be all right," he promised, meaning it. "Now where would you like to eat lunch?"

Startled, she looked up, as if not entirely certain she'd heard correctly. One corner of her extremely kissable mouth quirked. "Thanks for that," she said. "Quite honestly I was bracing myself for a barrage of questions I didn't want to answer."

"I wouldn't do that to you," he stated.

"I know." Her smile widened. "And for lunch, there's the Home Cooking Café on Main Street I've been dying to try. Let's go there."

When they pulled up in front of the little café, Garth made a snuffling sound.

"That's his prelude to a full-out cry," Eric informed her. "It's time for him to eat. I warmed some formula in the motel microwave and put it in my YETI. It should still be the perfect temp."

As soon as they were shown their booth, he dug out a bottle from his bag, poured the formula from the stainless steel cup and offered it to his son. Garth latched on eagerly.

"He was hungry," JJ said, marveling. "Such a determined little face."

"We Mikkelsons like our grub." Eric grinned, gazing down at his son with adoration shining from his handsome face. JJ's heart stuttered.

As if she'd heard, a waitress came by and took their drink orders. "I can give you a few minutes to look at the menu," she said. "Unless you already know what you want."

"I don't know about you," Eric said to JJ, "but I'm in the mood for a big bacon burger and fries."

Her mouth watered and her stomach growled at the thought. "Oh, that sounds amazing. That's what I want, too!"

The waitress grinned. "We have fantastic burgers. I think you'll both be pleased." She hurried away to turn in their order.

"I can't remember the last time I had a hamburger," JJ mused. "I try so hard to eat healthy, but every once in a while…"

Garth had finished his bottle. Lifting him to his shoulder, Eric began to burp him. "In California, just about everyone is obsessed with clean eating. I always felt like I had to sneak away when I wanted to eat red meat or fast food."

"Around here it's just the opposite," she told him. "Red meat is absolutely focused on." Because there were so many Pack members, though she didn't say that out loud.

Garth let out a healthy burp, chortling afterward, which made Eric smile. "That's a good boy." Pride rang in his voice.

The waitress brought them their drinks, cooing baby talk to Garth before straightening and promising them their food would be out soon.

Their meal arrived and, true to the waitress's word, the hamburgers were amazing. JJ ate slowly, trying to savor every bite, while Eric wolfed his down. Watching him, she hid her smile, enjoying the gusto with which he did most everything.

She had to wonder if that gusto extended to making love.

Chapter 12

As soon as JJ had the thought, accompanied with a vivid picture of him naked and on top of her, she pushed it away and focused on finishing her meal.

Having lunch with Eric relaxed her. The entire drive to the café, she'd been stressed. The way Greg had acted had unsettled her, to say the least. It had made her feel she'd stepped back into her old life, her old world.

Now, sitting across from Eric and Garth, she swore she could feel the tension draining out of her. The Realtor, though he looked nothing like Shawn, had acted just like her former boyfriend and most of his friends. If Eric hadn't been there, she knew darn good and well Greg would have kept on badgering her until she'd finally given in. It had been, after all, the same tactic Shawn had used.

Before Shawn—or BS, as she liked to think of it— she'd viewed herself as a reasonably confident person. In the three years she'd been with him, he'd managed to not only erode her confidence, but to somehow make her feel as if she *deserved* to be treated like dirt.

Now, she felt like herself again. "Thank you for lunch," she said, smiling.

"You're welcome. I think next I'll drop you off at Rhonda's and let her know I'm going to keep the motel room." Eric buckled little Garth back into his carrier.

JJ nodded. "I really wish you'd reconsider, but I understand why you'd rather not stay."

It wasn't long before they pulled up in front of Rhonda's. JJ couldn't help but glance next door at her house. Where before she'd thought the white frame structure looked cozy, it now looked damaged and sad.

Rhonda appeared at her front door the instant they got out of the car. "I was getting worried about you two," she said, smiling tightly.

"I'm sorry." JJ smiled back, uneasy again. "We met with Eric's Realtor and had lunch. I hope we didn't affect your plans or anything."

"Of course not." Rhonda hugged her, a quick, fierce movement more perfunctory than comforting. She turned to Eric, her smile wider. "I'm very excited to have you three staying with me. It gets lonely living by myself sometimes."

"About that…" Eric scratched the back of his neck. "I've decided Garth and I will continue to stay in the motel. I appreciate your kindness, but I really can't impose myself—and my baby—on someone I don't know."

"I wouldn't have offered if I thought it was an imposition." Rhonda's voice wavered. "Seriously, what kind of neighbor would I be if I didn't try to help you? Why waste money paying for a motel room when I have three perfectly good, empty bedrooms?"

Eric looked down.

As Rhonda stood there blinking at him, JJ realized the other woman was about to cry.

"It'll be okay, Eric," JJ told him. "If it doesn't work out or if Garth is too fussy, you can always go back to the motel."

Two against one. When Eric raised his face and met her gaze, JJ realized she should have stayed out of it. The expression in his eyes said he'd had her back with Greg, and she should have done something similar with Rhonda.

Except it wasn't the same situation. Rhonda was just trying to help, not force him to date her.

"I guess I can give it a shot," Eric finally said. "Let me go back to the motel and grab my stuff and check out."

Slowly, Rhonda nodded. "Only if you're sure," she sniffed. "I don't want you to do anything that makes you uncomfortable."

"I can watch Garth for you if you want," JJ offered.

He exhaled. "That'd probably work. Come on."

Following him to the SUV, she glanced back and saw Rhonda had gone inside.

"Look." JJ grabbed his arm. "I'm sorry. If you don't want to stay here, there's no reason you should. I should have done better to back you up."

The tightness in his jaw relaxed. Gazing down at her, his blue eyes crinkling at the corners, he smiled. For one skip of her heart, she thought he might actually kiss her, but then he looked away and the moment passed.

She raised her hand to her lips, unsurprised to realize they were trembling. As he unhooked Garth's infant carrier, she reached past him for the diaper bag.

"Thanks for this," he said, handing her the carrier. "I'll be back as quickly as I can."

Nodding, she turned and carried Garth to the front door, waiting until he'd driven away before going inside.

"Rhonda?" she called, standing in the foyer and feeling uncertain.

"In the kitchen," Rhonda said. "All the way back to your left."

JJ remembered. She hefted Garth's carrier and went to the large and bright kitchen. Sniffing appreciatively, she smiled. Rhonda had bread baking in a bread machine and a large pot of something that smelled like chili simmering on the stove.

"Do you want a glass of wine?" Rhonda asked as she turned around. Her smile faded as she took in the baby.

"No, thanks." JJ's chest felt tight again. Maybe Eric had been right to want to stay in the motel. "It smells amazing in here," she said. "I had no idea you liked to cook." Of course, she didn't actually know Rhonda very well at all.

"I love to cook." Rhonda sighed. "I thought I'd make a special meal to welcome you both to my home. But your tenant acts like it's going to be torture for him to stay here."

"Oh no, I'm sure he doesn't. He really just didn't want to impose. Babies are noisy and you're used to having peace and quiet…"

Rhonda motioned to one of the kitchen chairs. "Please, sit." She pulled out her own chair and dropped into it.

JJ took the seat across from her and began unbuckling little Garth to lift him out of his carrier. As she did, the baby started to cry.

Rhonda winced. "What does he need?" she asked. "Is he hungry? Thirsty? What can I do to help?"

Rocking him gently, JJ smiled. "I need to change his diaper, that's all. He ate when we did. Is there somewhere I can take him to do that?"

"Sure. Follow me." Rhonda led her down a hallway toward a bathroom. "This is the guest bathroom. You and Eric will be sharing it. Will this countertop work?"

"It will." Relieved and feeling more confident that everything would be all right, JJ smiled her thanks.

"I'll be in the kitchen when you're finished."

Once Rhonda had gone, JJ made short work of changing the baby's diaper and cleaning him up. Funny how she'd become almost expert at this, despite having known Eric and Garth only a couple weeks.

Still holding the little one, she picked up the carrier and made her way back to the kitchen. When she took a seat, she moved Garth to her shoulder so he could look around.

Rhonda poured two glasses of wine and brought them over, placing one in front of JJ, despite her earlier refusal. Amused, JJ restrained herself from shaking her head and simply smiled.

"Any word on what caused the fire?" Rhonda asked, taking a small sip of her own wine.

"They think electrical. My insurance company promises to have someone out tomorrow, and after that, I'm hoping I can get things to kick into gear fast. It's bad enough that I'm displaced, but poor Eric. His furniture is scheduled to arrive any day now."

Rhonda narrowed her eyes. "He has furniture? I sort of got the impression he was one of those drifter kind of men. You know, a free spirit, moving from town to town as the mood struck him."

Surprised, JJ shook her head. "No. He used to be a college professor. He took a leave of absence when his son was born."

"Seriously? He doesn't look…academic at all. I bet all his students had crushes on him."

"Probably." The subject made JJ uncomfortable. Mainly because she didn't like gossiping about someone she considered a friend. She decided to change the subject. "Did you do anything interesting when you went into the city?"

Rhonda crossed her arms. "Why?"

"Just making conversation," JJ retorted. "You've been acting weird ever since you returned. Is everything okay?"

"Just fine. And I'm not acting weird. It just scares me that my house could have caught on fire and I wouldn't have even known."

Such a strange comment. But then, maybe Rhonda had been homeless before. Who knew? One thing JJ firmly believed was never judge other people without knowing what they personally had gone through.

"I get it," JJ finally said.

The hard look on Rhonda's face faded. "Thank you. But I don't think you do. How could you? Actually, I got some bad news about a friend of mine while I was gone. They say she committed suicide, but I don't believe that. I think she might have been murdered." She looked down. "Anyway, I apologize if I was acting off. I've been trying to deal with the news the best I can."

Shocked, JJ stared. "I am so sorry. Now I feel awful."

"Don't." Rhonda shrugged. "I don't really want to talk about it anymore, so let's change the subject." Considering, she brightened. "Hey, I know we've discussed this before, but I thought I'd go ahead and double-check. Sort of like giving you a heads-up. If you're not interested in Eric, now that he'll be staying here I'm definitely going to make a play for him big time. So speak up now or have no regrets."

Horrified, JJ searched for the right words. If she didn't claim Eric as hers, then he'd definitely—and rightly—feel like she'd sold him down the river.

While Eric wasn't a hundred percent certain staying at Rhonda's was a good idea, he hated to let JJ down. Clearly, she'd really wanted him to stay. Not only did he have the absurd instinct that he should protect her, but the Rhonda who'd returned from her time away seemed a hell of a lot more tightly wound than the one whose driveway he'd shoveled a week ago.

Quite frankly, he had to wonder what had happened to her while she'd been gone. Not that it was any of his business, unless her behavior affected his son.

He shook his head. Worrying too much had always been one of his flaws. He'd hoped he'd left it behind when he'd traveled across the country, but maybe not.

After gathering up his and Garth's meager belongings from the motel room, he checked out and paid. With her attention focused on the television, the motel clerk barely acknowledged him. A quick glance revealed she was watching some kind of news conference.

"What's going on?" he asked.

"A burned and dismembered body was found near the performing arts center," she said. "And one of the college students has been missing. The police haven't identified the body yet, but everyone thinks it was her."

"Here?" he asked, still not understanding.

"Yes." Her tight lips, worried expression and the fear in her eyes told him this hit too close to home. "The girl that's missing…she was—is—my friend." Abruptly, she handed him his receipt and disappeared into the back room.

Once in his vehicle, he heard the rest of the story on the radio. Several small wild animals had been found, ripped apart but not eaten, as if they'd been killed just out of cruelty.

A chill snaked up his spine. As if on cue, his cell phone rang. When he saw caller ID, his stomach clenched.

"There are reports of a possible Berserker near you," Detective DeLeon said, his tone casual. Too casual. "You wouldn't happen to know anything about that, would you?"

"Of course not. I just learned about what happened. I'm as shocked as anyone else."

"Are you? What are the odds?" Instead of waiting for an answer, the other man continued. "You remember I told you we didn't think Yolanda was acting alone. And since Jason's cell phone never turned up, there's a good chance one or more of these cult members has made their way to Forestwood looking for you and your boy. While we're investigating, I wanted to give you a heads-up. Watch your back and, especially, keep an eye on your son. We've got people in the area, but our resources are stretched too thin to offer you a protection detail."

"Thanks, Officer DeLeon."

"Frank. You can call me Frank." With that, the other man hung up. Heart pounding, Eric dropped his phone into the console and started the engine. Damn. The man had a point. And worse, Eric had left his son alone with a woman he'd known for only two weeks, and another woman he barely knew who'd been acting strange.

He made it back to Rhonda's house in half the time it would have taken if he'd driven the speed limit. Luckily, no police officer stopped him to give him a ticket.

After he pulled up in front of Rhonda's house, he slammed on his brakes, completely forgetting about the potential of icy patches. The rear of his truck fishtailed, which made him feel slightly foolish.

Still, he needed to calm his racing heart and then go inside and act as if nothing was wrong. Though he'd started to trust—and like—JJ, for now all bets were off. He'd watch her like a hawk. And make sure neither she nor Rhonda were ever alone with Garth again.

When he walked up to the front door, uncertain whether he should knock or just walk in, he heard the sound of the television and figured they were just learning about the girl's murder. Instead of interrupting, he opened the door and went in, making a mental note to talk to Rhonda about locking the place up.

Both women's gazes were glued to the television, though JJ waved a quick hello. She was holding Garth, rocking him back and forth gently. From the broad smile the baby wore, it was clear he loved it.

For a second, Eric felt bad for suspecting JJ. But then he reminded himself how he'd once trusted Yolanda, too. Until the cult members were caught, he could trust no one. Still, the attraction sizzling between them would be no less difficult to resist.

A commercial came on.

"Wow," Rhonda commented. "In our little town."

"Did you hear about this?" JJ asked him.

Before answering, he reached down and took Garth out of her arms.

"I saw a news report at the motel office when I was checking out, plus that's all they were talking about on the radio," he said. "It's awful. Just awful."

"Yes, it is." Rhonda bowed her head. "One of my friends in the city recently died. Too much death and suffering so close together."

He offered his apologies, understanding now why she'd been acting so strange. Maybe he had been overthinking things.

"Looks like you had a beautiful day to run errands." Smiling sadly, Rhonda changed the subject.

"It was nice," he replied. "I hope it stays this way for a few days longer. While I knew winters could be brutal in the Northeast, I hadn't expected to be slammed by one major snowstorm after another, with barely a break in between."

Rhonda laughed. "It's not usually like this." At his unconvinced expression, she laughed again. "You'll get used to it. Either that, or you'll go back to the West Coast, where it's always warm."

The West Coast? He tensed up. "How did you know where I'm from?" he asked, keeping his voice casual.

"JJ told me."

No doubt picking up on his distress, JJ flashed an apologetic smile. "I'm sorry, I didn't know it was a secret."

"It's not," he assured her. Then, addressing Rhonda, he managed to smile. "I have no intention of going anywhere, no matter how awful the winter becomes. I like having four seasons, which is one of the reasons I chose to move here. Cold, I can deal with. Snow, I usually enjoy as well, especially considering my ancestors are from Norway. I still have family there."

"Norway?" Rhonda asked, arching her brows. "Wow. That's pretty cool."

"More similarities to Thor," JJ chimed in, flashing a quiet, quirky grin that he found sexy as hell.

Though his heart flip-flopped, he ignored that. "I just need the movers to be able to get through, even though I'll have to store everything at my shop until the house is ready. Is that too much to ask?"

Apparently taking pity on him, she squeezed his shoulder. While the gesture had been meant to be friendly, her touch seared him. He fought the urge to pull her close for more.

Oblivious, she smiled. "It's going to be okay. They've revised the forecast. The arctic front went back up north. No more snow is predicted for the next week at least. I know they said it would only take a week, but the weather has managed to double it. Your stuff will be here before you know it."

He hoped she was right.

After a rather uneventful evening, Eric claimed exhaustion and went to bed early, letting Rhonda know Garth was an early riser. She smiled sweetly and told him not to worry, but he still sensed something off about her. JJ, too, though he knew his overactive imagination had probably kicked in.

In the morning, he woke to sunshine pouring through his window. He jumped up and rushed to his window. Since the city had finally cleared the last of the snow dropped by the "storm of the century," Eric had been hoping Mother Nature would take a break for a while. Today, it appeared the skies would remain clear and sunny, with the weather cold, but dry.

Fortunately, he had a lot to do that would keep him out of the house. JJ informed him she had to stay there to meet the insurance adjuster.

He'd had Greg rush the closing, which was doable since it would be a cash deal. It was scheduled for that day, so he hadn't had to lease the space until the papers were signed. He'd be able to store most of his belongings there, until JJ's house was deemed livable again.

Last he'd heard, the moving truck with all his stuff on it had gotten stuck somewhere in Ohio. The nearly three thousand mile trip, originally projected to take a week, had already stretched into two weeks due to crazy winter weather all across the country. He made a quick phone call on the way to the closing, and the moving company promised him the truck would arrive tomorrow as long as the good weather held.

Luckily, all the forecasters continued to agree it would. He swore they sounded disappointed when they delivered the "no snow expected" forecast.

Relieved, Eric hummed as he drove. As if picking up his father's good mood, Garth waved his chubby fists and chortled from his carrier in the back seat, which made Eric smile. His son would never remember living in California, or experience the pain of knowing his mother had abandoned him. So far, no one but Frank DeLeon and his merry band of Pack Protectors knew Eric's story. And for at least right now, Eric planned to keep it that way.

This whole experience of moving East had been different than he'd expected. In so many ways.

Chapter 13

With Eric gone and the claims adjuster not scheduled to appear until that afternoon, JJ decided to take advantage of the good weather and roads and head into town herself. She climbed into her car, feeling odd when she realized she actually missed having a baby to fuss over in the back seat. Before starting the engine, she sat and looked next door at her poor house. Soon, she told herself. Soon repairs would begin and before too long everything would be back to normal.

While she was sitting in her car, her cell phone rang, startling her. When her mother's name came up on caller ID, she felt a nugget of worry. Just a tiny one, but it was there nonetheless. Her mother never called twice within a month, never mind within two weeks.

"Hello, Mom," JJ answered. "Is everything all right?"

"No, everything is not all right." Anita sounded both furious and afraid. "Shawn has been calling me. A lot. At all hours. I finally had to block him, but then he called from a different phone. I'm going to have to get a new number."

"I'm sorry."

"He's been threatening me," Anita continued, as if JJ hadn't spoken. "He says unless I tell him where you are, he's going to hire a hit man and have me killed."

Briefly, JJ closed her eyes. She knew Shawn, and sensed that while this was terrible, he'd only escalate it from here. Next he'd be talking dismemberment, and how he'd dispose of the body parts. She shuddered. How she'd ever thought she loved such a man astounded her now.

Of course, he hadn't revealed his crazy side until she'd been deeply involved in the relationship.

"Have you gone to the police?"

"Yes. And I'm going to have my number changed next. I'll make sure it's unlisted, if they do such a thing for cell phones."

JJ had no idea. "Mom, he's not going to hurt you. You're all the way over there in Australia. He's just using scare tactics to try to get information out of you."

"Well, it's working."

A shiver of foreboding skittered down her spine. "You didn't tell him where I was, did you?"

"Of course not." Anger vibrated in Anita's voice, pushing out the earlier fear. "I'm not an idiot. Judging from the horrible things he's been threatening, I'm really glad you got away from him. At first I thought you'd made a mistake. He seemed like the perfect man."

"I know. But that's all on the surface." Though she tried, JJ couldn't keep the shudder from her voice. "He's dangerous. I have no doubt that he'd eventually have killed me if I'd stayed with him."

Her mother went silent. When she spoke again, hurt rang in her voice. "Honey, why didn't you ever tell me? I'd have done what I could to help you. You could have flown here to Australia to live with me."

Which was probably what Shawn thought she'd done. Not wanting to frighten her mother, JJ kept this thought to herself. She wasn't even sure if she should mention the fire.

"Do you have a restraining order against him?" Anita asked shakily.

"I don't. Because if I did that, it would only make him angrier and more determined to make me pay. He considers me his belonging, not my own person. That's why I was so relieved to be left this house. I made sure to put the deed in my real name." Which wasn't Julia. Julia was her middle name. Her first name was actually Anabelle.

"He doesn't know your name?"

"Nope. He doesn't know a lot about me. That used to bother me, but now I'm just really grateful."

"Me, too." Anita's heartfelt response made JJ smile. "You know what? I'm glad you're not hiding stuff from me anymore. I can take it, you know. I think maybe I don't give you enough credit sometimes. You've gotten really good at handling whatever challenge life throws at you. I'm proud of you."

JJ winced, glad her mom couldn't see her. Now she had to tell her about the fire. "Uh, Mom?" she began, then hurried through the rest of the story.

Anita was silent for a few seconds after JJ finished. When she finally spoke, her voice was heavier. "Julia, you weren't going to mention any of that, were you?"

"I didn't want you to worry." Truth, but a pitiful excuse.

"I'm your mother. It's my job to worry about you." Anita stated the words matter-of-factly. "But it sounds like, once again, you have this under control."

"I do." And with a dawning sense of wonder, JJ knew that she did. "I was worried about my tenant, but he's worked out everything, too. Now all I need to do is get the place repaired so I can move back in."

"Good. I'll call you with my new phone number as soon as I have it."

"Okay. Stay safe, please. And, Mom? I love you."

"I love you, too."

After ending the call, JJ started the car and put it in Drive. She needed some retail therapy, though she couldn't spend too much money. Maybe a new top or a new pair of jeans. Or boots. She'd always loved boots.

As she drove slowly up Main Street, she tried to decide where to go first. The local bookstore, Nook of Books, caught her eye. There! She'd been planning to visit ever since she'd seen the place. There was nothing she loved better than perusing stacks of books looking for her next read. And she'd noticed an alarming absence of books in Rhonda's house. Maybe she could even get Rhonda reading. Heck, that was what friends were for, right?

After parking right in front, she killed the engine and, with her spirits up for the first time since the fire, went in. A little bell tinkled above the doorway, signifying her arrival.

Inside, the place even smelled like books. Paper and ink and…heaven. JJ stopped, turned in a circle and inhaled appreciatively.

"Can I help you find something?" An older woman, her silver hair arranged in a neat bun, approached. Her softly glowing aura proclaimed her a shifter. One thing JJ had noticed about this place was that just about everyone she met seemed to be. As far as she could tell, shifters outnumbered humans five to one.

JJ smiled. "No, thanks. Searching is half the fun."

The woman blinked. "You're new here. Are you visiting or…?"

"I just moved here. My aunt was Olivia Jacobs. I inherited her house."

"Oh, Olivia. We all loved her. I'm Gracie Cordell." She held out an elegant, long-fingered hand. "Welcome to Forestwood."

"I'm Julia Jacobs, but everyone calls me JJ." After shaking hands, JJ gestured at the well-stocked shelves. "I'm so glad to find an independent bookstore here. I didn't want to have to drive into Kingston and visit a chain store at a mall."

Gracie smiled and nodded. "Everyone's been really supportive of this place. We only opened up six months ago, but we're doing well. I'll leave you alone to browse," she said. "I'll be up front if you need anything."

"Thank you."

Time flew by. JJ couldn't believe the selection, which rivaled the big-box bookstore she used to visit in the city. By the time she headed to the cash register, she'd settled on two novels, one hardcover and one paperback. Though she hadn't read anything by the authors, the stories sounded interesting. A nonfiction, self-help book had also caught her eye, so she decided to get it, also since it was about making a career out of the things you loved doing. JJ figured she needed all the help she could get with that. While she'd truly enjoyed walking other people's dogs— and made quite a bit of money from it—that had been in the busy city. She wasn't sure there'd be a market for that in a small town. So she'd need to figure out some other way to earn a living, even though she'd have income from having a tenant.

"Good choices!" Gracie exclaimed as she rang up the two novels. When she got to the other book, she studied it for a second, before ringing it up and putting it in the bag. "Are you looking for work?"

Startled, JJ nodded. "Not actively, but I'll need to start soon. I'm just not sure what I want to do."

"I need a part-time clerk," Gracie told her. "I can't afford to pay too much, but it would give you spare time to look for something full-time."

"That's very kind of you. Working in a bookstore would be my dream job," JJ blurted, stunned. "Though I'd have to be careful not to spend all my paycheck on books."

"Then it's settled. I'll need you on Monday, Wednesday and Saturday, ten until six, with an hour for lunch. Will that work for you?"

"Of course." Though JJ knew she shouldn't look a gift horse in the mouth, she had to ask. "I'm wondering why, though. You don't even know me. How do you know whether I'd make a good employee?"

Gracie smiled. "I'm an excellent judge of character. Plus anyone who speaks about bookstores the way you do is meant to either work in one or own one. Since you can't do the latter, you might as well take the job."

"Thank you. I will." Bemused, JJ paid for her purchases and turned to go. "I'll be here at ten."

"Sounds good." Tilting her head, Gracie considered, her brown eyes sharp and assessing. "Every winter, one or two times when the weather permits, all of the Pack residents residing in Forestwood have a major hunt. I can see from your aura you're a shifter, though I don't know if you're Pack—nor do I want to know. But if you are, we're all meeting in the woods at the hill north of town on Saturday night. You're welcome to join us. It's a great way to get to know your neighbors."

JJ didn't bother to hide her shock. "Um, thank you?"

This made Gracie laugh. "I take it you're not used to people talking about what we are."

JJ couldn't help it; she looked around to make sure no

one was listening. Since nobody else had entered the shop since her arrival, the two of them were still alone. "You're right. I'm not. It's just not done in the city. Though we can see the auras, we might nod in recognition, but it's never spoken of out loud."

"Well, Forestwood is not only small, but shifters outnumber humans something like five to one. Most of us are Pack. Those that aren't, well, we don't know what they are and we don't ask." Continuing to smile, Gracie twisted an ornate, antique-looking ring on her index finger. "We do this several times a year. The solstices, for sure. And any time there's a full moon, you can always find a group putting together a hunt. We like the camaraderie. It brings us all closer together."

JJ nodded. A sense of community, something she'd always ached for… Longing filled her, though she took care to hide it. She couldn't imagine what it must be like to grow up in a place like this. Where she would have felt she belonged, rather than feeling like an outcast.

"I might be interested," she said. "My new tenant might want to go, as well. Is it okay if I mention it to him?"

"Of course." Grinning, Grace reached out and patted her hand. "The more the merrier."

All the way home, JJ couldn't stop smiling. Not only did she now have a job, but she had a communal hunt to look forward to. When she was a child, her mother used to regale her with stories of neighborhoods shifting and hunting in a community pack. JJ had always wondered what such a thing would be like. Now she'd get to find out for herself.

And maybe, just maybe, Eric would join her.

At the thought, she felt a shiver of longing. The sexual arousal after shape-shifting back to human was well known, and most times—unless by mutual agreement—politely ignored.

Being aroused around Eric was definitely not something she'd want to ignore. In fact, she could picture him, hard and huge and ready. Her being his friend, and available, might make him put his scruples aside and indulge in a moment of spontaneous passion.

And then she realized something else. Rhonda was also a shifter. If she attended the hunt, she'd be concentrating on staying close to Eric, JJ knew.

When she pulled up to Rhonda's house, she saw Eric's SUV parked out front. Rhonda's car was nowhere to be seen, which was probably a good thing, at least for Eric. Of course, JJ figured he could take care of himself. Guys who looked like him had to be used to being propositioned by women.

Making a mental note never to become one of those women, she went inside. Eric was in the living room with Garth. He was sitting on the couch, watching TV with the sound down really low and playing with his son.

Unable to contain her happiness, JJ greeted the baby, before showing Eric her purchases. She told him about her new job and also about the communal hunt.

"Anyway, I'd love it if we could go together," she finished, trying to ignore the way he'd lowered his brows in a thunderous frown.

"I'm sorry, I can't go." With that, he turned away, suddenly finding something fascinating in a brightly colored plastic baby toy. Garth's blue eyes followed the movement and he chortled.

Meanwhile, JJ struggled to process Eric's abrupt declination.

"I'm asking you as my friend. This will be my first time changing with a group of people I don't know." She wasn't begging, not quite. "It would really help to have a friend there with me among all the strangers."

"I can't go," he repeated, his voice hard, his expression closed off. "Can't. If I could I would. Believe me."

Perplexed, she eyed him. "Why not?" she finally asked, daring to push the limits of her courage. "What if you only stay for, like, an hour?"

"JJ." He rounded on her, his handsome face fierce and dark and something else, something that sent a shudder of raw need snaking up her spine. "I can't go. Because I'm not Pack."

After Eric's dramatic announcement, JJ hadn't known what to say. She'd mumbled something conciliatory, picked up her bag of books and hurried to her bedroom, closing the door quietly behind her. She sat down on the edge of the bed, wondering why she felt like crying.

She should have known. All along, she'd realized he was different. If he'd been Pack, she imagined his wolf would be larger than other men's, stronger, a better hunter. Beautiful, in the heavy, masculine way of him.

But since he'd stated definitively he was not Pack, not wolf, the question that begged to be answered was what? What form of beast did he become when he changed his shape?

She tried to picture him; she knew of many large feline shifters—panther and lion, tiger and cheetah. Most of them tended to avoid large settlings of Pack, and she couldn't imagine why Eric would want to live here rather than closer to others of his own kind.

But then she remembered what he'd said about the Drakkor. Their little town had gained a bit of notoriety when a female dragon shifter, or Drakkor, had been outed as living in a lakeside cabin and pretending to be their famed "lake monster" for many years. The entire town had embraced Libby, and her story had been published in several shifter periodicals.

Maybe he was Drakkor. That would explain his interest and his reasoning for moving here. Anyway, it didn't matter. Or it shouldn't. Because despite her best intentions, it seemed she had become one of those women who propositioned men. Even if only to ask him to hunt with her as a friend.

JJ's crestfallen expression tugged at Eric's heart. He'd given her the truth, trusted her with part of a secret he hadn't intended to reveal and managed to hurt her in the process.

He understood her request and wished he could have honored it. But the one thing he couldn't do was change with a bunch of wolves. He also couldn't reveal his true nature to JJ. No one except DeLeon and a few of his cronies knew what Eric was, and he intended for it to stay that way.

For centuries, his kind, his people, had been vilified and avoided, all because of a rare genetic mutation. Tests were unable to reveal it, and as a result, more and more bears had stopped having children. They were too afraid of bringing a monstrosity into the world. The bears' numbers had begun dwindling, and they tended to live in isolated communities, all of them in the North. Alaska, Canada, Russia, Norway and Sweden were the largest groupings. The farthest south Eric had heard of a settlement had been high in the Rocky Mountains.

When he'd been growing up, his grandparents and the rest of that family had been part of a group in Norway. But when one of the elders in the church, a kind and giving man, had been falsely accused of being Berserker by a small group of his detractors, his own friends had turned on him rather than defending him. Things had gotten so bad he'd feared for his family. He'd sent them to California to live, and once they were safely away, he'd hanged himself from the tallest tree in the village square.

The group had imploded after that, drawing up sides. Poisonous accusations, anger and eventually violence had flared. When, as if they'd known, Eric's parents had shown up to take them away, they'd all fled to California.

Now both his parents were truly gone. Eric and Lars had learned from a stranger that, a few years after they'd vanished from their sons' lives, they'd died in an airplane crash, slamming into the side of a mountain during a blizzard up in Alaska. The subsequent fire had been what actually killed them. Lars had gone back to Norway after that, leaving Eric with no family and only the company of the few other bear shifters he'd met. Yolanda had been one of them.

Living so far from others of his own kind wasn't easy. Eric envied the easy acceptance that Pack members enjoyed. The communal hunts, the knowledge that Protectors would always be there to have your back if you needed them… The freedom to mate and procreate when you wanted, without worrying about the consequences of a deadly gene mutation appearing one day without warning…

Eric didn't know what he'd do if it appeared in his son. He shook off the thought, refusing even to consider such a possibility.

Now, sitting alone in an unfamiliar bedroom in a virtual stranger's house, he acknowledged he may have made another major mistake. He'd allowed a petite and curvy redhead to get under his skin, to come too close. No one had ever said isolation would be easy. Maybe he should seriously think about finding somewhere else to live rather than waiting for JJ's place to be repaired.

Chapter 14

True to the company's word, the moving truck pulled into Forestwood at eight o'clock the next morning. The drivers called Eric once they were inside the city limits. He agreed to meet them at his shop, glad he'd already fed and bathed little Garth. He'd decided to store everything there until the house became livable again. The excitement of finally getting his familiar belongings, not to mention his car, had him moving fast.

After putting Garth's coat on him, Eric shrugged into his own parka, grabbed his keys and headed out. He didn't see either Rhonda or JJ, which was good, since he was too impatient for conversation or explanations.

He made it to his shop in ten minutes, glad for clear roads and good weather. Once he'd parked, he carried Garth inside the small office and set his carrier down on the massive wooden desk the previous owner had left.

Walking outside, Eric caught sight of the large moving truck rounding the corner. It was towing a trailer with the most precious cargo of all—his Camaro, still properly covered.

After winter had gone for good, that car would be the best advertisement for his fledgling business. He'd spent four years in his spare time restoring and customizing it, using only authentic parts. The time and love he'd put into making it absolutely perfect showed. He'd even entered it in a few custom car competitions, both times winning top prize. Anyone who wanted a car or truck restored would, after seeing his Camaro, know immediately that Eric was the man they wanted for the job. He was banking on that.

The first thing he had the movers do was unload his car. After they'd uncovered it, he inspected the exterior from front to back. Once he'd satisfied himself that the Camaro was still in perfect condition, he backed it into the first of the three bays and closed the door. The rest of his belongings would be stored in the middle bay. He'd purchased and installed security cameras, despite Rhonda shaking her head and claiming they were unnecessary. As if Forestwood had zero crime.

Once the men had finished unloading, Eric thanked them. He stood outside, holding Garth, and watched as the big truck lumbered away. He then closed all the doors and went back in. He planned to spend the rest of the day going through his things and taking out whatever he could use to make Garth's life—and his—easier.

The day of the community hunt, JJ half hoped Eric would ask her to come help him sift through more of his boxes. She would have agreed immediately, even though she had a meeting with a contractor at ten, and hoped to pin the man down on an actual date the repair of her house could start. But Eric didn't. In the kitchen, pouring herself another cup of coffee, she managed to smile at Rhonda as if nothing was wrong.

"Are you and Eric still having problems?" Her neighbor asked.

JJ shrugged. "I'm not sure. Why?"

"Because there's something I need to tell you." Rhonda looked around, as if afraid someone would hear her. "He's *wanted*, JJ." Her loud whisper came out both shocked and worried.

JJ crossed her arms. "Wanted for what? Where are you getting your information?"

"I have a friend who's a Pack Protector. Eric's ex-wife and best friend were both murdered under suspicious circumstances."

"What?" JJ couldn't help it; she gasped. "When? Where?"

"In California. I'm not sure when. But recently, like, within the last ten days."

Some of the tension drained from JJ's shoulders. "Well, Eric hasn't left. At all. If something happened in California, it couldn't have been him. He's been here longer than that."

Grimacing, Rhonda shrugged. "I could have the timeline wrong. Maybe it was before he got here. All I know is when I was in the city the night your house caught on fire, I met my friend for dinner. We were talking about fugitives and I asked him if the Protectors had their own top ten most wanted list. They do. He showed me on his phone. I saw all of their faces and their crimes. I recognized Eric immediately."

JJ swallowed. "Did you say anything to your friend?"

Rhonda gave her a calculating look. "No. Not yet. I don't know about you, but I confess, I'm intrigued. I like my men dangerous. It's so sexy."

Sexy? "That's crazy!" JJ gasped, the words bursting from her before she had time to reconsider.

Narrow-eyed, Rhonda pursed her lips. "Do you think so?" Her silky voice carried a thread of anger. "Or are you just saying that because you want him for yourself?"

For a heartbeat JJ couldn't find any words. When she finally spoke, she took a deep breath first. "Rhonda, stop. Neither of us knows much about Eric, but I think we at least owe him a chance to explain himself. I, for one, don't find murderers or criminals sexy. Or appealing. Yet I've been around Eric for a good while. You've seen how great he is with that baby. I can't believe he could have done what you claim he has."

"*They* claim, not I." Rhonda shook her head. "And has it ever occurred to you he might have offed the kid's mother so he could get custody?"

Now JJ felt naive. And gullible. Yet even with that, she couldn't help but feel Rhonda's friend had the wrong information. "If they're Pack Protectors, you'd think they'd have been able to locate him. I mean, he hasn't tried to hide himself. He even registered his new business under his name. I know, because I saw the paperwork."

"I don't know." Seemingly unconcerned, Rhonda shrugged. "I guess just keep your eyes open. As for me…" She flashed a sly smile. "If I get a chance to get close to him, I'm taking it. So I might need you to make yourself scarce. Or better yet, take care of the baby while I take care of Eric."

"What are you two talking about?" Eric asked, walking into the room. JJ jumped, feeling her face heat. Rhonda just continued to smile, letting her gaze travel leisurely over Eric's body, as if she could undress him with her eyes.

"Why, you, of course," she purred. "I was hoping JJ

would babysit little Garth tonight so I could take you out to dinner at my favorite Italian restaurant."

His quick—and alarmed—glance at JJ was almost comical. "JJ and I already have plans." His eyes begged her not to contradict him.

"Really?" Rhonda's disappointed pout seemed calculating. "Then how about tomorrow night?"

JJ barely kept from rolling her eyes. While she still liked Rhonda, and could understand her wanting Eric, her comments about criminals and murderers being sexy seemed creepy.

And no matter what Rhonda thought, no way was Eric either of those.

"I don't think so," he finally said, his voice kind. "I'm not really interested in dating anyone right now."

"Even JJ?" Rhonda asked, her hands on her hips and her color high. "Because it seems to me you and my friend there have been dating quite a bit."

"We're friends," JJ interjected, before Eric could comment. She actually felt sorry for Rhonda. While she didn't understand why Eric wasn't interested in a petite, curvy blonde, she was glad he wasn't.

"Yes, friends," Eric echoed.

"With benefits?" The bluntness of her neighbor's question shocked JJ. Again, her face heated. Just once she wished she didn't turn red every time she got embarrassed.

If he noticed, Eric gave no sign. "That's out of line, Rhonda. I think you owe JJ an apology."

She lifted her chin but said nothing.

Hurt, JJ lowered her head. She'd known all along that Rhonda had been interested in Eric, but hadn't thought they'd become enemies over it.

"Actually—" Rhonda finally spoke, giving JJ hope that this could all be smoothed over "—I think you're the one who owes JJ an apology. You didn't inform her she'd be harboring a criminal when she let you rent half her house."

Then, while both Eric and JJ gaped at her, she continued. "As a matter of fact, my suggestion is that you turn yourself in before she gets hurt."

It took a moment before Eric could speak. "Are you threatening me, Rhonda?"

Rhonda's perfectly shaped brows rose. "Of course not. Why would you think that?"

"Because that sounds like a threat." He crossed his arms. "I don't know where you're getting your information, but I'm not a criminal and I'm not wanted for anything."

"But—"

"No buts. I'm in constant communication with Pack Protectors. Believe me, if I were wanted for a crime, they'd know exactly where to find me." With that, he stalked from the room.

Rhonda remained silent for a few more seconds. "I don't know what to think," she said.

"Maybe you just looked at whatever you saw wrong. It sounds like the Pack Protectors are protecting him rather than hunting him."

"Maybe so. Either way, there he goes again." Rhonda jerked her head toward the window. Outside, Eric was buckling Garth into his infant seat. Briefly, JJ debated hurrying outside to talk to him, but then didn't move. Maybe they needed a little time and space before they could resume their friendship.

Friends. As if that was all she wanted. Deep down, she knew she longed for more, and she'd never been one to lie to herself. Clearly, since that would never happen, she needed to put it out of her mind. Right now, she wasn't even sure if their new friendship would survive.

Shortly before ten, she told Rhonda she'd be right back,

and went next door to her own house to meet the contractor her insurance agent had recommended. Since he'd be dealing directly with the insurance company, he took a look around and promised to submit a quote to them. Once they'd agreed, he promised to start immediately. She considered that a win.

After that meeting, she went back to Rhonda's house. Needing something else to occupy herself until the hunt, she cleaned the kitchen and the bathroom. Then she ended up back in the kitchen, rummaging through the cupboards until she found enough ingredients to make a cake.

Rhonda wandered in as she was stirring the batter. "Sorry," JJ said. "I can't sit still. I'm a bundle of nerves."

"Why?"

"The group hunt tonight. I'm so stressed, I'm almost at the point of chickening out and changing my mind about going."

"Humph," Rhonda snorted. "If you want to fit in around here, you need to get to know people. That sounds like a good way to do it."

Pouring the batter into the cake pan, JJ nodded. "I know. That's why I'm telling myself that no matter what, I have to make my way to the woods tonight. Are you going? Maybe we could ride together."

To JJ's surprise, Rhonda shook her head. "I'm not. I've got way too much to do," she said vaguely, by way of explanation.

"Like what?" Though she knew she probably shouldn't, JJ pressed the point. When Rhonda wasn't at work, she did little other than watch TV and drift around the house.

"Fine. If you must know, quite honestly, I've never liked those things. Too much random togetherness."

JJ shrugged, not wanting to admit she'd never experienced it. She might end up feeling the same as Rhonda, but wouldn't know until she tried it. Or so she told herself.

When her phone rang, she answered, even though she didn't recognize the number. It was her soon-to-be new boss, Gracie Cordell.

"Are you going tonight?" Gracie asked. JJ replied in the affirmative, though she was a little nervous.

Gracie chuckled. "It'll be fine. I tell you what—how about I meet you there? I'll watch for you. That way, at least you'll know someone. And then, when you start work at the bookstore on Monday, at least we'll have that shared experience between us. What do you say?"

Grateful, JJ thanked her. They agreed on a place to meet, and ended the call. Rhonda, who'd stayed in the kitchen, unabashedly listening to JJ's side of the conversation, shook her head and left the room.

JJ went back to making her cake. She was relieved by Gracie's friendliness, though she couldn't help but wish Eric was going. Which went to show how deluded she could be. He could no more change his species than she could.

What she hated more than that was the way Eric had been acting. He'd been remote and distant ever since telling her he wasn't Pack. He'd taken to spending a lot of time at his shop, and while she knew there was work to be done to get it ready, he didn't ask her to accompany him or even to watch Garth.

It hurt more than she wanted to think about. So she didn't. While her cake baked, she got busy making something else.

While Gracie had said the group was gathering at dusk at a spot deep inside the forest, she'd instructed JJ to meet her at the entrance to one of the hiking trails. Luckily, the weather had held. Even though cloudy and gray, the sky didn't even shed a single snow flurry. The temperatures hovered slightly above freezing. JJ dressed in layers, choosing each item of clothing by how easily it could be shed. The idea of stripping and changing in front of total strangers unnerved her, but she figured it would be pretty easy to find a bush or thicket to hide in for a few minutes.

The thought of hunting in a pack—a genuine pack of wolves—excited her.

Her enthusiasm warring with nerves, JJ arrived early. Since she'd never hiked a day in her life, she settled for pacing the parking lot. Relief flooded her when another car pulled up. The green four-door sedan parked next to JJ's car and Gracie waved from inside.

"Are you ready for the best hunt of your life?" she said in greeting as she exited her vehicle.

"Sure," JJ answered, aware she sounded anything but. "Listen, I'm wondering…for first-timers, is there a private area we can go to when it's time to strip off our clothes and shift?"

Gracie grinned. "You sound like you've never done this before. Don't worry, it'll be just like any other group hunt you've done, just with a bunch of different people."

Though she debated internally, JJ finally told her new boss the truth. "Actually, I've never done a group hunt."

"Never?"

"Nope. I've lived in the city among humans for most of my life."

Gracie shook her head. "Where did you go to change?"

"Central Park. I snuck out, usually in the middle of the night. Sometimes I could hear other shifters, but I never actually met up with one."

"You'll be fine." Patting her shoulder, Gracie pointed to where a small group of people had begun to gather near

a huge oak tree. "Those are the organizers. Let me introduce you around."

Inwardly balking, JJ nodded and let her new boss lead
her over. Two of the men swept their gazes over JJ appreciatively and openly, making her want to cross her arms
in front of her in self-defense. Of course, soon everyone
would let go of all human inhibitions, strip off their clothing and change into their wolf form. Then none of this
would matter in the slightest.

At least not until the time came to shift back to human.

Maybe this had been one awful, huge mistake.

As the crowd of people grew, Gracie stayed by JJ's
side. Finally, a tall man with a shock of gray hair blew a
whistle. "It's time. Everyone move into the woods. We're
going for the herd of deer that's been spotted on the other
side of the ridge."

JJ's heart skipped a beat. She couldn't seem to make her
feet move. As if she somehow understood, Gracie grabbed
hold of her arm and tugged her.

"Come on. We'll find you a nice little private glade so
you can change."

As they walked deeper into the woods, others already
began yanking off their clothing. Impervious to the cold,
several naked men dropped to the forest floor and began
the process of becoming wolf.

JJ stared, fascinated. When Gracie tugged at her again,
she wrenched her gaze away.

Ahead of them, several large wolves bounded off to
begin the hunt.

"It's time." Excitement rang in Gracie's voice. JJ could
see that her inner wolf obviously battled for release.

"You go ahead," JJ assured her. "I'm going to go that
way and find a semiprivate place. I'll meet you on the
hunt."

"Thank you." Her voice almost a growl, Gracie hurried away, shedding her clothing as she went.

JJ turned. All around her were people in various states of undress, and wolves. Lots of wolves—more than she'd ever seen in one place.

Growls and grunts and the occasional whine filled the air. Together in small groups, they loped off into the forest, joining larger groups. They'd hunt, working together, no doubt bringing down several deer. They'd feast on their kills, sharing equally. And when they were done, they'd return to this place and shift back to human.

After that, she could only imagine what would happen. Naked plus arousal equaled...

Panic jabbed her. She didn't want this. Not now. Not ever. She simply couldn't do it. Spinning on her heel, she took off at a dead run for the parking lot and her car.

Chapter 15

Eric couldn't stop thinking about JJ, stripping off her clothes to change in front of a bunch of strangers. Her smooth, pale, freckled skin, the lush curves her clothing only hinted at, on display for anyone and everyone to ogle. Another man would hold her close, breathe the slight sweetness of her lavender scent and run his hands over her curves. Eric didn't like it, not in the slightest, though he was well aware he didn't have a right to protest.

Though bears rarely hunted in groups like wolves, he'd done group hunts, too, though not recently. Not in years, in fact. Those had occurred only in his younger, more rowdy days. He well remembered the uninhibited group sex that always followed those things. He'd thought of mentioning this to JJ, but figured she had to know. Everyone—without exception—experienced sexual arousal after reassuming their human form.

His body stirred just thinking about it. Resolutely, he forced his thoughts away.

Because he hadn't wanted to be alone in the house with Rhonda, he'd packed up Garth and headed to his shop. He'd been spending a lot of time there, setting up his tools and his office. All Garth's things were there, too: his playpen, stuffed animals and brightly colored toys. Eric had brought only a few things to Rhonda's place. He couldn't wait until JJ's house was fixed. Luckily, she'd said the contractor would be starting work on Monday.

He stayed at the shop until his growling stomach forced him to go in search of food. Most of downtown Forestwood appeared to be shut down—he guessed they were all at the hunt. Finally, he found a small Chinese restaurant and scarfed down some delicious sweet-and-sour chicken.

Since Garth had already eaten and had played most of the day, he slept through dinner. Eric suspected he'd lucked out with such a calm baby. He counted his blessing there.

When he finished up, he reluctantly went back to Rhonda's. He wished he'd kept the hotel room. With lights turned down low, she had several scented candles lit in the dim room, filling the air with something that smelled like pears. Watching TV in the living room, she offered him a beer and invited him to watch with her. Though tempted, he didn't want to have to fend off any advances, so he claimed exhaustion and retreated to his room. At least he had a good book to read. Settling back against his pillow to do so, he fell asleep almost immediately, waking later to shut off the light and climb in between the sheets.

The morning after JJ's communal hunt, Eric went to make coffee shortly after sunrise. He'd taken to rising early—Garth woke up at six, anyway—and showering, planning on having coffee and breakfast before anyone else got up. When JJ strolled into the kitchen midway through his first cup, he greeted her warily.

"Did you have a good time last night?" he asked, dividing his attention between her and his coffee mug.

"I did." Her sleepy smile made his man parts twinge. "At first, it was a bit weird," she continued, shaking her head. "Interesting, watching so many people so comfortable with themselves they could shift next to virtual strangers."

"Did you like it?" he asked, unable to help himself, the intensity in his voice revealing feelings better left hidden.

"Not really." She swallowed. "I finally realized it wasn't my cup of tea and left. I was too embarrassed to come back here, so I went into town and had a drink at a bar. Downtown was pretty deserted. Mostly only humans there, but it was all right. As for the hunt, I think they were planning to bring down a couple of deer."

Fierce joy bloomed inside him. She hadn't done it. He couldn't imagine her passing up the chance to take down a deer. The bear inside him woke at that, shaking off the last of his sleepiness with a rumbling yawn. He himself needed to change and hunt, the sooner the better. Except then he'd have to ask JJ to watch Garth. Part of him still balked at that.

Still a bit stunned, he wasn't sure what to say. Should he commiserate with her or congratulate her? He settled on simply nodding and saying nothing.

After fetching her own cup of coffee, she pulled out the chair across from him and sat. "I start my new job tomorrow. That is, if my new boss, Gracie, isn't mad at me for disappearing. The bookstore is a couple of blocks away from your new shop. Maybe we could have lunch together sometime?"

Her earnest expression made him smile. "I'd like that," he said. "Once you get settled in, we'll decide on a day and a place."

At his response, her entire body sagged with relief.

Surprised, he cocked his head. "Are you all right?"

"I am now. I've been worried about our friendship, especially after I asked you to hunt with me."

He swallowed hard. "Please don't mention that again."

Though her lovely green eyes widened, she nodded. "I won't. I just wanted you to know I'm glad we can still be friends."

Friends. He still wanted so much more. About to comment, he closed his mouth when Rhonda strolled into the kitchen.

"Morning, you two." Her cheery voice made him wince.

"Good morning," he and JJ answered in unison. Surprised, they looked at each other and laughed.

Rhonda stared. "Did I miss something?"

"No." Shaking her head, JJ continued smiling. "We were talking about me starting my new job tomorrow."

"In the bookstore, right?" Rhonda worked in the large bank downtown as a loan officer. She, too, worked close enough to have lunch with JJ. Though tempted to point this out, he held his tongue. If JJ wanted to invite her friend, she could do it herself.

Walking to the pot, Rhonda poured herself a cup of coffee and carried it to the table. After she'd taken a seat, she scooched her chair closer to Eric. It took every ounce of self-restraint he had to keep from moving away.

"Working in a bookstore sounds kind of boring," Rhonda commented.

Her expression shocked, JJ shook her head. "That's only because you don't like to read."

"How do you know?" Rhonda countered, taking a long drink of her coffee.

"Because you don't have a single book in the house, at least that I can tell."

Glancing back toward the living room, Eric realized JJ was right. He hadn't noticed, but not even a coffee table book graced the room.

Rhonda laughed. "I only read e-books."

"Oh." JJ's face turned pink. "I didn't think of that. I read e-books, too, but there's nothing like the feel of a real book in your hands."

When Rhonda shrugged, Eric changed the subject. "I finally have all my stuff stored in my shop until the house gets repaired. Do you have any idea how long that will take?"

Before she could answer, the front living room window shattered.

JJ screamed. Rhonda whirled, growling and baring her teeth. Eric leaped for the baby, aware only of the need to protect his son.

"A brick." Outrage in her voice, Rhonda stalked toward the window, her shoes crunching on shattered glass. She picked the brick up, holding it high as though she was considering lobbing it back out the window.

"There's a note or something tied to it." Still snarling, Rhonda jerked loose the small slip of white paper. "Freakin' cowards."

Eric raised his head, still sheltering his son with his body. He cursed, an unintelligible Norwegian word he remembered hearing his grandfather use.

"Get him out of here," JJ urged.

She was right, but he hated to leave both women unprotected. "JJ, you take him and go to the back. Please."

After a second's hesitation, she nodded. Crossing to him, she grabbed the baby carrier and hurried off toward her bedroom.

Frowning, Rhonda watched her go before handing the

note to him. "I don't understand what this means," she complained. "It doesn't make any sense."

Scrawled in red ink were three words. *Abomination. Valor.* And *Sacrifice.*

Only once the Forestwood PD arrived did JJ feel safe enough to venture from her bedroom with the baby. They took Rhonda's statement, and after handing Garth over to Eric, JJ helped her sweep up shards of glass. Rhonda passed her the note and together they puzzled over the meaning of the words.

The police left after taking the report and a photo of the note, promising to make sure to patrol the area more frequently. They'd also taken photos of the footprints in the snow out front, just in case. Meanwhile, the room had grown cold, with frigid air coming in through the broken pane.

"We'll need to nail plywood over that," Eric commented. Both JJ and Rhonda looked at him.

"I've got some in the garage," Rhonda said. "If you'll help nail it up, I'd appreciate it."

"How big is it?" he asked. "If you plan to nail it, it'll have to be big enough to cover the entire window."

"It is." Rhonda sounded surprisingly upbeat, considering someone had attacked her home.

"Sure. If JJ will agree to watch Garth for a few more minutes."

Tempted to tell Rhonda she'd help nail up the plywood, JJ took the baby instead. She watched as Eric followed Rhonda to the garage to retrieve the plywood. Though it took only a few minutes to locate it and move it into place, the interior temperature felt like it had dropped another twenty degrees. JJ had taken Garth into the bedroom and left him there. She'd closed the door to keep the heat in.

Finally, they had it up. When they came back inside, Rhonda was shivering, telling Eric in a wounded little voice how cold she felt.

If she'd been hinting at him in the hopes he'd warm her up, Eric didn't appear to notice. JJ read the note again, out loud this time.

"'Abomination, valor, sacrifice.' Does anyone have an idea what that means?"

Scowling, Rhonda shook her head. "No clue. But when I find out who's messing with me, they'd better be careful. I don't get mad, I get even."

JJ chanced a glance at Eric. A muscle worked in his jaw and the bleak, haunted fury in his eyes told her he might have an idea what those words meant. Clearly, she'd have to ask him privately.

His next words surprised her. "I think Garth and I need to move out."

Both JJ and Rhonda gaped at him. "Because of the brick?" Rhonda narrowed her eyes. "You know what the note means, don't you?"

Instead of answering, he took Garth from JJ and headed toward his room. "We'll pack immediately. Thanks for the hospitality. If you have a deductible or something, I'll be more than happy to pay it."

Once he'd gone, JJ looked at Rhonda.

"Do you know, too?" Rhonda asked.

"I have no idea." JJ's heart pounded and she took a deep breath. "But I'm going to try and find out."

Determined, she hurried down the hallway, hoping Rhonda wouldn't follow her. When she reached Eric's room, she knocked on the closed door.

He opened it a crack and peered out. "What?"

"Can I talk to you?"

"I don't want to discuss it," he replied, and started to close the door.

Surprising herself, she stuck her foot in the gap like she'd seen in the movies, keeping him from shutting it. "Please."

To her relief, he let her in. "Just you, no Rhonda, right?"

She glanced back over her shoulder to make sure. "Right."

He closed the door behind her and turned the lock. He had his duffel bag on the bed and had clearly been throwing in clothes.

"You're really leaving?"

Meeting her gaze, he nodded. "It's not safe here anymore. Garth's safety has to come before anything else."

"So the brick really was aimed at you? What's going on?"

"The less you know the better."

"No." She moved closer, until they were standing toe to toe. "I'm involved already, whether you like it or not. I can't help you if I'm not in the loop."

His eyes darkened as he gazed down at her. "It's a long story."

"I've got time."

Another heartbeat passed with their gazes locked. Finally, he exhaled. "Come for a drive with me."

"Where are you going?"

"My shop. I'm going to stay there. It's got a rudimentary kitchen and bathroom. The security is much better, too, since I installed cameras and an alarm system. I'll just need to find someplace to take showers."

"I'm sure you can use Rhonda's house," JJ offered.

He shook his head before she even finished speaking. "Not happening." His tone told her not to ask why.

Once he'd packed everything, he did a double check

of the room to make sure he hadn't left a single piece of clothing before putting on his parka. "Come on," he said.

"Okay." She followed him out into the hallway. As they went past the living room, Rhonda jumped up to intercept them. Her gaze immediately went to his loaded duffel bag.

"You're really leaving?" The alarm in her voice had JJ eyeing her.

"Yes."

"I wish you wouldn't." Somehow Rhonda managed to get in between them and the door. "If you go, you'll be leaving both JJ and me completely unprotected."

He froze, and then shook his head. "This attack wasn't about either of you. Once Garth and I are out of here, no one should bother you again."

Rhonda's eyes widened. She looked at JJ, who nodded. "Are you going, too?"

With all her heart, JJ suddenly wished she could say yes. "No. I'll be back."

Eric started moving again. When he opened the front door, he looked back over his shoulder at JJ and then continued walking away.

As JJ started after him, Rhonda grabbed her arm. "Don't go."

Jerking herself free, JJ snagged her coat off the rack and headed after Eric. "I'll be back, I promise."

Outside, she hurried to catch up with him. Buckling the baby into the infant carrier, he looked up and inclined his chin toward the passenger seat. She got in and clicked the seat belt.

As they pulled away, she watched him, waiting for him to speak. Instead, he stared straight ahead, hands tight on the wheel, silent. Most likely he wasn't entirely sure he wanted to involve her in any of this.

"Well?" she finally demanded, when he showed no sign of wanting to talk. "What was all that about?"

Jaw still tight, he barely glanced at her. "My son is in danger. The Pack Protectors want me to go into a sort of witness protection program with him."

She swallowed, shocked. Noting her reaction, he nodded. She couldn't believe how incredibly painful she found the idea of never seeing him again.

"Are you?" Clearing her throat, she tried once more. "Are you considering doing that?"

"I'd prefer not to," he admitted. "But I've got to consider what's best for Garth."

"What kind of danger? I assume the Protectors are looking for the person who's a threat to you two?"

"They are. But until then…" The bleakness in his tone told her he'd already considered the alternative.

"What did that note mean? Abomination, valor, sacrifice? It doesn't make sense."

"For reasons I can't go into, they consider Garth both an abomination and apparently full of valor. They want me to give him up, to sacrifice him to their cause."

"Sacrifice?" Horrified, she tried to comprehend. "I'm struggling to make sense of your words, but I can't. I just don't understand. The idea that anyone wants to kill a sweet, innocent baby? What kind of monster would do such a thing?"

"Oh, they don't want to kill him," he said. "They want to take him from me and eventually test him to see if he carries a particular gene mutation. If he does, they want to try and breed him, so they can get more of the same type of mutation."

His words puzzled her. "I'm afraid I don't understand," she began.

"They know where I am," he continued, as if he hadn't

heard her. "That's why I'm moving to the shop until I decide what to do. At least there I have security."

"What about your business?" she asked. "How can you run a business that's open to the public? Especially since you seem to have no idea what this person or people look like."

His expression disgusted, he shook his head. "Good point. I hadn't thought that far ahead. I might have to take the Protectors up on their offer, at least until they're able to contain the threat."

"But why?" She studied him. "Why are they willing to do this for you? It's not like you're a key witness to some horrific crime, are you?"

"No." He smiled. "I'm not."

"Then why? Can you at least tell me that? From what I know about the Pack Protectors, they'd need a darn good reason before offering you their assistance."

Her comment appeared to surprise him. But then again, she had no idea what kind of shifters he and Garth were. His answer reconfirmed that.

"Not only were they part of a dwindling number, but the Protectors wanted to keep a close eye on Garth to make sure he didn't develop into something dangerous. And I don't blame them, to be honest. While I completely discount the possibility, they also know I'd lay down my life to protect Garth. No matter what the circumstances."

Interesting. "What are they worried he might become?" she asked.

"Let's just say my baby is very unique and special," he told her.

"That's not a real answer," she protested.

"It is and it isn't. But I assure you, it's the truth."

She eyed him for another moment. Then she took a deep breath and touched his arm. "Let me go with you."

Chapter 16

Stunned, Eric nearly drove off the road. He gripped the wheel and corrected enough to get them back in their lane. Then he pushed back the leap of excitement he felt at her words. "What?"

"I want to go with you and Garth if you decide to go into hiding. I can help you with him. Plus, your cover story will be more convincing if you appear to be a family rather than a single dad with a baby. That's fairly unusual and might make you more noticeable."

She made sense. Instead of immediately discounting her offer, he let himself consider her words. "I don't have any idea how long it might be."

"That's fine. I don't know when my house will be livable again."

By then he'd pulled into the parking lot of his shop. He parked by the entrance and, instead of killing the engine, left it running. "Why?" he asked quietly. "You barely know me. Why would you want to give up your life and go into hiding with me?"

There were several different responses she could give to that question. He waited, interested to hear what she'd say.

"Why not?" she countered. "I have no home, at least until it's fixed. I'm staying with Rhonda, and I don't really know her, either."

Gaze steady, he continued to eye her.

"Look, I like you. And Garth. You rented a house from me and you'd barely moved in when it caught on fire. I owe you."

Frowning, he didn't bother to try and hide his disappointment. "You're saying you feel *obligated* to disappear with me, due to a fire? You had absolutely no control over that."

She lifted her chin. "True. But my life is kind of on hold right now. And honestly, I think you and Garth could both use my help."

While he pondered her words, she sat very still and quiet. In the back seat, Garth let out a wailing cry. "His hungry cry," she said, proving her point.

"Yes." Finally, Eric turned the key and shut off the motor. "You do pay attention. Come on, let's go inside and I'll see about getting my boy fed."

She climbed out and stood on the sidewalk, waiting while he unbuckled Garth. Eric could tell from the way she kept opening and closing her mouth that she wasn't sure if she should continue to press him for an answer. Good. After all, he hadn't even decided what course of action to take. Instinctively, she probably knew he'd much rather stay and fight. But he had more to consider than merely himself. His first priority had to be keeping Garth safe.

Though JJ had asked to go with Eric impulsively, the more she thought about it, the more she knew it was exactly what she needed to do. If he wanted her, that is.

Eric's cell phone rang. "It's the Pack Protector, calling me back. Would you keep an eye on Garth while I take it?"

She nodded. Eric turned away while he took the call. After answering, he went outside.

When he finished his phone call, he came back into the room. Expression serious, he stopped and studied his son before lifting his gaze to meet JJ's.

"I'm going to stay," he said quietly. "I've already done more running than I ever wanted to do in my lifetime. I can protect Garth. I'm not sure, however, that I can protect both of you."

Her heart skipped a beat. "You won't have to protect me," she told him. "I'm pretty damn good at protecting myself."

As she spoke the words, she knew with a sense of astonishment that they were true. When Shawn had first started his abuse, she'd been stunned and shell-shocked. While she hadn't defended herself due to the fact that the only way she could was to shift into wolf, she'd gotten out of the situation and started a new life. Looking back, she realized her experience had made her stronger.

At first, Eric didn't respond. Finally, he shook his head. "You know, I think it might be better if you stay away from me and Garth until this is over."

For whatever reason, this infuriated her. She'd been willing to go on the run with him, had offered to help him any way she could. And all he came up with was asking her to stay away?

"I don't accept that," she said, even if she didn't have the right. "How about you fill me in on what's going on? I can be much better prepared if I know what specific circumstances you're facing."

"I can't tell you," he answered, as she'd known he would. "It would go against Pack law."

And there he had her. If his statement was true, that is. "There aren't too many laws they're stringent on these days. So unless you shape-shifted and revealed yourself to a human, or hurt a human while in your other form, I'm thinking we're safe."

He wasn't able to hide the flash of surprise crossing his face at her words. "What about your job?"

The abrupt change of subject momentarily stumped her. "What about it?"

"You just took a job working in that bookstore. If we went on the run, you wouldn't be able to work there. And I doubt the store owner would hold it for you, especially since you'd be up and disappearing."

"I'm sure once I explained—" she began.

"No. You couldn't explain anything. That's what going into a protection program is like. You just go. There isn't time for explanations. You don't get to call anyone and let them know you're safe. You just disappear, like you never existed."

She hadn't really considered all of that, but in the end, she didn't mind. Because something inside her told her she had to be with Eric and Garth. While JJ hadn't known him very long, she felt as if she'd known him forever. She couldn't imagine life without him somewhere in it. Though she hated to disappoint Gracie, she'd do whatever she had to in order to keep Eric and Garth in her life. "I'd still go," she answered, lifting her chin stubbornly.

He eyed her. "Are we really that important to you?"

The question hung in the air. Admitting this might make her feel exposed and naked, but she didn't think she could respond any other way. "Yes," she answered. "Yes, you are."

He kissed her then. The kind of kiss that shook her all the way to her soul and made her want to melt into him.

His kiss promised more than any words could, and her response let him know she would welcome all of it.

When they broke apart, she could barely stand. Not bothering to hide her disappointment, she sighed. "I want—" she began, aching with need and unfulfilled desire.

"Shh." He smoothed her hair back away from her face. "I'm going to call them and tell them to come get us. We're going to go into the protection program."

Her heart stuttered. "Okay," she managed to reply. "I'll need to call Rhonda and let her know."

She realized what she'd said at the same time he did. They both laughed, more of a nervous chuckle, actually.

"I can't, can I?"

He shook his head. "No. And this will be your last opportunity to change your mind. Once I make that call, you're involved, whether you want to be or not."

Although she'd feel a lot better about her decision if she knew exactly what the danger was, she nodded. "I'm ready," she said. "But I don't have any clothes or makeup or anything. I'll need shampoo and deodorant and lotion, at least."

"I'm sure they'll provide it. I was told all I need to do is give them a list of what I want and they'll get it."

After that, things proceeded at a breathtaking pace. Less than thirty minutes after Eric made the call, a black sedan with tinted windows pulled up to the shop. Eric opened up the third bay and the vehicle drove in.

Once the door had closed, with the car inside, Eric hurriedly transferred several bags of baby provisions to the trunk. He also removed the infant carrier from his SUV and installed it in the back seat of the sedan.

After buckling little Garth inside, he crossed over to JJ and took her hand. "I'm going to sit up front until we're

safely out of town. I want you to stay as close to my boy
as possible."

Suddenly tongue-tied, she nodded. "That's fine. Where
are we going? Do you have any idea?"

He shook his head. "No doubt they'll inform us once
we're on the road."

She climbed into the back seat to be with the baby and
Eric got into the front. The driver opened the bay, climbed
into the car, and pulled out and parked, leaving the engine
running. He then got out and went back to close everything up and lock it. Eric went with him, leaving Garth
in the car with JJ.

Watching them, JJ felt a pang of misgiving, imagining
Rhonda's worry when they didn't return. She had promised
to go back, after all. Maybe she could sneak in one little
phone call to reassure her neighbor. She could let Rhonda
know they were safe, without revealing any pertinent information about their location.

Since she knew both Eric and the Protector would frown
on this idea, maybe she could ask someone to at least get
word to Rhonda and Gracie. The idea of being a no-show
at the bookstore Monday turned her stomach. Not to mention her mother's worry when JJ appeared to drop off the
face of the earth.

Had she made a mistake? Was she staking everything
on a possibility that might never come to be?

Priorities, she told herself. Once all this—whatever *this*
might be—was over, she'd be able to explain, and hoped
they'd understand.

Once Eric had double-checked to make sure everything
at his shop would be secure, he and the driver turned to
head back to the car.

As they did, another vehicle came screeching around
the corner. When she heard the first *pop-pop*, JJ realized

they were under fire. Immediately, she went into protect-baby-Garth mode, ducking down and crawling over the seat to cover him with her body.

Heart pounding, and trembling as she was, her unusual action and utter terror communicated themselves to the baby. He began to wail. "Shh!" she told him, frantic to keep him quiet. "It's all right. Daddy will be back in a second. Please hush."

Of course, he understood none of this, and continued to cry.

More shots rang out. Someone shouted—was that Eric? When the car door opened, she prayed it was him. It wasn't.

She had one second to register that the man wore a black ski mask before he yanked her off Garth and tossed her to the pavement. Somehow, she lurched back up and went after him, with only one thought in her mind: *protect the baby.*

As she flung herself at her assailant, he turned and punched her. His fist connected with her jaw. She knew one instant of blazing pain before everything went dark.

When he came to, Eric rolled over, wincing from the pain of the wound in his leg. Belatedly, he saw that he'd been shot and was still bleeding. Next to him, the Pack Protector lay covered in blood. The dark sedan remained where they'd left it, engine running. The other vehicle was gone. Baby Garth. Where the hell was his son?

Pushing up, he tried to stand. The pain and loss of blood made him dizzy. Somehow, he got his scarf off and used it to tie a makeshift tourniquet around his leg. Then he crawled toward the Pack Protector, who didn't move. Eric checked him for a pulse. There wasn't one. The other man, whose name Eric hadn't even gotten, was dead.

JJ? Though the entire world tilted when he tried to

move, he managed to drag himself toward the sedan. He registered JJ lying on the cement next to the car, either unconscious or dead. The open back door revealed the seat was empty, infant carrier and all. Garth was gone.

Heart pumping, Eric could feel himself weakening. He couldn't pass out, not before he made it to JJ. His vision blurred as he reached her, but he summoned up every ounce of remaining strength he possessed to check her pulse. To his relief, the steady beat of her heart told him she lived. Unconscious, but the lack of blood meant she hadn't been shot. Good.

His phone. Dimly, he registered that his cell was in his pocket. Pulling it out slowly, wincing with every movement, he managed to type in 911. When the operator answered, he gave his location. After that, he let the blackness win and take him.

When he next opened his eyes, he found himself in a hospital bed. His leg had been bandaged and all around him machines beeped quietly. An IV had been placed in his arm.

As memory came flooding back to him, he sat up. "Garth!" Aching grief and worry and terror threatened to overcome him, but he pushed all that away. He had to focus on finding his son.

"Hey." JJ's voice. He swung his head in her direction. Anxiety that mirrored his own sparked in her eyes. "They took Garth," she said. "I tried to stop them, but I couldn't." Her voice wavered. "I'm so very, very sorry. I let you down. Worse, I let Garth down."

Somehow, despite the tubes and cords, he managed to put his arms around her. They held on to each other as if drowning. He drew strength from her, and suspected she might have felt the same way.

Someone cleared a throat from near the door. "Excuse me." A tall woman in a neat pantsuit entered the room. She had fashionable, horn-rimmed glasses and wore her dark hair in a tidy bun. "I'm Linda Felts and I'm with the Protectors," she said, keeping her voice low. "I know the human police will be here any moment to ask their questions, but our man was killed, so I needed to get in and go first."

JJ pulled away. Eric wanted to catch her arm and ask her to stay close, but he didn't. "Where's Frank DeLeon?"

JJ started, though he wasn't sure why.

"He was assigned to meet you at the safe house. He's en route back here as we speak. For now, I'm in charge of this case."

Eric nodded. "What was his name, Linda?" he asked. "The agent who was killed. What was his name?"

"Dan Pendarki." She swallowed hard. "Thank you for asking. He was newly married, and he and his wife have a baby on the way."

Grief once again stabbed Eric. "He was the second Protector to die, because of my case."

"It's not your fault," she told him, her voice once again crisply professional. "They knew the danger when they signed up for this job." Her eyes watered, but she lifted her chin. "You weren't the one pulling the trigger. Now we've got to find out who did this and get them."

"And find my son," he declared, equally fierce. "I need to get out of here. Every second we waste is dangerous to him."

"We already have people searching." Linda looked from Eric to JJ before refocusing her gaze on him. "I've read the file. We have a pretty good idea who kidnapped your boy and why. What we don't know is where they are now. But we will find them. I assure you of that. We have people everywhere. And we're good. Damn good."

Worry for Garth clawed at him again. Aware he'd be absolutely useless unless he forced himself to focus, he pushed it away. His inner bear grumbled at that. Eric didn't blame him. After all, he couldn't just lie there and do nothing.

"The human police will put out an Amber Alert," JJ interjected.

"Yes, and that can be very helpful to us in locating them." Linda glanced back at the doorway as if expecting the human police to come in at any moment. "Any sightings will be relayed to us, as well as human law enforcement. We just need to make sure we get there before they do."

"I agree," Eric said. "As a matter of fact, I need out of here. The sooner I can start looking, the better."

JJ exhaled loudly, drawing both Eric's and Linda's attention. "Look, I'm embroiled in this now. Deeply. And I still don't know what's going on," she said. "Now that I've become involved, maybe it's time to fill me in? Starting with who is DeLeon?"

For the first time, Linda appeared flabbergasted. Her brows rose as she looked at Eric. "You didn't tell her?"

"We're not mated," he said. Everyone knew shifter law expressly forbade revealing too much about species unless the individuals were personally involved.

"You know I'm Pack," JJ said.

"Everyone's Pack," he retorted. "And I told you I wasn't."

"So I know that you're something else, but not what. Drakkor, maybe? And I assume Garth is the same. I'm going to also guess that's why the Protectors are involved, since the Drakkor are nearly extinct."

"Not Drakkor." That was as much of an answer as he wanted to give.

Pursing her lips in disapproval, Linda shook her head.

"You need to fill her in," she said. "We've all got to be on the same page."

"Okay, so you know, too?" JJ's wounded tone matched her expression. "Everyone knows what Eric is but me?"

Jaw tight, Eric looked down. Though he dreaded telling JJ, he had no choice. He knew how she'd respond. After all, he'd seen how other shifters reacted to his kind. Too many times. Seeing that look of revulsion in JJ's beautiful green eyes would kill him.

But finding Garth mattered more. And if JJ could help, he'd give her all the truth she could handle.

"I'm Vedjorn," he said, using the Old Norse word. "A bear shifter. As is my son." Bracing himself for her reaction, he waited.

Chapter 17

Eric held his breath. JJ eyed him, her gaze thoughtful rather than condemning. "A bear, huh? I've never met one before. I didn't know there were any bear shifters in California."

"My family immigrated there when I was very young. Originally, we're from Norway." Which JJ already knew, but he figured maybe Linda Felts didn't.

"Okay, so you're a bear. Rare. I get it. And the Pack Protectors are helping you. What I don't understand is why did someone kidnap Garth? He's just a baby. He can't even crawl yet." The anguish in JJ's voice mirrored Eric's own feelings, making him realize JJ loved Garth, too. "Does this have something to do with those three words that were written on the paper attached to that brick that came through Rhonda's window?"

"Yes." Linda answered for him. "There are a group of people, a cult, actually, who want you to offer the baby to them as your sacrifice, we think. They want to raise him, until they can see if he'll become Berserker."

"We know that already. What we don't know is what they'd plan to do if he doesn't," Eric said.

Linda continued on as if she hadn't heard him. "What we do know is these people appear to worship the Berserkers. They seem to be an odd mixture of many disillusioned shifters. We're not sure if they already have a Berserker in their midst or if they're merely hoping to breed one." She swallowed hard, glancing sideways at Eric before continuing. "Since Garth's mother might have been Berserker, you are aware that there's a good chance the baby will be one, as well."

"He won't," Eric insisted, his tone fierce. "And Yolanda wasn't. She was crazy, yes. Strung out on drugs and alcohol. But I shifted with her many times, and she wasn't a Berserker. Garth will be fine."

"You won't know that until he's old enough to shapeshift," Linda said smoothly. "But I agree, it's not something we need to worry about now. What we do need to worry about is his safety."

"Agreed." Again Eric tried to sit up. Dizziness made him freeze. Hoping no one had noticed, he eased his head back onto the pillow and willed his strength to return.

JJ looked sick. "What do they want to do to him? He's only three months old. Surely they won't hurt him?"

"Hopefully not," Linda interjected, her tone soothing. "We don't know exactly what they want to do with him."

"Even the possibility of anything happening is unacceptable." JJ glared at Linda before turning to Eric. "We've got to find them. And him. Now." She grabbed Eric's arm. Startled, he winced.

"Sorry." Releasing him, she took a deep breath. "Are you strong enough to leave? Because we need to save

Garth. We have a better chance than anyone. No one else cares about him like we do."

"I know." He spoke with grim certainty as he ripped out his IV, an action that hurt like hell. "Help me get out of here. I need to find my clothes."

"They had to cut your pants off you," Linda told him. "And you need to stay put, at least until you've answered the human police's questions."

He was about to argue, but closed his mouth as a nurse appeared, no doubt alerted by the frantic beeping of the machine. "You pulled out your IV?" She shook her head. "Now we'll have to start a new one in your other arm."

Though his entire body vibrated with impatience, he managed to nod. "Sorry. I got a little bit agitated."

She bustled out, promising to be back in a minute with the supplies she needed.

"We don't have much time," Linda said, speaking in a low, urgent voice. "The police will be here at any moment. Right now, you just need to claim ignorance. You have no idea why anyone would abduct your son. As far as you know, it could be totally random."

"I feel like all this is just wasting time," he grumbled. "I need to *do* something."

"Our people are on it, I promise. And we need the help of all the human law enforcement agencies, so you've got to cooperate."

Though he didn't like it, he could see her point.

True to Linda's predictions, both the Forestwood police and the FBI came by and questioned him. Since there'd been a kidnapping and Garth was so young, not only had an Amber Alert been issued, but the FBI had assigned extra people to the case.

Eric stuck to a limited version of the truth. After all, it was no lie that he frantically wanted his son back. And though he—along with the Pack Protectors—had a theory, in reality he wasn't sure why anyone would want to go to such lengths to snatch a three-month-old infant.

Both the local law enforcement and the FBI agent promised to do everything within their power to bring Garth home.

After they left, Linda returned. "If you're ready to go, we've got a car out back." She handed him a pair of men's black slacks. "You're probably going to have to cut a slit in these so they'll fit over your bandage."

Accepting them, he thanked her. He motioned for JJ to close the curtain around his bed and wait on the other side of it with Linda. It was a struggle, but he managed to get the slacks on. "What about a shirt?" he asked. "I think mine should be around here somewhere."

"I brought another one." Linda stuck her hand inside the curtain and tossed a red sweatshirt on the bed. "It should fit you."

It did.

"Are you ready?" Linda asked.

When he answered in the affirmative, she yanked back the curtain. "Then let's get out of here."

"Don't we have to wait for the doctor to discharge him?" JJ asked.

"We'll handle that." Linda pursed her lips. "Just follow me and do exactly what I say."

While Eric felt he and JJ would do better on their own, for now he knew he had to trust the Pack Protectors to help. "Okay. Where are we headed?"

"The two of you need to go back home—to that woman's house where you are staying. Act like everything is normal—"

"That's impossible," JJ interrupted. "Rhonda's going to notice we're missing the baby."

Linda shot her a quelling look. "As I was saying, go there. Go straight to your room and gather up whatever belongings you want to bring with you. I will send a vehicle for you half an hour after you're dropped off."

Eric nodded. "We'll have to stall Rhonda. Maybe we'll luck out and she won't be there."

"But what if she is?" JJ sounded doubtful.

"Then you distract her long enough for me to get to my room and close the door. If she sees my leg…"

Eyes wide, JJ looked at him. "What exactly do you want me to tell her?"

"Anything but the truth," Linda stated. "No civilians need to know anything about this, understand? We keep this to ourselves."

Which made sense, he supposed. Especially since they had absolutely no idea who they could trust.

As they drove back to his shop, both Eric and JJ were silent. He couldn't stop worrying about his son. The mental images that kept flooding him were the stuff of horror movies. He had to forcibly expel them from his head.

Instead, he tried to concentrate on what he'd do to the bastards who'd kidnapped Garth. In this, he thought like his bear self, because he wanted to rip them apart with his bare hands.

When they pulled up in front of his shop to retrieve his SUV, the first thing he saw was the bullet-ridden sedan, still parked where he'd last seen it. His gut twisted and bile rose in his throat.

"Why is that still here?" JJ wondered out loud.

"Right now, it's still evidence," Linda answered. "All the law enforcement agencies are going over it with a fine-toothed comb. It'll stay until they're finished with it."

"Who's it registered to?" Eric looked away from the car. The last time he'd seen his son had been when Garth had been securely strapped in his infant carrier in the back seat. "Surely the FBI will want an explanation of why we were even in that car instead of my SUV." He frowned. "I'm surprised they didn't ask me. Or did they?"

"They already did," Linda said. "You were kind of in and out, so JJ answered for you."

The mention of her name brought JJ out of whatever deep reverie she'd gotten lost in. She blinked. "What?"

"We were talking about that car." Linda pointed. "Eric was wondering what we told the Feds."

"Oh. I told them we were going on vacation with a friend. Exactly like you said."

"Vacation?" Eric needed to know how well thought out the Protectors had gone with their story. "Where?"

"Tybee Island, Georgia," JJ promptly replied.

"Good job." Linda flashed an approving smile before she turned back to look at Eric. "Now, I want you both to go back to Rhonda's and try to act normal. If she sees the leg, tell her you got hurt at the shop."

"I still think she's going to notice we don't have the baby." JJ's voice broke midway through her statement.

"Make something up. Remember, you have thirty minutes before we come back for you. Pack what you need."

JJ sighed. "Fine."

"Half an hour, people." Linda looked from one to the other. "Surely you can stall this Rhonda person for that long."

Eric nodded. "We'll figure something out."

"We will," JJ echoed.

"Good." Drumming her fingers on the steering wheel, Linda considered them both. "I'll pick you up around the corner. The two of you will have to pretend to be going for a walk or a drive or something. Just don't tell anyone anything."

Eric nodded. "I'd prefer to take my own vehicle."

"You can't."

"I'm not leaving it parked in her driveway. How about we meet you back at the shop?"

"I like that idea," JJ agreed. "As long as I drive."

After a moment of silence, Linda finally nodded. "Fine. Half an hour. Don't be late. I don't want to have to come looking for you."

Eric wondered if she knew she sounded like a mother chiding her two small children. The quick glance JJ shot his way told him she was thinking the same thing.

"Understood," he said. "We'll meet you at the shop in one hour."

"See you then." Linda started to walk away. She looked back over her shoulder and sent them both a casual wave.

"Right." He nodded, clenching his jaw. Actually, he had no intention of meeting anyone. He planned on heading out immediately to find his son. JJ would be welcome to come with him if she wanted. If not, he'd tell her he understood.

Rhonda met them at the front door when they walked in. "What happened to you?" she asked, eyeing his bandaged leg.

He muttered something about an accident with a piece of machinery at the shop, and hurried away to his room. Once he'd closed the door behind him, he listened while JJ attempted to make small talk with Rhonda. After a few moments, he heard her coming down the hall and closing the door to her own room.

His cell phone pinged, indicating a text. Checking, he saw it was JJ, wondering how much longer she had. He texted back, asking her if she could be ready in ten minutes rather than thirty.

She replied in the affirmative, saying she'd meet him

outside. He wondered if she had an inkling of his plans. He rather hoped she did. Together, he and JJ made a pretty good team.

As she hurriedly tossed random bits and pieces of her remaining clothes onto her sheet, as Eric had suggested, JJ wondered what he was up to. Asking to meet earlier could mean he simply wanted out of the house, was eager to get started…or he had another plan in mind. Whatever it might be, she'd be on board with it.

Because the most important thing in all of this was saving Garth. Still, the surname of DeLeon was one she'd hoped never to hear again. Surely it was only a coincidence. She'd ask again, as soon as they were safely away from here.

Once she had enough to wear for a week, she tied the sheet up as best she could. Now the trick would be getting out of the house. Rhonda had a nose for intrigue and she'd soon sense that something was up, even though she hadn't yet noticed baby Garth's absence. That would only be a matter of time. JJ didn't want to involve her neighbor if she could help it. Rhonda had already done more than enough to help.

Her phone pinged. Another text from Eric. Go out the window. Great idea.

After lifting the sash, she tossed her makeshift bag out before climbing over the sill.

Once outside, she prayed Rhonda wouldn't glance at the yard and see her. She hurried to Eric's SUV, relieved to see he was already inside, in the passenger seat, with the engine running. She gave one last glance over her shoulder before climbing into the driver's seat. No sign of Rhonda. Good. The less she knew, the better, especially in this situation.

"What's your plan?" she asked. "I know you must be up to something, since you wanted to leave much earlier."

As she pulled out of the driveway, he didn't answer at first. Instead, he directed her down the street and around the corner before asking her to pull over to the shoulder and park. "Look," he said, turning in his seat to face her. "You have a choice here. What I'm about to do might be wrong, but I feel in my gut it's what I have to do."

Somehow she knew what he would say before he said it. "You want to search for Garth alone."

One brow rose. "Exactly. I think I'll have a better chance if I don't have to play by the same rules law enforcement does. Plus they'll keep looking, with or without me, so there'll be double the chance to locate my son."

Slowly, she nodded. "You know they'll be furious."

"Yes. And they'll expend time and resources to locate us, because they'll think we know something we didn't tell them."

She liked that he included her by saying *us*. As if he knew she was with him, no matter what. "Do you not trust them?"

"Right now, I don't trust anyone." He shook his head. "Except you. I appreciate you being in my corner and wanting to help, despite barely knowing me."

Deciding to be honest, she gave him her truth. "I feel like I've know you forever."

When he grinned, she couldn't help but notice the attractive way the corners of his eyes crinkled. "Exactly. I'm not sure why that is, but I'm awfully glad we're friends."

Friends. Talk about quickly deflating her ego. Still, in a way, she knew he was right. The attraction remained, simmering beneath the surface, but they were definitely friends.

"Are you with me?" he asked. "Because we need to put

as much distance between us and Forestwood as we can before they realize we're not going to show."

Feeling a low thrum of excitement in her belly, she nodded. "Let's go."

As she was about to shift into Drive and pull back into the street, Eric covered her hand with his. "Thank you," he said. "I don't know what I'd do without your support. I can't stop worrying about him. I'm praying he's safe. If they so much as touch one single hair on that baby's head…"

"They won't." She squeezed his hand hard. "Don't even allow yourself to think it. They clearly need him for breeding or something."

He exhaled. "Thanks again. I needed to hear that." He took another deep breath. "I need to drive."

"No. You have a wounded leg and you just got out of the hospital."

"I don't drive with my left leg." His grin showed he knew she'd give in. "And I know where I'm going. Please."

The please did it. With a sigh, she got out and switched places with him.

"Thank you," he said. Pulling out into the street, he headed east. "I'm going to pick up 87 and go south."

Surprised, she eyed him. "Where are we heading?"

"Poughkeepsie. My ex-wife has family there. I figure I'll start with them."

"Why? I don't understand. You said she gave up all rights to Garth shortly after he was born."

"She did." His grim expression told her there was more. "But then, after a month went by, Yolanda changed her mind. But she was unstable, using drugs, and when I refused to cooperate she began harassing me. She made horrible accusations, trying to get me arrested and thrown in jail. All so she could get her hands on our son."

"Is that why you traveled clear across the country to Forestwood?"

"Yes."

"And you think your ex is behind Garth's kidnapping?"

He exhaled. "Yolanda was killed shortly after I got here. She attacked a Pack Protector and shot him, then turned the gun on herself. She didn't die, but vanished from the hospital, and they found her body in an exploded car a few miles away. At least, that's what they think. No one has actually given me verification on that."

Struggling to absorb this information, JJ shook her head. "That sounds like the plot from an action-adventure movie. What happened to the Pack Protector?"

"Unfortunately, he died, too. He was one of my friends."

"I'm sorry." Staring, JJ didn't know what else to say. The craziness Eric had been living with since his son was born seemed unimaginable.

"Who's DeLeon?" she asked, trying to sound casual.

"One of the Pack Protectors assigned to the case."

Immediately, relief filled her. Shawn was human. He might share the same last name, but no way could he be the same DeLeon Eric knew.

"Why?" Eric queried.

"I used to know someone with that last name," she said. "My ex, actually. But he's human, so they're not related. Which is what I expected, but still…"

"With all the crazy things happening to me, you never know. Anyway," Eric continued, "before I left California, Yolanda's mother and sister were making noises about wanting to see the baby. It's entirely possible one of them might have been behind this."

"But they live here in New York?"

"Her mom does," he admitted. "But they've been estranged since before we married. I have no idea where the sister lives."

"Yet you still moved here?"

He sighed. "To be honest, I didn't even consider her mother when I chose Forestwood. I'd almost completely forgotten about her. It wasn't until Garth was kidnapped and I started racking my brain that I remembered."

The thought that his ex's estranged mother might have taken his son seemed staggering, but JJ guessed the reality of Eric's life made it a very real possibility. "Do you really think…" She couldn't finish.

"I do." His grim tone matched the tenseness in his jawline. "Especially if they're even half as crazy as Yolanda was. At the very least, it's a possibility I don't want to discount. So we're going to Poughkeepsie to pay them a visit."

Chapter 18

They were a few miles south of Kingston when JJ's cell phone rang. "It's Rhonda," she said, frowning. "I feel terrible sneaking out of her house like that. I should tell her something."

"Don't answer," he urged. "We'll fill her in later."

Though her stomach churned, she let the call go to voice mail. "She's going to worry, you know. And she's been a good friend."

"How long have you known her?"

"Not long. I met her when I moved to Forestwood a little over a month ago." She glanced sideways at him, just as her phone beeped to tell her Rhonda had left a message. "Why?"

He shrugged. "Just making conversation. Rhonda's been great. She seems like a nice woman. A bit flirty, but nice. But I promise you, the less she knows, the better. In about an hour, Linda Felts and the others are going to descend on her, wanting to know where we are and if she's heard from us."

"Which is going to confuse her."

"True. But how much better if she doesn't feel compelled to lie?"

He had a point.

"I left a message for my new boss, explaining I was going to have to pass up on the job. I told her I was sorry and that I'd try to come by and explain later. At least that way she won't be expecting me."

"Good idea."

They stopped for gas in New Paltz. After filling up, Eric typed an address into his GPS. Once he'd finished, his cell rang. "It's Linda Felts. I'm going to have to ditch my phone. As a matter of fact, you should, too."

Wondering if he might have gone a little crazy, she eyed him. "What? Why?"

"Because they can track our phones. They don't even need a warrant." He cruised to a stop on the shoulder and got out. When he climbed back in, he smiled. "I put my phone under the front tire. When I go forward, the car will crush it. Let me have yours." He held out his hand.

"No. I'm kind of attached to this one." She cradled it protectively. "It's new. I just got it when I moved to Forestwood."

"I'll buy you a new one."

She didn't like the idea of being without a phone. "But all my numbers are in here."

"I'll take out your SIM card. When you get a new one, we'll use that card to retrieve all your info."

Reluctantly, she handed over her cell. Again, he stepped outside, and walked around to the other front tire. When he returned, he squeezed her shoulder. "It's going to be okay."

Though she nodded, she couldn't help but wonder if she'd made a huge mistake.

When he put the vehicle in Drive and pulled forward, she covered her ears with her hands. Childish, maybe, but she didn't want to hear the awful crunching sound when her iPhone was destroyed.

As they continued on, following the directions given by the dashboard GPS, JJ tried to relax.

"You're really attached to your phone, aren't you?" he asked.

She shrugged. "I am. I like knowing if I get in trouble, I have a way to reach help."

"Look inside the glove box," he said. "There are two budget cell phones in there. Pick one. And yes, it's only temporary. For now, it will have to do."

After doing as he asked, she removed the plastic case from one of the phones. "When did you get these?"

"Before I left Cali. You never know when something like that might come in handy."

Finally, they pulled up in front of a modest raised ranch. The robotic voice of the GPS announced they had arrived at their destination.

Suddenly nervous, JJ eyed the house. "Now what?"

"This is where Yolanda's mom lives. I'm going to ring the bell and, once she answers, introduce myself."

"Do you think she has Garth?"

Grim-faced, he shrugged. "I don't know. But I figure I'll be able to tell from her reaction."

"Just in case, do you want me to go around to the back and scope things out?" Her stomach might have twisted at the idea, but if Eric thought she should, she'd do it.

"Not yet. I don't know who all lives here. Just wait here and keep an eye out."

"Okay." She watched as he made his way to the front

door. More than anything, she hoped little Garth would be found safe. Here in the arms of his misguided but loving grandmother rather than with some demented cult intent on doing him harm.

The front door opened, though Eric didn't go inside. As he stood conversing with whoever had answered his knock, JJ guessed from the tense set of his shoulders that it wasn't going well. A moment later, the door closed and Eric made his way back to the SUV.

"Yolanda's mother, Sophia, answered, but she didn't even recognize me," he said as he climbed into the driver's seat. "Of course, we've only met once. Another woman who claimed to be her caregiver told me Sophia has dementia. If that's true—and I believe it is—there's zero chance she was the one who came after Garth."

"I'm sorry." JJ squeezed his shoulder. "I know this is disheartening. What do you want to do next?"

He blinked. "I'm not sure. I was so convinced she had Garth, and now..." Her heart squeezed as he hung his head and took a deep breath.

"You're tired and not thinking straight," she said. "Maybe you should get some rest. Things might appear clearer in the morning."

"I'd like to find a place to change," he said, surprising her. "This area has lots of woods and thickets. Sometimes being my other self brings clarity to my mind. Let's find a motel to stay for the night. Maybe one near a restaurant, so we can grab supper before dark. I don't want to hunt on an empty stomach. I'm apt to kill too many small animals, and that would be noticed."

Heart pounding, she took a deep breath. "Would you mind if I changed and hunted with you?"

Among her kind, this was a completely ordinary request. Wolves were by nature pack animals, and the more the merrier. She wasn't sure how that was among bears. It seemed to her that, in nature, they were much more solitary.

Eric appeared to be thinking while he drove. Though he didn't answer her right away, she had a feeling she'd crossed some forbidden boundary she'd known nothing about. Hurt stabbed her, swift and sharp, but she squashed it quickly. She had no right to expect him to do things just because her species considered it normal.

"Or do the Vedjorn not do that sort of thing?" she asked, more to give him an easy way out.

"Not usually," he admitted. "Though it's been a long time since I left Norway. In California, I mostly hunted alone. My ex came with me a time or two, but since our kind are few and far between, we'd both grown used to shifting by ourselves."

Hiding her disappointment, JJ managed a friendly smile. "It's okay. I understand. I guess you can go change, and then when you come back, I'll go out and do my thing."

Jaw tight, he shot a quick glance at her. "I actually wouldn't mind your company."

Her breath caught. "Okay. Sounds good then. Let's change before we find a motel and get dinner. After we hunt, we might not need to eat again."

Though he jerked his head in a nod, he didn't look at her. "Are you certain you…"

Since he let his words trail off, she tried to guess what he was asking. "Won't be intimidated because a bear and a wolf aren't normally running buddies? Of course not."

Now he glanced at her quickly, before returning his gaze to the road. "I was thinking more along the lines of won't find me repulsive. Believe me, I'm well aware of how the Pack regards my people."

"The Pack is a group of individuals," she pointed out.

"Not every single one thinks the same way as all the others. You know that."

At first he didn't respond. Finally, he gave a small nod. "Perhaps you're right." But his tone indicated he didn't believe her.

"Look," she said. "I've never met a bear shifter. But I've never been one of those who feel wolves are the best. Yes, there are more of us, but I recognize the others. Lion, tiger, panther, all the big cats—I'd love to meet one. And even though our town is well-known for harboring a Drakkor, I never witnessed her changing into a dragon."

His half smile made her heart do a quick flip-flop. Though still a long way from appearing happy, this was the best she'd seen him since Garth had been taken. "What are you trying to say?" he asked wryly.

"That my experience is limited, that's all. Heck, I've never even changed with other wolves before. Well, except for my mother. I have to admit that I'm very interested to see what it's like when you shift into bear."

"Probably much the same as when you become wolf." His expression grew serious. "You do know what happens after we change back to human, right?"

A tiny thrill went through her, settling into her core. "Yes," she answered, her face heating. "I'm aware." More than aware, actually. She actively hoped they could act on the fierce stab of desire they were sure to feel. As if she hadn't been fantasizing about doing just that.

"Don't worry, I can control myself," he said, dashing her hopes. "I won't touch you."

She wished she had the nerve to speak, to let him know she wanted him to touch her, aching for him with every fiber of her being. It had become a constant companion, this need for him.

They both were quiet as they drove to a large, wooded

park they'd passed earlier. Inside, JJ's heart pounded and she felt jittery, though she tried to seem calm and composed. She had no idea what Eric was thinking, whether he regretted whatever impulse had led him to agree to hunt with her.

They pulled into the deserted parking lot. At this time of the year, the woods were empty.

"Good," he said, sounding satisfied as he parked and killed the engine. "We have the place to ourselves."

Struck by a sudden attack of nerves, she opened her door and got out. "Let's do this," she said, sounding much more confident than she felt as she strode off into the woods. In the cold night air, her breath made little puffs ahead of her. Luckily, the waning moon provided enough light that they were able to make their way as humans. Once they became their beasts, their animal eyes would adjust much more quickly to the darkness.

He hurried to catch up to her. "You don't have to, you know. I won't think less of you if you want to back out."

"I get it." Slowing her pace, she exhaled. "If I seem a bit nervous, it's because of me, not you. I've never let anyone besides my mother see me shape-shift."

"Again, you don't have to. We can go our separate ways and meet up at a designated place when we're done, if you want."

"No." She stopped and turned to face him. "Let me have this experience, please. I consider you a friend and I'm looking forward to this." As she spoke, she felt a rush of expectation. Her words were true. Even if she wished Eric was more than a friend, at least she had that.

"Okay." He pointed to a narrow, apparently less used trail that veered off from the main one. "Let's try that way."

Suppressing a shiver, she did as he suggested. The cold had begun to seep through the soles of her shoes, chilling her bones. But that wouldn't last for long. Once she became wolf, her heavy winter fur would protect her.

Inside, her wolf paced. Already awake, her beast knew she would soon be let out to run. Anticipation overrode the last of JJ's human nerves.

Next to her, she sensed Eric's beast doing the same.

He caught her looking and nodded. "Raring to go. How about you?"

"The same." If only she could slow her racing heart.

Finally, they came to a small clearing and stopped. A large fallen tree off to one side would be the perfect place to stash their clothing. All around them were the faint sounds of nocturnal nature.

"Do you want to go first or shall I?" he asked.

The idea of stripping off her clothes in front of him and changing to wolf while he watched made her feel dizzy. "You, please. I want to see what happens when you become bear."

He stared at her hard, his face expressionless. "Okay. Whatever you do, don't let fear get the best of you. As bear, I'm pretty large and threatening, but I won't hurt you."

"I'll be fine."

At her response, he shrugged. "All right then. But don't say I didn't warn you."

Without waiting for her to respond, he peeled off his coat and placed it on the fallen tree. When he next proceeded to undo his belt, her mouth went dry. While a more polite person would have looked away, she kept her gaze trained on him, unwilling to miss a single second of this. For once, she wished for more light and less darkness, though she counted herself lucky that she was able to see him at all.

Next he removed his shirt, his skin gleaming in the moonlight. His muscles rippled with each movement, making her long to touch him. Luckily, her feet felt rooted in place as she waited for him to take off the rest of his clothes.

He stepped out of his shoes and socks without looking up. Now his jeans and underwear were all that remained. She held her breath, the anticipation building in her, even as her wolf snarled with impatience.

The jeans went and then, while she shamelessly ogled him, he dropped the boxers. She gulped and blinked. She had a few seconds' impression of him, impossibly large and already incredibly aroused, before he dropped to all fours on the forest floor and initiated his change.

Instead of the sparkling lights that surrounded a wolf shifting, she saw ripples of energy. Which made sense, because the change from human to bear had to be more powerful than human to wolf. While she watched, his perfect masculine body contorted. His bones stretched and elongated, and fur began to appear on his previously smooth skin.

And then, so suddenly she jumped back in surprise, a large brown bear reared up in front of her. Powerful, strong and breathtaking. It—he—eyed her for a moment before lumbering off into the underbrush.

Damn. Heart racing, JJ felt her fingers tremble as she fumbled to rid herself of her clothes. Finally, they were off, the frigid air bringing goose bumps to her naked skin. Like Eric had done, she also got down on her hands and knees, loving the feel of the damp earth and rustling leaves under her.

Once more she inhaled deeply, and she, too, began to change. Around her, the usual sparkling lights reassured her, even as she grimaced at the mild discomfort while bones lengthened and changed shape. For her, becoming wolf always felt like this, slightly painful and also invigorating. Though much smaller in body, she wasn't as fast as Eric, though once she gave herself over to her wolf she lost all sense of chronological time. As wolf, she lived in the moment.

Finally, her change complete, she lifted her muzzle to the wind to locate Eric's scent. Tangy and sharp as it was, she quickly located it, and loped off after him. When she caught him, he playfully rolled, inviting her to tag him with her nose. Once she had, she did the same, leaping and spinning in a manner more like a pup than a full grown she-wolf. It had been years since she'd felt this carefree and playful. Overjoyed, she grinned.

They played tag for a good while. Though he outweighed her by twice as much, Eric was gentle with her, careful of his massive claws and sharp teeth. For her part, she tried to do the same, though a couple times she nipped him in her excitement. He never protested or retaliated, making her wonder if he even felt anything through his thick fur coat.

If anyone had been watching, the sight of a massive bear and a good-sized wolf running together might have seemed like something miraculous. Or at least unusual. But as they chased each other and played, a deep happiness filled JJ's wolf self, a joyful contentment that even overrode her need to hunt. Once or twice, as a very young wolf pup, she'd played with similar abandon, until her mother had ended the hunt. She'd never thought she would feel this way again.

Her stomach growled, reminding her she hadn't eaten. She needed to hunt. Yet she was having too much fun to break it off, at least just yet. Her hunger pangs would have to wait.

Though not for long. A quick whiff of a scent had her turning, just in time to catch the flash of gray as a rabbit

raced past. Without a second thought, she took off after
it, leaving Eric to bring up the rear. Unlike wolves, bears
were omnivores, she knew, just as comfortable eating roots
and berries as meat. The need to hunt might not be as ingrained in Eric, but JJ felt compelled to follow the tantalizing scent of her natural prey.

Without heed to direction or distance, she crashed
through the brush, running low to the ground. Eventually, she lost scent of the rabbit, raising her head to find
she had no idea where she might be. Again, she lifted her
snout and scented the wind. Nothing. Odd, since Eric's
bear smell had been strong, almost overpowering.

Thinking hard, she remembered where the moon had
been positioned, and took off in the direction from which
she'd hopefully come. Several times she stopped and
sniffed, slightly worried that she still could not locate Eric.

Just as she felt confident that she'd almost reached the
clearing, she came across the same large boulder she'd
passed a few minutes earlier. Which meant she'd been trav-
eling in a circle. While wolves didn't get lost, as far as she
knew, her bad sense of direction as human had translated
to tonight's change.

No scent of bear reached her, but in the distance she
heard a crashing sound. Something big, moving fast. Bear
Eric? Or someone else? Instinct had her staying hidden,
low to the ground, at least until she ascertained whether
it was friend or foe.

The scent reached her at the same time as the snuffling
sounds. Bear. Eric. With a joyous woof, she ran toward
him, head-butting him hard enough that he staggered. Instinctively, he let out a startled snarl, which, had she not
known him, would have scared the heck out of her.

Her stomach growled again, loudly this time. Panting,
she wondered if Eric would object to one more hunt, a pro-

ductive one this time. But no, he shook his massive head, and then moved off, looking back at her as if asking her to follow him.

After a few minutes, they arrived back in the clearing where they'd left their clothes. Eric stopped, eyeing her. She knew he wanted to know if she wanted to change back to human first, or should he.

Sitting back on her haunches, she considered. She had no way to communicate other than by body movement, so she couldn't tell him she thought they should both shift at the same time. She dipped her head at him, aware he'd take the gesture to mean he should begin.

A second later, he did.

Inhaling sharply, she initiated her own change. This time, going back to her natural state, the pain seemed far less and was over much more quickly.

Just like that, she found herself lying in her human form, stark naked on the cold, damp forest floor.

Restless and stimulated, she stretched once, her nipples pebbling from the cold, and pushed herself to her feet. Anticipation making her heart pound, she looked around for Eric, eager to see the force of his own arousal, hoping it would match hers.

Chapter 19

To JJ's disappointment, Eric stood with his back to her, already stepping into his clothes.

"Wait," she rasped. "Not yet." Her quiet plea reverberated with longing. Slowly, he turned, holding his shirt over the part of him that she most ached to see.

"JJ, we discussed this." He shook his head, almost as if by doing so he could shake off the primal urge of his body's desire. "Friends don't take advantage of friends."

"Friends don't make friends beg." The words slipped out before she had time to consider them. Once said, she couldn't call them back, so she decided she might as well run with it. "You know I want you. And I'm aware you want me, too. What could be the harm?"

Turning away, he continued dressing, as if he hadn't heard her. While she stood shivering, naked and aching, refusing to let the sting of his rejection win.

Finally, he faced her again. Now fully dressed, even

in the shadowy forest he couldn't hide the desire blazing from his eyes. "Put some clothes on, please." He sounded as if he'd swallowed a mouthful of rusty nails. "You know I want you, JJ. But if and when we ever come together, it won't be because we've just shape-shifted. I want it to mean more than that."

Stunned, she lowered her gaze. How could she argue with that? Even though she knew coupling after shape-shifting was as natural as breathing.

No matter what words he used, she couldn't keep from feeling inadequate. As though her naked female form hadn't been enough to make him want her.

Dressing quickly, her movements wooden, she wondered how she'd ever face him again.

He must have sensed this. For whatever reason, Eric seemed unusually attuned to her emotions. But as soon as she'd finished dressing, pulling on her winter parka, he strode off, barking out a quick order to follow him.

If they hadn't been in an unfamiliar area, she would have done the opposite. Anything to keep from facing him and making herself realize he didn't need her, at least not in the way she did him.

Finally, they emerged from the trail into the parking lot. His SUV still sat there, under a streetlight. She kept as far away from him as possible. Once he'd used the key fob to unlock the doors, she climbed up into the passenger seat and turned her face toward the window.

Silent as well, he turned the key and started the motor. "The heat will take some time to come on," he said, his tone casual.

Small talk. She refused to acknowledge his comment, but continued to stare out at the dark parking lot and wait for him to put the SUV into Drive.

Instead, he reached out and squeezed her shoulder. Despite herself, she jumped.

"Come on, JJ. I don't break my word. Not if I can help it."

This got her attention. "Your word?"

"Yes. I promised not to touch you. No matter what. We discussed this, well in advance of what we both knew would happen."

She closed her eyes. She hadn't had the nerve to tell him earlier how much she would have welcomed his touch, and after what had just happened in the woods, she didn't know, either. "It's okay," she said, pleased her voice came out steady. "We're friends, nothing more. I was just overcome after shifting. It happens. It's all gone now." A tiny white lie, but completely necessary.

With his gaze shuttered, he nodded. "All right. Now let's find a motel and bunk down for the night. We'll head back home early in the morning."

Her stomach chose that moment to loudly protest. "I need to eat," she said. "I didn't have much luck hunting earlier."

"You know what?" His remote expression relaxed. "I do, too. Let's find a place to grab a late dinner."

By the time they'd located a restaurant and taken a seat in a booth near the back, JJ felt better. "Listen," she began, gathering up her courage to tell him the truth. "I—"

"Can I get you two something to drink?" the waitress asked, interrupting. JJ ordered a glass of wine and Eric a beer. Once the woman had hurried off to get their drinks, JJ opened the menu and studied it.

"You were saying?" Eric asked.

Suddenly glad she hadn't spilled her guts, JJ shrugged. "I don't remember. Whatever it was, it mustn't have been important. Now to decide what I want to eat. Everything looks so good."

Eric nodded, taking one more glance at his menu before closing it. "I'm in the mood for steak," he said, studying her. "How about you?"

She thought of the rabbit she'd been chasing in the woods and her mouth watered. "Since rabbit isn't a choice on the menu, I'm going with chicken."

After bringing their drinks and taking their orders, the waitress promised their food would be ready soon and took off again.

"I'm sorry," Eric said, reaching across the table for JJ's hand. "I didn't mean to insult you."

Though she had a fleeting urge to cover her embarrassment with a flip remark, JJ decided if he could be honest, so could she. "I'm trying not to take it personally, but it's difficult. It's just…" She gave a helpless shrug. "It's just what we do."

He nodded. "I'll be honest with you, JJ. I want you. But right now, with Garth missing, I can't focus on anything else. And if you and I—when you and I—ever get together, I want to be able to give you my undivided attention."

Though warmth flooded her at his words, she hoped she didn't show it. "You're good, I'll give you that."

His puzzled frown didn't seem feigned. "Good?"

"At sweet-talking." She flashed him what she hoped was a careful smile. "Thanks. And know this. We will get Garth back."

"Yes. We will." Because the alternative was not only unacceptable, but unthinkable.

Their food arrived and they each dug in. JJ had to pace herself, feeling she could have shoved the entire meal in her face and inhaled it. Even so, she cleaned her plate in record time. But looking up at Eric, she saw that he, too, had finished.

"I wonder if we set a new record?" She kept her tone light, though the fact that she had to stifle a yawn before she'd finished might have ruined it.

"Maybe so."

After paying the bill, they drove down the street and checked into a single-story motel. The room they were given was small but clean, with two double beds.

"Are you going to be okay with this?" Eric watched her closely. She couldn't help but wonder what he'd do if she said no. Offer to sleep in the car? Of course, the knowledge that he wouldn't be touching her would make any woman feel at ease, right? Even if she still, despite everything, wanted more, she'd get over it. She had to.

"I'll be fine." Another yawn. "I'm so tired I don't care where I sleep. I just need a place to lay my head."

Despite her exhaustion, falling asleep seemed impossible. Her body craved rest, but she couldn't shut off her mind. She'd made sure to slip in between the sheets well before Eric came out of the bathroom, and yet the heat suffusing her had her fighting the urge to kick away the covers.

He'd emerged from the bathroom fully dressed, clicking off the lights before divesting himself of his jeans. Every movement, every rustle, had her imagining him naked beneath his covers. She couldn't help but wonder what he'd do if she crossed the space between their beds and joined him there.

Sometime after, she dozed. She woke to a sound she didn't recognize, the faintest noise, muffled. Listening, she pushed herself up on her elbows, wondering if she should alert Eric, just in case. As her eyes adjusted to the dim light, she realized Eric had gotten out of bed and taken a seat in one of the armchairs near the window. She could barely make out his outline, but he appeared to be doubled over, hunched in pain. And then, with growing worry, she realized what she'd heard had been him, trying hard to silence the sounds of his anguish.

Her heart broke. Without a second thought, she hurried from her bed and went to him. Kneeling in front of him, she saw he'd covered his face with his hands, and his shoulders shook with the force of his silent emotion.

What else could she do but gather him close to her? "It's all right," she soothed. "I promise, it's going to be okay."

The instant she touched him, he froze. As she gently peeled his hands away from his face, she wasn't surprised to see the gleam of moisture in his eyes.

"I'm sorry," he muttered, his voice breaking. "I'm just worried sick about my baby boy."

She kissed him then, aware she could do little to ease his pain other than offer herself. As a distraction, maybe, or in sympathy… Either way, she knew her desire, her need, could help make him feel better, if only temporarily. As for herself, well, maybe he could heal her, too.

As their lips touched, the jolt of the connection sent warmth through her. Opening her mouth to him, she let her tongue spar with his, finding the taste of him intoxicating and arousing. She knew he claimed he couldn't want her, but she also knew he needed something to take away the sharpest edges of his pain. She was willing to be that distraction, giving them both what they desired.

He turned, she shifted, and then she found herself straddling him. A bit shocked as she settled herself over his arousal—Shawn had never allowed this—JJ found she quite liked it. The fact that she wore only thin panties, while Eric had on boxer shorts, made the contact almost as good as if they were naked.

He stroked her with his fingers. Already wet, her body became slicker. She moaned, unable to keep from clenching herself around him as he pressed inside her. At her fevered response, he arched himself, thrusting up.

"That's it," he growled. "The clothing has to go. I need you naked, touching me skin to skin."

Hooking one finger into the waistband of her panties, he tugged them down over her hips. She lifted herself, stepping out of them as he hurriedly divested himself of his cotton boxers. His body, hard and thick, rose to meet her hungry gaze.

Heart racing, she couldn't resist touching him. As she closed her hand around his shaft, he groaned. His body throbbed. Frantic, she rose, settled over him again, then lowered herself slowly, until she'd sheathed him deep inside her. The feeling of fullness, of completion, so stunned her that she froze, unable to move, unable to breathe.

And then, beneath her, he brought himself up, going even deeper. She gasped, and rocked in response. Together, they danced the age-old movements of mating. As the pleasure built nearly to the point of explosion, he went still.

"Don't. Move." He sounded as if he spoke through gritted teeth.

Though the order had been clear, she could no more resist moving than she could stop her heart from beating. Though she tried to go slow, the frenzied need built inside her. This time, he didn't try to stop her. Instead, he let himself go along for the ride.

When her desire finally peaked, she shuddered again and again, as pleasure rippled through her in waves. A second later, he groaned and pushed himself even deeper inside her, his body pulsing with his own release.

As they held each other, sweat-slickened bodies gradually cooling, she realized they hadn't used protection.

Their lovemaking had been too spontaneous for either of them to think about such a precaution. Foolish, but even worse, she wasn't on contraceptives. Though with Shawn she'd always vigilantly taken her birth control pills, she hadn't refilled the prescription last month, after she'd run out. She hadn't thought she'd need them, with no man on the horizon.

Keeping her concerns to herself, because Eric definitely had enough on his mind, she finally rolled away and headed to the bathroom. When she returned, she went to her own bed, feeling slightly awkward, a whole lot sore and way more satisfied than she probably should.

He got up slowly and, on his way to the bathroom, stopped and kissed her cheek. While she lay there dazed and ridiculously pleased, he continued on, closing the door quietly behind him.

Turning on her side, she shut her eyes and tried to will herself to sleep.

The next morning, Eric wasn't sure whether to be angry with himself over his shocking lack of self-control or to push it to the side until he had the strength of mind to deal with it. Right now, worry and fear for Garth consumed him, though JJ with her generous spirit and earthy sensuality had managed to make him forget temporarily. Despite what he'd told her earlier, turning away from her splendidly naked body in the forest had been one of the hardest things he'd ever done. Only the knowledge that giving in to a moment's intense desire could ruin their friendship had stopped him. He didn't know what he'd do without JJ's help and support. He could only hope the previous night's lovemaking hadn't managed to wreck everything.

After cleaning up in the bathroom, he'd walked past JJ and gone to sleep in his own bed, though he would have liked nothing better than to crawl in next to her and hold her. But while he knew he would have drawn comfort from the simple touch of her, doing such a thing might hint at promises he wouldn't be able to keep. Not now, maybe not ever. He refused to do that to her. In his mind, that would be an even worse betrayal than what had already occurred.

Somehow, despite his inner turmoil, he'd managed to sleep. When he next opened his eyes, sunlight spilled around the edges of the light-blocking curtains. In the other bed, JJ sat up and stretched, glancing over at him while he lay motionless and watched her through half-closed eyes.

When she got up and headed to the bathroom, he stayed in bed a few minutes longer, trying to calm his instantly roiling gut. If Garth had been here, Eric would have been the first one up, changing his son's diaper and warming a bottle. The thought made him ache all over.

JJ emerged a few minutes later. He tried to smile at her, aware his weak attempt probably resembled a grimace.

"Your turn," she said, her voice brisk. "Do you want first shower, or shall I?"

Grateful that she didn't want to talk about what had happened between them, he exhaled. "Do you mind if I go first?" he asked quietly. As usual, worry and fear continued to simmer within him, but he refused to give in to it again, as he had last night. "It'll just take me a few minutes and then the place is all yours."

"Okay." She seemed unusually shy. "I'm going to turn the TV on and see if there's anything interesting on the morning shows. Maybe I can catch the local news."

He took his shower the way he always did—hot and quick and furious. Once he'd toweled off, he felt at least fairly ready to face the day. While JJ showered, he planned to try and firm up his plans to find his son.

After he'd dressed, he emerged to find her standing

motionless in front of the television. Something in her posture alerted him.

"What's up?" he asked.

"Come here," she said. The panicked undertone in her voice had him hurrying. "Look. We're on the news."

"On the news? That doesn't make sense. We haven't done anything wrong." He moved closer.

"The authorities are looking for these two missing people," the announcer said, flashing both his and JJ's photos on the screen. And then, to Eric's disbelief and shock, a video began, showing the recovery of a missing infant supposedly tied to the two of them. The baby had been found with a woman who was apparently trying to cross the international border, into Canada. Her name was not mentioned. The newscaster finished up with the news that the baby was safe.

Garth. It had to be.

For a second, Eric couldn't force a single word past the lump in his throat.

"Garth," he said, staring at the screen, not quite certain he could believe his ears. "They found him."

JJ nodded. When she turned her face to his, tears were streaming in silver tracks down her cheeks. "He's all right," she sobbed, her voice catching.

"Come here." Emotion made his own sound rough. He held out his arms. With a choked sob, she launched herself at him, wrapping him in a fierce hug. He held on to her, feeling as if he'd been drowning and had gone under for the third and final time before being thrown a life raft.

"He's okay, he's okay," JJ kept repeating. And then she stiffened and pulled away. "Eric, we've got to find out where he is. We need to go get him."

"Exactly. And we will. Get ready, as quickly as you can."

After sending her off to the shower, he dialed Linda

Felts. Her voice mail picked up, so he left a message with his new number. He figured right now she was in the middle of a heck of a lot of craziness. He began packing up both his and JJ's belongings in preparation for checking out.

When JJ reappeared, her long hair still damp, she hurried over. "Well?" she asked. "What did they say?"

"I left a message. Let's grab breakfast on the road. I figure we'll head back to Rhonda's house and make it easy for them to find us."

They got food at a drive-through and ate while he drove.

They pulled up in front of Rhonda's shortly before eleven. The construction crews were busy working on JJ's house. She bit her lip, looking from her place to Rhonda's. "I think I'm going to go over and check on them," she said. "Want to join me?"

With impatience thrumming through his blood, he managed to nod, not wanting to have to make explanations to Rhonda alone. He kept his phone in his hand, silently willing Felts—or someone, anyone—to call back. If he didn't hear from her in the next half hour, he would make a repeat phone call.

JJ held out her hand and he took it.

Inside, the workers had made tremendous progress. The front entrance and hall looked completely repaired. It had even been repainted. The soggy smoke smell had vanished, also. The workers all seemed to be upstairs. He wasn't sure if that was a good thing or bad. Maybe that meant they'd finished repairing the downstairs.

"Wow." Eyes wide, JJ was turning in a slow circle. "Amazing."

His cell phone rang. He started, his heart pounding.

JJ froze. "Answer it," she said.

As if he needed urging. He already had it out of his pocket and his password typed in.

"Where the hell are you?" Linda Felts demanded once he'd answered. "We've wasted valuable resources searching for you and—"

He cut her off. "Where's Garth? I saw on the news that you found him. I want my son."

Silence. Then she sighed. "That's a long story."

His gut clenched at her ambiguous words. "I don't care. You can tell me the story later. Not right now. Just let me know where I can go to pick up my boy."

"We'll bring him to you," she said. "Eventually. We've got some questions we're hoping you can answer first."

Unease coiled in the pit of his stomach. "Is this some kind of a trick?"

"Of course not. There's simply a lot more than meets the eye. We need to talk in person rather than on the phone."

"After." He snarled the word. "After I have my son, then we'll talk. Not before. Do you understand?"

"We'll be there in half an hour," she said, and then ended the call.

Dazed, he stared at his phone for a second.

"What the heck was that?" JJ asked. "Is everything all right?"

"I don't know." Pushing away his despair, he shook his head. "That entire conversation was strange. I'm beginning to wonder if that video was fake."

"What?" JJ gasped. "Why would they do something like that? It makes no sense."

"I don't know."

Coming closer, JJ laid her hand on his shoulder. "Linda is a Pack Protector, and as such, is held to a higher ethical standard. She—they—wouldn't trick you. They're on your side."

"Are they?" He couldn't keep the bitterness from his voice. "She never definitely said they had Garth. Though she did say they'd bring him to me, eventually."

JJ cussed, a rarity for her. "Hand me your phone. I'm about to call that woman and give her a piece of my mind."

"It's okay," he said, even though it wasn't. Not even remotely. "I don't want to risk antagonizing her. She'll be here in thirty minutes. You can tell her in person."

Chapter 20

Rather than dealing with explanations to Rhonda, they elected to wait at JJ's house. Eric insisted they complete the inspection, forcing himself to care that the downstairs area—his living space—appeared completely finished. There was even electricity again. And water. "I wonder if this means Garth and I can move in again. Once I have him back, that is."

Though a shadow crossed her face, she nodded. "It probably does. I confess, I'm almost afraid to go upstairs and see my place."

Which right now was the last thing he wanted to do. He couldn't keep from checking his watch, dismayed to see only ten minutes had passed since Felts's call. "We've got time," he said grimly. Actually, he wanted to start pacing, outside, where he could see the Protector's car pull up. Waiting infuriated and worried him. Especially since he didn't know if they were really bringing Garth or not.

Judging from the nervous apprehension on JJ's face, she needed a distraction almost as badly as he did. "Let's at least go take a look. Then we'll wait outside on the front porch."

She didn't move. "I'd rather just go outside now. I can't take the suspense, the not knowing."

This he understood. But he also knew it would be worse if they just stood there staring at the street, waiting for the vehicle to appear. "Come on," he urged. "Upstairs. Let's take a look. We'll hurry."

Reluctantly, she followed him up the stairs. They'd just reached the landing outside her living space when the downstairs front door flew open, hitting the wall with a thud.

"Freeze," a male voice shouted. "No one move. We've got this place surrounded. Eric Mikkelson and Julia Jacobs, you're under arrest."

Eric's first instinct was to shield JJ with his body. He wasn't sure what kind of game the Protectors were playing, but he didn't want her risking her life for his mess.

"We're here," he shouted. "Upstairs, on the landing." The hammering in JJ's living area stopped, which meant the contractors had heard him. Perfect. It never hurt to have witnesses.

"Come down with your hands up," Felts ordered. Good, at least he wouldn't be dealing with a total stranger.

He glanced back at JJ. Her petrified expression warred with the outrage in her eyes. "Put your hands up," he told her quietly. "And don't lower them until they say you can, no matter what."

She nodded. "But why?"

"I have no idea." Turning, he raised his hands and began making his way, step by step, slowly down the stairs. "Stay behind me."

When they turned the corner, he saw Linda Felts, her weapon drawn, flanked by two others who, judging by the auras, were also Protectors.

"Where's my son?" he demanded, shooting her a hard look.

"He's safe." Her own hard glare infuriated him. "But we have a few questions for the two of you."

He'd already started shaking his head before she'd finished speaking. "Not until I have my boy."

"Are we being charged with something?" JJ asked, stepping out from behind him, in complete disregard of his instructions. "If so, you'd better charge us. And I'll be contacting an attorney, so if you do charge us with something, I'll be wanting to speak with her first."

After a quick, startled look, Felts shook her head and laughed. "Honey, we're Protectors. You know that. We are definitely *not* human law-enforcement. As Pack, we operate by our own rules, not the ones the human police and FBI have in place. You're under Pack law now. You don't get an attorney."

JJ swallowed, but to her credit, her expression remained undaunted. "I still have the right to know the accusations being made against me."

"Hello?" Rhonda was coming up the porch steps. "JJ, is everything okay in here? I saw you and Eric come back and then—" She stopped short as she entered the foyer and saw Linda Felts and her two armed agents. Fear flashed across her face, though she quickly hid it. "What exactly is going on here?" she demanded.

"That's what I want to know," JJ replied. "These people just showed up and claimed they're arresting us, but they won't say what the charges are. Not only that, but Eric's baby has gone missing and these people supposedly found him, but won't give him back to us. I think you need to call 911."

Involving the humans. Exactly the last thing the Pack Protectors would want. They'd really have a difficult time making explanations, since they couldn't tell humans the truth.

"Pack Protectors?" Her expression grim, Rhonda looked from one to the other. Linda Felts jerked her head in a grudging nod. She could tell by Rhonda's aura that she, too, was a shape-shifter.

"I thought your job was to uphold the law," Rhonda continued sternly. "Not break it. Stealing this man's child and now threatening to arrest them without good cause doesn't sound like the Pack Protectors we all know and love."

Wow. Even Eric was impressed by Rhonda's confident and authoritative tone. He saw the way Felts blanched, but the Protector stuck to her guns.

"This is none of your concern," she said coolly. "I suggest you simply turn around and march right back to wherever you came from. Unless you want to be arrested, too."

Instead of appearing worried by the threat, Rhonda laughed. "Just try it," she said. "I'm sure even corrupt Pack Protectors have to draw the line at cold-blooded murder."

JJ gasped. Clearly, the thought of being killed hadn't occurred to her. It had to Eric, though. And he knew he couldn't allow it to happen, because Garth needed his father.

"I'm not going anywhere," Rhonda declared, crossing her arms. "Not until I'm certain my friends here are safe."

Felts made a sound of disgust and holstered her weapon. "Stand down," she ordered, and the other agents did the same. Jerking her thumb toward Rhonda, she met Eric's gaze. "Who is this woman?"

"JJ's next-door neighbor. The three of us have been living with her while JJ's house is repaired."

"From the fire," Rhonda added helpfully. "Now I'm wondering if you Protectors had anything to do with setting that?"

JJ gasped again. "This is a mess" she managed to mutter.

"Isn't it?" Rhonda's voice was a mixture of gleeful and disgusted. She still seemed poised to attack at the slightest provocation. Inside, Eric's bear reacted to the hostility emanating from her and reared up, massive head cocked in interest. The urge to change, right then, right there, rocked Eric, but he managed to wrestle his other self quickly back into submission.

When he looked up, Rhonda was watching him with what he could only describe as a satisfied gleam in her eye.

"I don't understand any of this," JJ said quietly. "We were going to a safe house with your agent. Someone attacked us and—"

"Our agent was killed." Felts looked from JJ to Eric, her expression cold. "This is the second agent we lost while working with Eric. This time, we've received reputable intel that you two knew this was going to happen."

"That's ridiculous." Now furious, Eric glared at the Protector. "Explain our motives, please. And identify the source of this so-called reputable information. Because from where I stand, that is nonsense. It defies all logic. Not only was JJ knocked out, but I was injured in the shootout, and my baby was taken. How could you—how could anyone—possibly think I'd be okay with that?"

"It's not you we're concerned about." Felts swung her gaze around and pinned JJ with it. "It's her. One of the suspects we have in custody has told us Julia Jacobs did this in a twisted plot to gain control of your child."

Stunned into silence, Eric struggled to make sense of her words. JJ appeared equally shocked, already shaking her head. He waited for her to deny the accusations, but she remained silent. Even Rhonda now eyed her friend with suspicion and doubt in her gaze.

He thought about his ex-wife and how completely Yolanda had fooled him. Was it possible that he'd been tricked again, this time by a warm and giving redhead?

No. "I don't believe it," he declared, earning a grateful look from JJ. "If she wanted Garth, she'd had numerous opportunities to take him. She's been my friend and his, and she'd never in a million years do something like this."

"Thank you." JJ finally found her voice, gratitude and something else resonating in it. "He's right. I don't know what's wrong with you people, but I'm not the bad guy in this situation. I'm also a victim here."

"What have you lost?" Felts asked, her tone skeptical.

JJ stared at the other woman. "My home, for starters. Is it true? Were the Protectors behind the fire?"

"No." Of this Felts appeared certain. "You never even came onto our radar until you decided to tag along with Eric and his son."

"Speaking of my son," Eric interjected. "Do you really have him safe or was that a ruse to get us to come in? Because so help me, if he's still out there somewhere, in danger from a bunch of religious fanatics, I'll—"

"Garth is fine. He's being looked after by our people."

Eric sagged with relief. Meanwhile, Felts continued holding his gaze. "We've arrested two people for his kidnapping. Your ex-mother-in-law and her nurse."

"What?" He blinked. "I visited my ex-mother-in-law yesterday. There's no way she could have been involved. She has dementia."

"There is some cognitive impairment," Felts conceded.

"But she's still largely functional. We're still questioning her and the nurse. There are several more people involved in this. Julia Jacobs was specifically mentioned as one of them."

"By whom?"

"Does it matter?" Felts barked. "Why aren't you more concerned that your supposed friend apparently betrayed you?"

"Because I don't believe it." Deliberately, he reached out and gathered JJ close. "And you still haven't explained to me exactly why you do."

Clearly frustrated, the Protector grimaced. "There are other things in play that we aren't at liberty to reveal yet. When the time is right, we will."

"But my son is safe, right?" Even though they'd already said he was, Eric wanted to hear it again.

"Yes."

"Then why won't you let me have him back?"

"We have to deal with all threats first." Felts dipped her head toward JJ. "There's no way we're letting him around anyone who might mean him harm."

While he appreciated their concern, he didn't understand why Garth was suddenly so important to them. Something wasn't right with their story.

Aware now, more than ever, that he had to be careful, Eric swallowed. "Was there ever even a real cult who wanted him? Or was that some bizarre story you cooked up for whatever reason?"

Again Felts glanced at Rhonda, who watched the exchange with avid interest. "I'm not comfortable with discussing this in front of your neighbor."

He agreed. "Rhonda, you should go. JJ and I will fill you in later."

"Are you sure you two will be okay?" Rhonda asked.

"Yes. Please leave. The sooner I can get through this nonsense, the faster I can see my son."

Though she huffed, Rhonda turned and went out the front door. "I'll be in my kitchen if anyone needs me," she called. "Just shout. I've got really good hearing."

Once she was gone, Felts sighed. "Your ex-wife might not be dead."

Convinced he must have heard incorrectly, Eric asked her to repeat herself.

"I said we believe Yolanda is still alive. And she's behind the attempt to steal Garth. She wants her son, according to her mother. And she'll stop at nothing to get him."

He shook his head in denial. "But you found her body, with Jason's, remember? A positive ID was made, or so I was told."

"And you still haven't explained why you think I'm involved in all of this," JJ added, her arms crossed and her expression tight. "I didn't even know Eric until he rented the bottom floor of my house."

"Do you know a Shawn DeLeon?"

JJ's expression froze. "Yes." Her clipped response seemed at odds with the stark look of fear in her eyes. "What about him?"

"He has friends who are Pack Protectors," Felts began. "Actually, his older brother, Frank, is assigned to Eric's case."

"Brother?" JJ frowned. "How is that possible? Shawn is human and Frank is Pack."

"Shawn is Frank's adoptive brother. It turns out that his parents took him in when Shawn's mother was killed in a subway accident."

"Frank DeLeon is related to Shawn," JJ repeated, as if she didn't believe it. "The Pack Protector who is helping Eric with his case."

"Exactly." Now Felts sounded bored. "And if you have a problem with that, you'll need to take it up with Frank."

"If you want to, JJ, we will. I keep waiting for him to make a reappearance," Eric stated. "I'm sure he could help you sort through everything. Frank DeLeon's a good guy."

"Maybe so." JJ cleared her throat. "His brother, Shawn, is not."

Eric looked from her to the Protector. "What does De-Leon's brother have to do with any of this?"

"He asked his brother to help him locate you," Felts said, eyeing JJ. "He also gave us some information that led us to believe you are more involved in this case than you let on."

"I'd be careful of believing anything Shawn DeLeon has to say." JJ sounded brittle, as if made of glass and about to shatter at any moment.

Still not understanding, Eric caught JJ's arm. "Was he your former boyfriend?"

Swallowing hard, JJ held his gaze. "Yes."

"He said fiancé," Felts corrected.

"No. We lived together, but were never engaged. And I broke it off a couple of months ago."

"Again, not according to him." It almost sounded as if Felts was enjoying herself. "He said when he refused to allow you to get pregnant, you ran off. And that you are so desperate for a baby, he's worried you planned to steal one. Is that what happened here, with Garth?"

"No." Keeping her chin up, JJ swayed slightly. Then she squared her shoulders and met Felts's gaze. "He's not only a liar, but he's dangerous. I'm sure he's furious that I dared to leave him. After all, he regards me as his property. Please don't let him know how to find me."

Felts cocked her head. "I'm sorry to say it's a bit too late for that. He already knows."

Eric caught JJ as she slid silently to the floor.

* * *

When JJ opened her eyes again, a jolt of sheer terror made her gasp. She sat up, her head pounding and her mouth so dry it might have been full of cotton.

"Hey." Eric's voice.

Blinking, she tried to focus, finally succeeding as he moved closer, into her line of vision. She saw that they were still inside her house, downstairs in Eric's living room. He'd evidently carried her there and placed her on his sofa.

"You've got to get me out of here." She didn't bother to try and hide the panic in her voice. "If Shawn comes after me, I'm as good as dead."

"Are you serious, or...?"

"Or what? Being dramatic? I can't tell you how many times he's threatened to kill me if I ever left him."

"Is he human or Pack?"

"Human."

Eric shook his head. "Then you were never in any real danger. Any wolves can defend themselves against a mere human."

"What?" She couldn't help but stare at him in rising horror. "You know the edict. I can't harm a human while in my wolf form. I'd be hunted down by the Protectors."

"Not if it was in self-defense." He seemed too calm, his voice flat and rational, she realized. Almost as if he was humoring her.

Then she remembered the lie Shawn had told the Protectors. A falsehood Eric apparently believed. That stung, but then again, she wasn't sure she wouldn't wonder which was the truth if their situations had been reversed.

"I would never hurt Garth," she said. "And I promise you, I had nothing to do with his abduction."

Chapter 21

JJ held her breath while Eric studied her. Finally, his expression softened. "I know you didn't. I'm just puzzled as to why Felts thinks you did. I've got a call in to Frank DeLeon to see if I can get this cleared up."

She winced. "If Shawn is his brother, it won't matter what you or I say. Blood runs thick. He'll help him."

"I wouldn't be too sure of that. Frank takes his job seriously. And this Shawn person sounds like an all-around bad guy."

"He's a stockbroker. Well respected among his peers."

After pulling out a chair next to the couch, Eric took her hand. "How about you fill me in? I had no idea you were in an abusive relationship."

To her horror, her eyes filled with tears. Swiping at them with the back of her hand, she took a moment to gather her composure. "I didn't know," she finally said. "I grew up in the city, and met him right after college. I wasn't sure what I wanted to do, and since my degree was in business, I took a receptionist job at the finance company he worked for. He was tall and handsome and sure of himself. Everything I wasn't. He drew me in the way a bright light attracts a moth."

Saying nothing, Eric waited.

"It started with small things at first. He didn't like my outfit, or the way I fixed my hair. Soon I was scrambling to please him, because he was always so right, and I wanted him to love me."

Now that she heard herself speaking the truth of their life, she could only wonder how she hadn't seen it sooner.

"The first time he hit me, he apologized. But he also said it was all my fault. If I'd been better, prettier, less *me*, it would never have happened." She gave a self-deprecating laugh. "And I don't know why, but I believed him."

"Until one day you didn't."

She nodded. "Exactly. Until one day I didn't." Swallowing hard to get past the lump in her throat, she shrugged. "And now I'm here. My great-aunt passed away and left me the house in Forestwood. I made sure Shawn didn't find out, and I left when he was at work. I didn't take anything that wasn't mine, because I sure didn't want to be accused of stealing."

"Did you have a car?"

"No. I took the train." Thinking about it made her smile. "When I got here, I had to take a driving class and get my license. After I had that, I purchased my car used. My mother was so impressed."

"Your mother?" Gaze sharp, he watched her. "What about your mother? Did she know? Couldn't she help you?"

"Oh, she knows. And she tries, but since she lives in Australia, there's not a lot she can do from so far away. We talk once or twice a month on the phone."

"Well, at least Shawn couldn't threaten her."

"True." Try as she might, JJ couldn't manage to produce a second smile. "That's one advantage to not having her close, I supposed. But even so, the distance didn't stop Shawn from repeatedly calling and harassing her. The last time I talked to her, she was changing her phone number so he couldn't keep phoning her."

"Come here." Eric pulled JJ into his arms. "It's all going to be fine, I promise. I'll get Garth back, and I'll make sure Shawn leaves you—us—alone."

With his muscular arms around her, she could almost believe him. She'd been strong for so long, and though she'd settled into her new life in her new town, in the back of her mind she felt like she'd been on the run. And damn if she wasn't tired of running.

"I'd like that." She sighed. "What happens next? Where did Felts and her people go?"

"They had no concrete evidence and couldn't arrest you, so I asked them to leave. I'm still waiting to hear back from Frank DeLeon."

"What about Garth?" JJ searched Eric's face. "When can you go get him, or are they bringing him to you?"

"I'm still trying to get confirmation on that." He grimaced. "But Felts did let me see video of him, which proves he's all right."

Relieved, she nodded. "Good. As for me, I really don't want to hang around here and wait for Shawn to show up."

"I agree." Smoothing a few wayward strands of hair from her face, he followed up with a quick kiss on her forehead. "Are you strong enough to walk?"

"I think so." To prove it, she sat up and swung her legs over the side of the sofa. She waited, but everything remained in focus. "I'm not even dizzy. I'm not sure why I fainted, but I've heard shock will do that to you sometimes."

Despite that, he took her arm. "Come on."

Walking with him to the door, she resisted the urge to lean into him. Though she would enjoy it, she didn't want him to think her weak or unsteady. "Where are we going?"

"To Rhonda's. If Shawn DeLeon comes looking for you, no doubt he'll go directly to your house. We can see everything from Rhonda's, and we should be safe there."

He had a point. Plus she wanted to thank Rhonda for standing up for them the way she had earlier.

Once they reached Rhonda's house, they found the door locked. "I can't say I blame her," Eric commented. "Things have been a little crazy lately." Lifting his fist, he knocked three times sharply.

They heard the sound of Rhonda's heels as she hurried to answer. "Come on in," she said, peering around them as she ushered them past her. "Where's your police escort?"

JJ waited to answer until they'd reached the kitchen. As usual, the warm yellow walls and bright artwork cheered her. "They couldn't actually charge me with anything, so Eric made them go." She climbed up on her usual bar stool. Rhonda went around to the other side of the island, fiddling with a mixing bowl full of what looked like cookie dough.

"Oatmeal cookies," she said, smiling faintly. "I tend to bake when I get upset. It soothes me."

"Those are my favorite." Eric took a seat next to JJ, taking her hand in his.

"Listen, Rhonda," JJ began. "I wanted to thank you for standing up for us earlier. You haven't known me that long, but I appreciate your faith in me more than I can express."

Rhonda looked down, appearing almost shy. "You're a friend. Both of you. I don't let anyone talk that way about people I care about."

"Thank you for that." Eric echoed JJ's words. "And if

you need someone to help you dispose of those oatmeal cookies, I'm your man."

They all had a quiet chuckle at that. Rhonda began dropping dough by the spoonful onto a baking sheet. Once it was full, she slid it into the oven and set a timer. "In just a few minutes, you're welcome to have as many as you want."

As the delectable scent of oatmeal cookies baking filled the room, Eric inhaled. "I'll definitely take you up on that," he said.

"Good." Smiling, Rhonda filled a second cookie sheet to put in once the first came out. "Eric, I'm really glad they found your son. I'm sorry I didn't even notice he was missing. When are you supposed to get him back?"

"No worries." Eric checked his watch. "As a matter of fact, I'm waiting to find out when I will get him back. Actually, I'm tired of waiting." He stood, phone in hand. "If you ladies will excuse me, I need to make a call."

Both JJ and Rhonda fell silent, watching as Eric walked outside to the front porch. Once he'd gone, JJ filled Rhonda in on everything that had transpired after the other woman had left.

"A crazy ex-boyfriend?" Rhonda's brows rose. "Wow, I never would have guessed it. I'm glad you found the courage to get out of that situation. A lot of people don't."

JJ studied Rhonda's carefully neutral expression. "You sound as if you speak from experience," she said.

"Actually, I do." Rhonda grimaced. "I know exactly where you're coming from."

Before JJ could ask her to explain, several gunshots went off outside, one right after the other.

"Eric!" Jumping up, JJ ran for the door. Behind her, she heard Rhonda's oven timer sound.

"Wait!" her neighbor yelled. "What if it's Shawn? Don't go outside until you know what's going on."

Almost to the front door, JJ skidded to a stop. She turned as Rhonda rushed up behind her. "Eric's out there."

"I know." Shouldering in front of her, Rhonda pushed her back. "I'm an uninvolved third party. Let me go check things out. You hang back until I give you the all clear."

Before JJ could speak, Rhonda went out the front door. Stunned, JJ hesitated for all of three seconds before going after her. No way was she leaving Eric out there to fend for himself, not to mention letting her friend put herself in danger.

Heart pounding, JJ at first didn't see anything, squinting as she was into the bright winter sunlight. Rhonda's front yard was empty. Next door, though, at JJ's place, a small crowd of people had gathered. She spotted Rhonda's fuchsia sweater on the fringes and ran over to join them.

Rhonda turned as JJ reached her. "It wasn't a gunshot," she said, her voice relieved. "One of the construction workers had an accident with one of the nail guns. He's hurt and an ambulance is on the way."

"I'm so sorry." Feeling bad for the worker, JJ nonetheless couldn't help searching the area for Eric. Sirens grew closer and an ambulance pulled up, lights flashing. As the paramedics got out and began administering first aid to the wounded man, most of the neighbors dispersed, heading back to their homes. And still no sign of Eric.

"Rhonda?" JJ caught her friend's arm. "Have you seen Eric? I know he came outside to make that call."

Rhonda frowned. "No. But his SUV is still here. Maybe he went inside to his own place."

Breathing a sigh of relief, JJ nodded. "You're probably right. I'm going to go check on him."

"I think you should leave him alone. He's going through

an awful lot right now." Rhonda's tone sounded a tiny bit sharp. "Give him his space. He'll come back when he's ready."

Maybe Rhonda was right. After all, Eric had wanted to talk in private. JJ didn't want to intrude by barging in on him. Still...she couldn't shake the feeling that something might be off. She wasn't sure what or how, but even as she turned to follow Rhonda back to her house, she questioned whether or not she was doing the right thing.

"Come on," Rhonda urged. "Those oatmeal cookies might still be warm. And if they're not, I've got another batch ready to put into the oven."

Eating cookies was the furthest thing from JJ's mind, but she managed to smile and nod. "I'm game," she said.

As she followed Rhonda down the hall toward the kitchen, she wished she could shake the ominous feeling that something was very, very wrong.

Once Eric had informed Frank DeLeon's assistant that he'd hold until the Protector was located, the woman took him up on his offer to do exactly that. He held, listening to tinned Muzak, and held, and held, until he wanted to throw the phone against the wall in a fit of anger.

After the first fifteen minutes, about to hang up and dial again, he heard a commotion outside. A nail gun, maybe. Then sirens indicating an ambulance. Curious, he went to the window to check it out, just in time to see one of the construction workers loaded up to be taken to the hospital.

Then Frank came on the line. "What's up?" he barked, his voice stressed.

Immediately, Eric tensed. "I'm calling to get an ETA on my son's arrival," he retorted. "Infants his age don't do well away from their parent for too long."

The silence on the other end stretched on for the space

of several heartbeats. "Uh, yeah," Frank finally said. "We're working on that. It'll be soon, that's all I know."

"This is ridiculous." Letting his frustration show, Eric muttered a curse. "Damn it, I just want to see my boy."

"Look, I've got company here. I'll have to call you back." And the Protector hung up the phone.

Eric cursed. While normal social niceties might demand he wait to hear back from the other man, this was not a normal situation. He punched Redial, listening as the phone rang and rang. Finally, voice mail picked up.

Well, two could play that game. He punched Redial again. Voice mail. And he tried once more. Voice mail. Whatever the hell DeLeon was up to pissed Eric off. And worried him. Until he had Garth back, he couldn't take anything for granted.

Just as he was about to try calling again, his phone rang. "What the hell, DeLeon?" Eric snarled. "Now is not the time to play games."

"I just had a visitor," DeLeon began.

The hair on the back of Eric's neck stood up. "Your brother?" he asked. "Shawn?"

"How do you...? Never mind. Yes, Shawn. We've got a major problem. There's a bit of a situation."

"Involving Julia Jacobs? Because Felts and her crew already questioned her. Your brother has a personal vendetta against her and his intel can't be trusted."

"I know." Exhaustion and strain warred with each other in DeLeon's voice. "That fact has recently been hammered home. This is my adoptive brother, damn it. But what he's done this time... Listen, I might as well level with you. I had one of my people drop Garth off here so I could personally return him to you. Shawn tied me up and took off with the baby. My assistant walked in and just freed me."

"Took off with... Why?" Feeling his heart drop, Eric

struggled to make sense of it all. "What the hell does your brother want with my son?"

"That's just it. He doesn't want Garth at all. He says he'll exchange the baby for the girl."

At first Eric didn't understand. "The girl?" Then, as he realized what Shawn DeLeon wanted, horror filled him. "You mean JJ?"

"Yes. And he wants it to go down in an hour, right after dark. At the crossroads of Fifth and Elm, near the cemetery. He says if we don't do what he asks, the baby is as good as dead."

And if JJ went to Shawn, he'd kill her. Rage filled Eric. He muttered something along the lines of he'd call DeLeon back later. Jamming the phone into his pocket, he ran outside and hurried next door to Rhonda's house.

"JJ!" he called, rushing up the steps, inside and down the hallway. "JJ, where are you?"

He found her in the kitchen with Rhonda. Both women looked up as he ran in. "I need to talk to you privately," he said, grabbing her arm. "Sorry, Rhonda."

"It's okay." JJ shook off his hand. "Rhonda's on our side. You can talk in front of her. What's going on?"

Breathing hard, he took a second to catch his breath. Then he told her what DeLeon had said. "And he wants you in exchange for Garth. He's demanded we meet tonight, near the cemetery at Fifth and Elm. In less than an hour. It's already dark outside."

Eyes narrowed, Rhonda stepped in front of JJ as if to protect her. "You're not seriously thinking of doing this, are you?"

At first he didn't answer.

"You are, aren't you?" Rhonda shook her head. "Men. You're all alike."

JJ moved around in front of the other woman. "It's

okay," she said. "Actually, I think Eric needs our help to come up with another plan."

Relieved, he nodded. "Exactly. And that's why I wanted to talk to you alone."

"I'm glad you didn't." Rhonda came around the other side of the island, a heavy cast-iron skillet in her hand. "Because now I know what I have to do."

She swung. He felt an instant of blazing, red-hot pain before he fell.

JJ jumped back, her heart pounding as Rhonda slammed her skillet into the back of Eric's head. He went down like a bowling pin hit by a heavy ball. As she rushed to Eric's side to check on him, she cradled his head in her hands and checked for a pulse. His heart beat steady and strong, despite the egg-sized knot coming up on the back of his head. "Rhonda!" She glared up at her friend. "You didn't have to do that. He wasn't going to overpower me and drag me to the cemetery."

"No, he wasn't." Something in Rhonda's tone made everything inside JJ tighten. "But I will."

JJ saw Rhonda swing the skillet right before it hit her.

Chapter 22

When JJ came to, her head aching, she was in the back seat of a car. Trussed and tied like a Thanksgiving turkey, she could barely move. But she was able to lift her head just enough to see Rhonda in the driver's seat.

"I don't understand," JJ managed to say. "Rhonda, please. Tell me what's going on."

They made a right turn and Rhonda slowed, finally pulling over. "We're at Fifth and Elm," she said, her voice an odd mixture of both sad and satisfied. "I'm bringing you here to exchange you for Eric's baby."

Once again, her friend had managed to surprise her. "You knocked both me and Eric out to *help* him?"

"No." Rhonda sighed. "I'm not exchanging you for Garth to get the baby back to Eric. The baby's mother— a lovely woman named Yolanda—contacted me shortly after Eric moved into your house. After listening to her story, I agreed to help her. Whatever wrongs she might have done, whatever mistakes she made, those don't give him the right to deny her access to her own child. She's been broken up about this."

"You're helping Yolanda, someone you barely know?" JJ struggled to understand. "I considered you a friend."

"I am your friend," Rhonda said decisively. "Believe me, you'll thank me when this is over."

"Thank you? For delivering me to a man who's surely going to kill me? For taking an infant away from a father who loves him? How could you possibly think I'd thank you for that?"

Rhonda sighed. "Because there's a lot more going on here than you know. I know you've heard the term *Berserker*, but are you aware what it really means?"

Slowly, JJ tried to shake her head, wincing at the pain. "Crazy killer, is my guess," she said. "Though Eric insists Yolanda wasn't one."

"Berserkers stem from an affliction among bear shifters. When they change, they become a focused killing machine. Nothing can stop them. Nothing except death. Little Garth is believed by his own mother to be a Berserker. Of course, no one will know until he's old enough to shapeshift, but he must be safeguarded until then. Yolanda will protect him."

Still struggling to make sense of Rhonda's words, JJ swallowed. "Protect him from what? And if you have no way of knowing whether or not such a tiny infant is going to become this Berserker, how can you possibly hold it against him until he's a teenager? I believe bears are just like the rest of us. Children can't change their form until they're in their teens."

"This child is different. Yolanda said she'd seen him start to shift. She knows they'll kill him once they learn what he is. She's only trying to save her son."

"Yolanda is lying. I've spent a good bit of time with Garth. Not once did he ever act like anything other than a normal, three-month-old baby. He certainly isn't shape-shifting."

As she stared down at her silently, Rhonda's expression told JJ she didn't believe her.

"Please don't do this." JJ let her fear and worry sound in her voice. "Please, Rhonda. I'm begging you." There had to be something more, something she was missing. Because otherwise, Rhonda's desire to help a woman she barely knew made absolutely no sense. "What is it you're not telling me? There has to be more to this than you're saying. Otherwise, I don't understand what you're doing. Help me understand." Even talking hurt. She wondered if Rhonda's skillet had dislocated her jaw.

Rhonda went silent for so long JJ feared she wouldn't answer. "I've been there," she finally said. "Where Yolanda is now. But my ex took my daughter overseas. I never saw her again. She'd be a teenager now." She sighed, the sound heavy. "So I couldn't let another woman go through what I did. Eric seems like a nice guy, but what he's doing is wrong."

"Except you don't know all the facts, do you? All you're going on is what Yolanda told you. You've never discussed any of this with Eric. You don't have his side of things. He's told me a little about all of this, and Yolanda was doing drugs and partying. She got involved with a group of people that sound like a cult. They're wanting little Garth—our sacrifice for their greater good, as they see it. Remember that brick that came through your window? The note read 'Abomination, valor and sacrifice.' That was from them."

For a moment, Rhonda appeared torn. "How do you know this? Are you a hundred percent certain?"

"The Pack Protectors are involved. They're trying to protect Garth. Eric, Garth and I were on our way to a safe house when someone attacked us and one of the Protectors was killed."

Rhonda closed her eyes. "Now I'm not sure. Everything seemed so clear. Listening to you has done nothing but confuse me. You've gone and muddied the waters."

This gave JJ hope. Maybe, just maybe, Rhonda would change her mind before handing her over to Shawn. She shuddered, well aware of how powerful his need for revenge would be. Still, she'd gladly walk into the bowels of hell if by doing so she could save Garth.

"Maybe I should reconsider." A note of panic had crept into Rhonda's voice and she rubbed her temples. "I need a little more time to think about this."

A sharp rap at the window made her jump. Heart pounding, JJ saw Shawn's face pressed against the glass. When he spotted her, a slow smile spread across his patrician features. "Good. You tied her up for me. Thank you. And you're early. Come with me and I'll take you to the baby."

"Don't do it, Rhonda," JJ urged in a low voice. "Once he gets you outside alone, he won't honor his bargain."

"That's where you're wrong," Rhonda said. Her smile chilled JJ's blood. "Because he has no idea what he's dealing with."

Eric came to, his head throbbing. He sat up too quickly as he remembered what Rhonda had done. Everything spun. She'd knocked him out. But why? Pushing to his feet, he held on to the kitchen counter until the room stopped moving. Moving as fast as he could, he checked out every room. No sign of either Rhonda or JJ. Which could mean only one thing. Rhonda had taken JJ to the cemetery to make the exchange. He'd have to figure out the why of it all later. For now, he had to get out there now.

Though it felt as if a sledgehammer relentlessly slammed into his head with every step, he ran to his SUV. Jumped in, found his keys and sped toward the cemetery. Once there, he figured he'd play it by ear. If worst came to worst, he'd shape-shift and let his bear self deal with Shawn De-Leon. The human wouldn't know how to react to a massive grizzly looming over him.

Traffic was light and he made it to the corner of Fifth and Elm in record time, turning on Elm to pull into the first entrance and park. The cemetery took up two blocks on Elm, stretching all the way to Third. This time of the year after dark, the place was deserted, which no doubt was why Shawn DeLeon had chosen it.

Now Eric had to find Rhonda, JJ, and hopefully Shawn and Garth.

Getting out of his car, he considered his next move. JJ had seen him as bear, so she wouldn't be alarmed. He figured shifting would only be to his advantage.

He stepped behind a huge oak, stripped off his clothes, dropped to the ground and initiated the change. He pushed his body to shift as quickly as possible.

Slam. It hurt like hell, especially with his still-aching skull, but he did it. Then, using his powerful bear nose, he lifted his massive head to the wind and tried to catch a whiff of anyone's scent.

Nothing. Just damp earth, decaying leaves and a bite of winter. Disappointed, he began moving, aware they had to be here somewhere. He hadn't been unconscious long enough for Rhonda to have already handed JJ over to Shawn.

A sound reached his ear, a faint wail that seemed to come from underground. It was almost unearthly, if he hadn't been so familiar with the cry. His heart skipped a beat. Garth. On all fours, Eric raced in that direction, keeping all his animal senses on high alert.

As of yet, he saw no sign of any of the others. While Garth was his first priority, no way was he letting Shawn DeLeon get his hands on JJ if there was anything he could do to stop it. And Rhonda. He had no idea how she was involved, but she had gotten in the middle of a mess.

The eerie sight of so many tombstones and trees, along with fading mementos left by loved ones, would have been spooky to a human, stumbling along in the dark night without a flashlight to guide his way. The waning moon provided little light, especially with the cloud cover. Luckily, his bear eyes could see better in the dark than when human. Again, he heard Garth cry. He went utterly still, moving only his gaze across the desolate landscape, trying to get a bead on the cry. Again, the sound seemed to come from under the ground. Had Garth been buried alive? If Shawn DeLeon had harmed that baby in any way, laws be damned. Eric would rip him apart, limb from limb.

Someone screamed, distracting him. Male or female, he couldn't tell, though part of him hoped it had been Shawn. JJ might have been captured. Rhonda, too. But JJ had one distinct advantage over any human. If she'd use it.

Another scream sounded, softer this time. At least he'd been able to pinpoint the direction. He started off, moving swiftly on all fours, keeping as low to the ground as possible.

Scent reached him first—the overwhelming musky smell that always signified humans. Then a light floral odor that he recognized as JJ. Rhonda, too, along with a masculine, too-heavy cologne that had to be Shawn. The one scent he most wanted to detect—the baby powder and milk of Garth—seemed oddly absent.

As Eric drew closer, their words drifted to him on the breeze. They were arguing. And when they finally came into focus, he saw Rhonda facing off against a tall, slender man who must be Shawn. JJ, who was either tied up or unconscious, lay on the damp earth in front of him.

"Look, you promised me the baby," Rhonda said, her voice low and furious. "I brought your ex-girlfriend, now give me the kid."

"I promised you nothing," the man sneered. "I made a deal with my adoptive brother, not you. If you chose to go around behind his back, that's your problem. I'm not turning the baby over to you."

Rhonda growled, the low and guttural sound a warning Eric well recognized. Shawn even stepped back, his eyes widening. Though he no doubt had no idea what that growl could mean, he knew enough to be aware it wasn't good.

JJ struggled to sit up. "Rhonda, don't." Her sharp voice told him she knew what Rhonda meant to do. "Shawn, I'm not going back with you until I know Garth is safe."

"You don't have a choice." Just like that, his confidence returned. "You're tied up, with no way to escape. So it's safe to say you'll go wherever I want you to."

This time JJ snarled. Eric knew if he didn't act fast, she'd shift to wolf and attack. And if she did, Shawn wouldn't reveal where he'd hidden little Garth.

With a roar, Eric reared up to his full height and lumbered into the midst of them.

Rhonda jumped back, clearly startled. Shawn froze, his mind apparently struggling to process what had appeared right in front of him. And JJ, looking up at him, started to laugh. "My knight in shining armor," she said, her words clear enough to let him know she hadn't been seriously injured. "If not a bear, he'd have been facing a wolf any second now."

Eric moved over and placed himself between her and Shawn. Shawn moved backward so quickly he tripped over his own feet and nearly fell.

As Eric opened his mouth to issue another threatening growl, Garth cried out again, his hungry cry. This time, Eric could tell the sound seemed to be coming from a few feet away, but *below* them. He bared his teeth.

"Where's the baby, Shawn?" JJ demanded, pushing herself up awkwardly into a standing position. Even with her hands still tied behind her, she faced the other man with her chin up. "Bring out the baby or I'll have the bear attack you."

Shawn's eyes darted from her to Eric. Unbelievably, he appeared undecided as to what course of action to take.

Rhonda chose that moment to step into the fray, grabbing JJ and spinning her around. "Is that Eric?" she demanded, jerking her thumb toward him. "Because if so, you need to be extremely careful what you ask him to do."

"You think?" JJ glared at her neighbor. "Considering you knocked both of us out so you could meet my ex here at the cemetery and become party to abducting a baby, maybe you aren't the one to be offering advice."

Garth's cries went from whimpers to out-and-out wailing, which meant he wanted a bottle *right now*. Glancing at JJ, who understood and nodded, Eric dropped to all fours and moved rapidly in the direction of his son's cries.

"Stop him," Shawn ordered. "Don't let your pet maul the kid."

As he got closer and closer to Garth, Eric was able to pinpoint where the cries were coming from—a massive stone crypt, ancient and covered with dying moss. Circling it, he used his shoulder to push on the door to see if it would open. It did not.

Spinning around, he gave a furious roar.

"He wants you to open up that crypt," JJ said to Shawn. "And Rhonda, do you think maybe you could untie my hands now?"

Instead of rushing over, Shawn began to edge away in the opposite direction.

"Hold on," Rhonda shouted, rushing to block his exit. "You're not going anywhere, buddy."

Even as bear, Eric could have predicted what would happen next. Shawn swung at her, clearly having no qualms about striking a woman. With moves worthy of a professional boxer, Rhonda arched away, narrowly missing his blow.

And then, with a furious snarl, Rhonda dropped to all fours, still fully clothed, and began to initiate a change.

JJ reacted from pure instinct. "No!" she shouted, slamming herself into Rhonda before she could shape-shift. Changing in front of a human who wasn't one's mate was a crime punishable by imprisonment or even death.

Surprised, Rhonda rolled. "What the hell was that for?" she demanded, launching herself to her feet, fists up, looking as if she wanted to go a few rounds in a boxing ring.

"You know." JJ glared right back. "Now untie me so we can go rescue the baby."

To her surprise, Rhonda did as she asked. Once her wrists were free, JJ shook them to try and get the circulation going again.

"You know if you go into the crypt, he's going to lock you inside with that baby," Rhonda said. "Which is why I'm not going in there."

"Maybe." JJ shot her ex a disparaging look. Next to Eric as grizzly, Shawn didn't seem nearly as intimidating. "Or you will. I'm not an idiot. Which is why Eric there is going to make sure that doesn't happen."

Nodding his huge head in agreement, Eric crossed the

space between them and the crypt, taking a position next to Shawn.

"Thanks," JJ said. Then, in case he hadn't figured everything out yet, she jerked her head toward Rhonda. "She tried to exchange me for Garth, just so you know. Apparently, she and Yolanda worked out some sort of agreement. Yolanda wants her son back. Rumors of her death appear to have been greatly exaggerated."

Eric's bear blinked, which she guessed was his way of letting her know he understood. Meanwhile, poor little Garth had worked himself up into a frenzy, hiccuping in between frantic cries. Her stomach knotted. They needed to hurry up before the air ran out.

"Now, Shawn, show me how to get into the crypt," JJ barked. She couldn't help but notice the way he gave a little start before shooting the bear a worried glance.

Reluctantly, and moving slowly enough that JJ suspected he was working on an alternate plan, Shawn shuffled over to the crypt. He reached behind a stone marker and twisted something—obviously some sort of hidden lever—and the massive door began to slide slowly open. As it did, Garth's cries sounded clearer and much closer.

It took every ounce of self-discipline she had to keep from rushing inside the crypt for the baby.

"How did you find out about that?" Rhonda asked, the admiration in her voice infuriating JJ.

Shooting Eric yet another assessing glance, Shawn shrugged. "I watched a documentary on old graveyards. They featured a crypt similar to this one. When I arrived here early, I couldn't figure out where to put the kid. So I checked out a couple of crypts. This one had the gears to open it up. Perfect place to stash him."

"Yeah, until he ran out of air," JJ said. Shawn's frown told her he hadn't even considered that horrifying possibility. "Then you would have been guilty of murder in addition to kidnapping."

"I'll be fine," Shawn retorted. "My adoptive brother is in law enforcement. FBI, I think. He'll take care of me. He always does."

"Not this time." JJ took great pleasure in saying those words. The crypt was finally open. "Eric, I'm going in," she said. "Watch my back."

Chapter 23

The giant grizzly nodded. As JJ took a deep breath and stepped into the dank darkness, little Garth stopped crying. She froze, uncertain now which direction to move. She didn't know what she'd do if she bumped into a skeletal body or a coffin or whatever they put inside these things.

"Garth?" she called out, using the singsong voice he always responded to. "Where's my little Garthy-poo?"

He made that little snuffling sound, with his small fist in his mouth, that she loved so much. Which was enough for her to judge how close he was. Had Shawn placed him on the frigid ground or on, heaven forbid, a cement ledge, shelf or a casket?

Taking a deep breath, she tried not to think about where she was or how awful it would feel to get locked in this place. Luckily, little Garth had no idea—all he knew was cold and darkness.

Hands in front of her, moving slowly, she called the

baby's name again. This time, apparently still hungry and most likely wondering why she wasn't feeding him, Garth let loose with his impressive lungs.

Perfect. Crossing the space between them, she focused on the sound. "Here you are." Picking him up, she clutched him to her. At least he'd been bundled into his coat, though his tiny hands were icy cold.

She turned around and carefully made her way toward the opening. "I've got him," she called as she stepped out of the darkness. To her shock, Shawn had vanished.

The instant JJ disappeared inside the crypt, Shawn took off, sprinting toward the parking lot as if he truly believed he could outrun a grizzly bear. Except in this case, Eric had no plans to chase him. No way was he leaving JJ and Garth alone with Rhonda. Since she'd admitted to attempting to help Yolanda get Garth back, he figured he knew exactly what she'd do. Attack JJ and steal the baby.

He glanced at her, to find her watching him with a half smile on her face. "You need to change back," she said. "Before the authorities get here. I know you've got Pack Protectors helping you, but they just might send the human police or FBI. You know there's no way you can explain a grizzly bear in the cemetery."

Just then, JJ emerged from the crypt holding a quiet Garth. Eric immediately forgot everything besides getting to his son.

"Here he is," JJ announced.

Immediately, Eric knew he needed to change back to human so he could hold his little boy. But his clothes were a good way off, and the last thing he wanted was both Rhonda and JJ there to witness the expected arousal that always came with the change.

JJ seemed to understand the problem immediately.

"We'll walk to where you left your clothing," she said, shooting a hard look at Rhonda. "While you change, I'll make sure she doesn't try anything foolish."

"Really?" Rhonda drawled, apparently unable to resist. "And how, exactly, are you planning to do that?"

"Tie you up, of course," JJ responded sweetly, as she reached down and picked up the rope previously used to bind her.

"That's not really necessary," Rhonda began.

But JJ shook her head. Carefully placing little Garth at Eric's furry feet, she walked over to Rhonda. "Hands behind your back," she ordered. "And count yourself lucky I don't hit you upside the head and knock you out."

Once Rhonda's hands were secured and JJ had picked up Garth again, Eric led the way back to the place where he'd changed. His discarded clothing remained in a pile at the base of a tree.

With a quick jerk of his head, he indicated JJ should stand with Garth on the other side of him, away from Rhonda. Even though her hands were bound, he didn't entirely trust her not to try something. She was a shifter also, and could easily change to escape her ties.

Of necessity, he planned to make this the fastest shift back to human he'd ever done.

Dropping to all fours, he initiated the change, pushing his body hard. Pain knifed through him. Ignoring it, he continued. As soon as he'd regained his human form, he turned his back to the two women and grabbed his clothes.

"You know, you and I are more alike than you realize," Rhonda said. "I didn't put two and two together until you appeared in your bear self here, but now I understand much better. I thought Garth got his nature from Yolanda, but if both of you are Vedjorn, the chance of him becoming

Berserker is that much more likely. You know this, which is why you went on the run."

"I went on the run, as you put it, to protect my son. And what do you mean, like you?" Though he suspected he knew. Hoped it wasn't so, but figured Rhonda would tell him.

Still moving fast, he yanked up his jeans to cover his arousal. He winced as he tried to close the zipper. There'd been other times in the past when he'd wished there was a way to turn off this particular occurrence, but never more than right now.

Rhonda didn't answer, which could be good or bad, depending.

Once he'd donned his shirt and his parka, he yanked on his gloves before he finally turned to face her. Holding Garth, JJ remained on his other side. "Are you planning to answer?" he asked. His breath made plumes in the frigid night air.

"A bear." All bundled up herself, she came closer. "I saw you shift back to human. And I know what happens after that. I'm available," she purred. "If you want to slake your body's need."

Though his arousal stirred, he didn't move. "No, thank you," he began, before the rest of her words dawned on him. "You're a bear shifter, too?"

"Yes. I came here five years ago to hide out." She licked her lips, not a wise move in this kind of cold. "My father was put to death for being a Berserker. And you know how they feel that trait is hereditary, so my mother packed me up and shipped me off. She wanted to protect me, the same way you think you can protect your child."

She took another step, her gaze fixed on his somehow still conspicuous bulge. He yanked his parka down over it.

"Come here," she urged him, her voice seductive, despite the fact that she knew JJ stood right behind him. "I know all too well that burning need. You're as aware as I am of what we have to do."

"No." He straightened up, drawing all his strength and willpower into himself. While to any other man her offer might have been tempting, the only woman he wanted was JJ. This realization so astounded him, he froze.

Which turned out to be a huge mistake. With her hands still tied, Rhonda barreled into him, knocking him down into the damp leaves. On top of him, she bared her teeth as if she meant to bite him. When he recoiled, she began fumbling with his clothes.

Eric pushed. Hard. He might have used a lot of his energy changing and hunting, but he still had enough strength to move a determined woman off him. She flew backward, landing on her behind in the snow.

"No," he said again, loud and clear, just in case she'd somehow missed it the last time. He pushed himself to his feet, glaring at her. She bowed her head, finally acquiescing.

Behind him, little Garth began to cry, his hunger pangs unabated.

Watching Rhonda carefully, JJ brought the baby to him. "He wants his daddy."

Relief and love flooded through him.

"Is he all right?" he asked, taking Garth from her and kissing his baby boy's forehead. "He looks okay."

"He seems fine. His hands are a little cold, but Shawn knew enough to put him in his winter coat and hat. He just forgot the gloves."

Eric carefully examined Garth's small fingers. Luckily, the sleeves of his jacket were long enough to keep them semiwarm. Though the dim light made it difficult to see, blood flow appeared good. He saw no sign of frostbite.

While he did all this, Rhonda stood stock-still, her head back up, her eyes glittering, watching. "You really love that little guy, don't you?" she asked, a note of wonder in her voice. "Maybe I was wrong to believe everything your ex-wife told me."

He wouldn't have put it past her to lie in the hopes of getting away with what she'd done. Or worse, attempting to trick them so she could make a move to grab Garth. Over his dead body. Right now, dealing with Rhonda was the least of his priorities.

"Let's get out of here," he told JJ. "I want to get Garth home so I can check him over and get him fed."

"What about her?" JJ asked, eyeing Rhonda. "I'm guessing we should bring her with us. We can't leave her here."

Which actually would be what he preferred to do. But JJ was right. "We'll let the Protectors deal with her once we're back home."

"Let me take Garth," JJ offered. "That way your hands will be free to handle anything else that might happen." She meant Rhonda, who turned to grimace at her.

Because JJ was right, he handed over Garth. Ordering Rhonda to walk ahead of them so he could keep her in his eyesight at all times, they began to make their way back to the car.

Rocking the baby as she walked, JJ sighed. "I still can't believe Shawn found me. I'm not sure I can ever feel safe again."

"It'll be okay. He's probably looking at some jail time, since he faces human charges of kidnapping and attempted murder. Both Protectors and human law-enforcement will be looking for him. I'm pretty sure he won't do anything that might reveal his location right now."

"I wouldn't be so sure of that," Rhonda interjected,

her voice smug. "I don't know how you feel about your ex-wife, but that woman can be very persuasive when she wants to be."

He grimaced. It was true that Yolanda had a raw, animalistic sex appeal, at least when one didn't know she was crazy. No doubt someone like Shawn would be susceptible to her wiles.

"What about you?" he asked, more from curiosity than anything else. "Does Yolanda appeal to you, as well?"

"Not in that way." Her response came immediately. "Though I have to admit, *you* do."

JJ snorted. "Keep dreaming."

Staring directly at Eric, Rhonda ignored her. "Eric, you know you have a duty to our kind, don't you?"

The cold had begun to seep through his clothes, making him concerned for his son. They'd almost reached his SUV. Using his key fob, he unlocked it and then handed the keys to JJ. "Go ahead and get him inside and start the engine so the heat can warm him up. His car seat is still in the back."

JJ nodded, glancing from him to Rhonda before accepting the keys and hurrying to the car. He waited until she and Garth were both inside, with the motor running, before turning to face Rhonda. "I'm going to press charges," he said. "And I'll be urging JJ to do the same."

"For what?" Her indignant tone seemed to indicate she didn't feel she'd done anything wrong. "This is a Vedjorn matter, and as such, not subject to external laws."

Did she just make up her own rules as she went along? "We'll let the Pack Protectors decide about that."

"What is *wrong* with you?" she asked. With her hands still tied behind her back, she thrust her chest out. "I know I'm attractive. There are not very many of us here in the

United States. How is it that you aren't even interested in mating with me?"

Inwardly wincing at her complete absence of self-respect, he shook his head. "I'm not interested in mating with anyone right now."

"Right," she sneered. "You sure seem interested in JJ. Of course, you're aware that's not allowed."

"It's allowed," he said, before he thought better of it. "Just frowned upon. There's a difference."

"Forbidden," she insisted, glaring at him. "I know. I met a really nice wolf shifter a few years ago, but once he learned I was bear, he told me he got visited by the Pack Protectors."

"You revealed your true nature?"

"I can do what I want. Plus I thought he should know, since we were about to have sex together."

More wrongness, but what Rhonda did was not his concern. The Pack Protectors might decide otherwise. He took a deep breath. "Rhonda, you need to let this go. There will never be anything between you and me."

For a split second, he thought she might agree. But then she narrowed her eyes and advanced on him. "I claim you as mate," she declared. "You cannot refuse me. Join with me, now."

Eric stared in disbelief. That wasn't how it worked and she had to know it. Shaking his head, he gestured toward his SUV. "Get in. We're going back to the house. The Protectors will most likely be waiting for us there."

As he turned toward the vehicle, Rhonda let out a guttural roar. Full of rage and fury and something else: madness. Damn. Heart pounding, he realized she'd begun making the change to bear. Though her hands were tied, they wouldn't be for long. Since she still wore her human clothing, her jacket tore and her jeans ripped.

Not wanting any part of this, Eric began to sprint for

the car. Surely she wouldn't attack him from behind, bear against human. Surely not.

He grabbed the driver's side door handle, yanked it open and jumped inside, locking the doors behind him. Since the engine was already running, he shifted into Drive and hit the accelerator, making the wheels spin.

"She's coming at us!" JJ exclaimed. "I think she's going to ram the side."

As they pulled away, he looked back. A large brown bear, grizzly just like him, stood at the edge of the cemetery watching them go.

"I hate that she's getting away, too," JJ said, her voice shaky. "Now both she and Shawn are out there, free. And they could get together again with Yolanda."

Eric slowed so he could make the corner. Rhonda roared, the rage-filled sound reverberating around the cemetery and down the street. Loud enough to wake the dead.

One more backward glance and he kept going, his heart pounding in his chest. A word lurked at the edge of his consciousness, one he didn't want to even allow himself to think. Not now. Not yet.

And then…incredibly, the bear launched herself toward them, running full-out. Luckily, her top speed was only around 35 mph. Deadly for anyone on foot, but easily beatable in a car.

Still, despite having to know catching them would be impossible, Rhonda kept coming. Unbelievably gaining, until Eric accelerated and left her behind.

"She's crazy." JJ sounded both shocked and sad.

"No wonder she and Yolanda get along." He would mention this episode to Frank DeLeon and Felts for sure. Because he seriously wondered if it was possible Rhonda might be Berserker. And determined to make his innocent son one of them, too.

* * *

As they drove, JJ eyed the back of Eric's head and wondered when she'd fallen so deeply in love with him. She'd chosen to stay in the back with Garth, figuring he'd put a tied-up Rhonda up front.

Rhonda. A Vedjorn. No wonder she hadn't wanted to participate in the town Pack hunt. Thinking back to how often she and Garth had been alone with Rhonda, JJ considered it quite a miracle that something awful hadn't happened sooner.

"I can't believe your ex-wife contacted Rhonda and got her to turn against us," JJ mused. "But then again, if they're both bears, I guess that would automatically convey a sense of solidarity."

"It shouldn't," he said. "I regret the day I met Yolanda."

The dejection in his voice made JJ ache to comfort him. "But then you wouldn't have this beautiful baby boy. You know, I really think this is all going to work out in the end. Wait and see."

Though she'd really been offering that hope to cheer him up, after uttering the words she felt better.

They pulled up in front of her house. The construction workers were long gone, though they'd left her front porch light on. Next door, Rhonda's house sat dark. JJ wondered if the other woman would be going back home, or if she'd meet up with Shawn and Yolanda somewhere and begin plotting a second attempt.

The thought turned her stomach. "Eric?" Leaning forward, she squeezed his shoulder. "I'm thinking it might be better if you took Garth and went somewhere else. At least until they catch the three of them."

"We tried that, remember? Besides, I'm not going anywhere without you."

His words had her heart skipping a beat. Still… "Keeping Garth safe is first priority."

"Of course." He got out of the car and opened the back door, unbuckling a remarkably silent Garth from his car seat. "Right now, getting him fed is what needs to happen. After that, we'll deal with anything else."

But once they were inside Eric's living space and he'd heated a bottle of formula, the baby wouldn't take it. He moved his head from side to side, his mouth tightly closed.

"He looks kind of pink," JJ pointed out. She placed the back of her hand against Garth's forehead. "He's burning up. You need to take his temperature."

Looking worried, Eric did as she suggested. "He's got a fever of 104 and he's breathing fast. It's probably a result of being kept for who knows how long inside that crypt. We'd better get him to the ER."

They bundled him back up and headed outside. Midway between the house and the car, the tiny baby shuddered and went limp.

Eric froze, panicked. "Is he…?"

Chapter 24

JJ snatched Garth out of Eric's arms. "He can't be," she said, insistent in her belief. Then, as she lifted him, completely unsure of what action to take, Garth inhaled a deep, shuddering breath and began to cry. Even his voice seemed off, broken and weak.

"Let's go," Eric ordered. "Right now, before something else happens."

They made it to the hospital in record time. Eric pulled up in front of the ER and jumped from the SUV to help JJ and little Garth out of the back seat. They left the vehicle there and hurried in to the triage desk. As soon as the nurse heard what had happened, she sent for an aide, who promptly showed them to a room.

"A nurse will be in to take his vitals," she said. "And then a doctor will visit."

After that, things moved surprisingly fast. The nurse arrived, took Garth's temperature and blood pressure, and before she'd even finished making notations in her computer, a white-coated doctor arrived.

"You have a very sick baby," he said, looking from JJ to Eric and back again. "We think he might have bacterial pneumonia. He's going to need antibiotics and we're going to be admitting him."

"Pneumonia?" Eric frowned. "Would that have caused him to lose consciousness?"

"No. Are you sure you didn't imagine that?"

JJ bristled at the doctor's insinuation. But something about the way Eric was watching the man caused her to pay attention and keep her thoughts to herself.

Just as the thought occurred to her, several men in dark suits came into the room. A look of recognition flashed over Eric's face at the sight of one of them. "DeLeon," he said. "It's about time you got here."

Unable to help herself, JJ took a long look at the Protector. So this was Shawn's adoptive brother. Odd how Shawn had never mentioned him, not once in all the time they'd been together. But then that was Shawn, completely absorbed only in himself.

Another man, taller and heavier than the others, stepped forward. "I'm afraid we need to speak to you privately," he said, his voice deep and sonorous. "I have to ask you both to please come with us, right now."

"No." Eric didn't even have to think about his answer. "I'm not leaving my son."

DeLeon nodded as if he understood, but one of the other men grunted. He looked out of sorts in his rumpled, navy blue suit and tie. "Don't make us arrest you."

What the... Eric stood his ground. "On what charges?"

"Assault and battery," the other man said. "A Ms. Rhonda Descart is pressing charges against you."

JJ gasped, but Eric could only stare. "Descart? Are you sure that's her last name?"

"Yes. Why?"

They all watched him now. Even JJ, her eyes wide and still full of shock. "Because I know that name. I've heard Yolanda mention it. Descart is the last name of one of her best friends. A woman who moved away before Yolanda and I married, so I never met her."

"Rhonda?" DeLeon asked. "Was Rhonda your ex-wife's friend before moving here?"

He struggled to remember. "No, her first name wasn't Rhonda. It was something weird, like a seasoning. Sage. That was it. Sage."

He saw he now had everyone's full attention. "What?" he asked, directing his question to DeLeon. "What did I say?"

"Sage is Rhonda's middle name," DeLeon explained. "It's extremely likely Rhonda actually was—or is—Yolanda's best friend."

Which would explain a lot.

"There's more," Eric said, bracing himself for their reactions. "I suspect Rhonda might be Berserker."

DeLeon and the others all exchanged looks. "That's a weighty word to throw around," the Protector said. Then asked, "Are you telling us that Rhonda is also Vedjorn?"

"Yes."

"As is Yolanda," JJ offered.

"We know."

DeLeon's sharp reply didn't appear to faze her. "Do you still have to arrest him?" she asked. "Because I was there the entire time and Eric never assaulted Rhonda."

No one immediately answered.

Finally, the same agent who'd threatened to arrest Eric

spoke. "Excuse us a moment. We need to talk privately." At his gesture, the other agents followed him out of the room.

Except DeLeon. "I'm sorry about all this," he said, his expression miserable. "I'm glad you got your son back, though. I hope he's going to be all right."

"Me, too." Eric frowned. "He's got pneumonia, no doubt because Shawn stuck him in a crypt, with little protection from the damp and the cold. I have no idea how long my son was kept there, but evidently long enough to make him seriously ill."

"I'm sorry." Apologizing again, DeLeon heaved a sigh. "This is a mess. I'm not really sure how my brother got involved in this, but I hate that he's on the run now." He eyed Eric. "Why didn't you call and fill me in? I had no idea you even had your son back until Rhonda showed up, wanting to press charges."

"No time." Glancing toward the doorway, Eric spoke quickly, telling DeLeon everything that had happened since they'd last spoken.

When he finished, the other man stared, scratching his head. "You couldn't make this stuff up. Geez."

"I know."

"Let me get this straight. You're telling me Rhonda clobbered you, and then knocked out JJ? Using a…frying pan?"

"Cast-iron skillet," JJ corrected. "It's much heavier. In fact, I think we need to press charges against *her*."

For the first time since arriving at the hospital, DeLeon smiled. "You know what? That might work. At least it would shut those other guys down." He jerked his head toward the door. "They aren't real sure what to do right now."

"Who do they work for?" Eric asked. "I know they're shifters, from their auras. I thought they were Protectors like you. That's why I mentioned the possibility that Rhonda is a Berserker."

"FBI." DeLeon sounded glum. "The child abduction got them involved. Dealing with that agency can be a pain in the ass sometimes. At least we have enough contacts there to ensure they didn't send human agents to investigate."

Eric shook his head, returning his attention to Garth, who was still far too motionless. At least the machines hooked up to his tiny body showed that his heart still beat. That, and the steady rise and fall of his chest, reassured Eric that his son still lived. "I'm not leaving him," he repeated. "Not without a fight."

"Me, either." JJ came and stood next to him. "The only thing that matters right now is Garth. Once he's better, we can focus on catching Shawn and dealing with Rhonda."

"Actually, that's my job," DeLeon stated with a twisted smile. "Though they've asked me to step down from the case due to family being involved, so I should say that's the Pack Protection Agency's job."

"Can you do anything to keep Eric from being arrested?" JJ asked. She stood near enough to him that their hips bumped. He put his arm around her and pulled her even closer. When he looked back at DeLeon, the other man gave him a nod of approval.

"He won't be arrested now. If they push it, all you have to do is claim Rhonda assaulted you."

"It's the truth."

"I know." DeLeon sighed. "Let me go find them and see if we can work something out. You two focus on getting your baby well. I'll talk to you later."

Neither DeLeon nor the FBI guys ever came back.

Later, after Garth had been admitted and they'd moved him to a room on the pediatric floor, Eric gestured toward a recliner near the large window. "It's late," he said to JJ. "Why don't you try to get some rest and I'll watch over Garth."

"First shift?" She attempted to smile, but exhaustion tugged the corners of her mouth down. "I sleep for four hours and then you wake me so you can get some sleep."

Though he didn't plan to close his eyes until he knew for certain his son was out of the woods, he nodded as if he agreed. "Sounds like a plan," he said, taking the hard-backed visitor's chair next to the bed.

Wearily, JJ climbed into the recliner, pulling up the extra blanket a nurse had found. Within seconds, she'd fallen fast asleep.

Eric contented himself alternating between watching her and watching Garth. Staying awake was going to be a challenge, but he'd do it. He wished he'd had the foresight to grab a cup of coffee before JJ went to sleep.

DeLeon texted ninety minutes later.

All charges dropped. Though we had Rhonda in custody, we had to let her go. Let me know if either of you are serious about pressing charges against her. Right now, with both Shawn and Yolanda on the loose, I think it's better if we let her go. She might lead us to them.

Eric sent back his agreement. For now, he'd leave Rhonda alone. But if she came anywhere near him or his family—including JJ—all bets were off.

Sometime during the night he must have dozed off. He woke up with JJ gently shaking his shoulder. "Time to switch out," she whispered.

"What time is it?" he whispered back. He stood and stretched, trying to ease some of the kinks in his back.

"A little after three." She pointed toward the recliner. "Go rest. I'll try to watch him."

Though he hated to leave Garth's side, Eric knew he needed to catch a few hours' sleep if he hoped to have a prayer of being at his best later. And he trusted JJ to keep a good watch over his son.

Gratitude filled him. It had been a long time since he'd trusted anyone but himself.

With a thankful nod, he kissed JJ on the cheek and crawled into the recliner. He figured he'd be out like a light as soon as he closed his eyes.

His assumption must have been correct, because the next thing he knew, a too-cheerful nurse entered the room, warbling out a bright "good morning" as she flipped on the lights. Both he and JJ started. Garth still lay quietly, but his eyes were open and he appeared to be tracking the nurse's every move.

"I've got his bottle here," the woman said with a smile. "After I take his temperature, would Mommy or Daddy like to give it to him?"

Too tired to correct the misconception, Eric pushed to his feet. "I'll do it."

She handed him the bottle. Using a digital thermometer, she put it under Garth's arm and waited. "Perfect," she said, when it beeped. "His fever is gone. I'll let the doctor know. Let's see if he wants his bottle, shall we?"

To Eric's relief, when he offered, Garth latched on and drank hungrily.

"Wonderful!" the nurse exclaimed. "I bet if he keeps improving, the doctor might let him go home this afternoon."

Eric blinked away the sudden rush of moisture to his eyes. "He's going to be okay?"

"Of course he is," she chided. "The antibiotics are doing their job. Call me if you need anything."

Once she'd gone, JJ hurried over and wrapped her arms around Eric's waist. They stood together while Garth finished his bottle. When he had, Eric carefully lifted him up and burped him.

"He needs a diaper change," JJ pointed out. She located a stack of disposable diapers and handed him one.

Contentment and joy filled Eric as he changed his son. Reluctant to let him go, he sat on the edge of the bed and simply held him.

The nurse had been correct. After the doctor made his rounds, he informed Eric he'd be sending Garth home with antibiotics. He gave instructions that they were to follow up with a family physician, unaware that they'd need to locate one first since they hadn't been in town long enough to have one.

By the time they left the hospital, both Eric and JJ were starving. She'd made a quick run earlier to the hospital coffee shop and gotten them each coffee and a sweet roll, but he went to a drive-through on the way home and picked up a box of fried chicken, along with two sides.

JJ realized something once they'd arrived back at her house and were comfortably ensconced in his warm kitchen. This was how it felt to be a family.

After they'd eaten and Eric had given his son his afternoon bottle, Garth went down for a nap. Eric joined JJ in the living room. "You know you're staying here until your place is livable," he said. "No arguments."

"There won't be." Tight-lipped, she glanced out the window at Rhonda's house. "I have nowhere else to go."

"I wonder if she went home," Eric mused. "Since no one filed any charges."

"I doubt it. She's probably with Shawn and Yolanda, plotting their next move." JJ took a deep breath. "Don't you think it's odd that both our exes are working together against us? Even though they both want different things, it's crazy."

"Extremely odd. It's even weirder that your ex happens to be related to the Pack Protector assigned to my case."

She tried for a smile, though she had the feeling it looked more like a grimace. "One of those instances where truth is stranger than fiction. You couldn't make this stuff up."

He agreed. "I just want it to be over, so we can all get back to normal."

Normal. Eric had no idea how much she'd hoped moving to Forestwood would give her that. She'd started down that road, too—settled in to her house, even found a job. And while she'd never intended to fall for her handsome tenant and his adorable infant, she had. She could only hope once all this craziness ended, normal would still be a possibility for them all.

That night, JJ slept on the couch. Eric tried to offer her his bed, but she insisted he stay close to his son. In the morning, she got up first and made a pot of coffee.

Since he'd had to throw away everything in his refrigerator when the power had been cut off, she rummaged through the cupboard to see if there was anything she could make for breakfast. She found some pancake mix, the kind that needed only water added, and an unopened container of maple syrup. They wouldn't have butter, but this would be better than nothing.

After breakfast, she showered, then watched over Garth so Eric could do the same. Once he emerged, his blond hair still damp, she took a quick trip to buy groceries. Even though Eric asked if she wanted to help him bathe Garth, she felt she needed to get out of the house to reclaim her equilibrium. This sudden enforced coziness had the potential of causing great emotional distress if she allowed herself to get too comfortable.

Because Eric—and Garth—were everything she'd ever yearned for, everything she'd ever dreamed of. The shining possibility of a future with them made her dizzy with longing.

At the store, she loaded up on meat and produce, plus essentials like milk and butter and cheese. Trying not to wince at the total, she paid and wheeled the cart with her bagged groceries outside. Of necessity, she took extra precautions—scoping out the entire parking lot before she went too far, car keys in hand, and being vigilant about checking out her surroundings. But she didn't relax until she had everything loaded in her trunk, cart put away, and her doors locked with the engine running. Now to drive home.

Home. Even though her floor still wasn't finished, staying with Eric felt the same as being home. Except better.

When she got back, Eric came out and helped her bring in the groceries. Catching sight of the receipt, he handed her two hundred-dollar bills. "Thank you," he said, ignoring her weak attempts to refuse. "This should stock us up for a little while."

Over the next few days, they settled into a sort of domestic routine. Mundane, actually, but one JJ found satisfying. The only thing that would have made it better would be if Eric would welcome her into his bed. They'd shied away from any kind of intimacy since that night in the motel room. Often, she found herself watching him, aching with suppressed desire and need, and wondering if he felt it, too.

Eric kept in touch with Frank DeLeon. So far, five days in, no trace had been found of Rhonda, Yolanda or Shawn. JJ wondered about Shawn's job—he'd been zealously dedicated and well compensated there. His brother informed her that Shawn had taken two weeks' vacation, and as of yet, his position wasn't in any danger. Of course, that would all change once he returned. The Protectors were watching and waiting for that to happen.

"We just need to be careful not to get lulled into a sense of false security," Eric told her over dinner.

About to take a bite of the fried chicken she'd prepared, JJ nodded. The construction company had given her a ten-day estimate of when they figured the work would be done in her place. Once everything passed inspection, she'd be able to move back in. She and Eric hadn't discussed this yet, mostly because she was hoping all the craziness would be over by then. Surely, the Protectors would be able to close Rhonda and the others down.

"You'd think," Eric agreed, when she mentioned this to him. "The main problem seems to be that they've gone into hiding. Until they make a move or someone spots them, we're kind of stuck in this limbo. DeLeon assures me that they're working every lead. There's a lot we're not privy to going on behind the scenes."

She nodded. His restlessness that evening was a new thing and made her feel jittery. Eric insisted on cleaning up after their meal, since she'd cooked, so she let him, but afterward he prowled around the small living room like a wild animal confined to too small of a space.

"Are you all right?" she finally asked, as she realized what might be his problem. "I can watch Garth for a few hours tonight if you need to change."

The grateful look he shot her made her smile. "How did you know?"

Secretly pleased, she shrugged. "How could I not know? You're acting like a grizzly trapped in a cage. Go hunt. Garth and I will be fine."

Brows lowered, Eric stopped his pacing long enough to consider her words. "I don't know," he hedged. "I'm still afraid to leave you and Garth unprotected. And I can't take you with me, because the last thing he needs is to be outside in the cold while he's recovering."

"We'll be fine." She smiled at him. "I'll lock the place up after you leave and won't sleep until you get back. Remember, I always have my own secret weapon. Wolves have sharp teeth and claws. Besides, unless they're watching us, they'll have no way of knowing you're gone."

Still he hesitated. Full of love, she couldn't keep herself from going to him and wrapping her arms around his waist. Eric stiffened for an instant, but then relaxed enough to hug her back.

They stood that way for the space of a few heartbeats, while she battled a surge of desire. About to look up and pull him close for a kiss, she instead stifled her disappointment when he pulled away.

Chapter 25

Some of JJ's disappointment must have shown in her face.

"Do you have any idea how much I want you?" Eric asked, his voice low and rough. When she shook her head, he grimaced and dragged his hand through his hair. "I haven't stopped wanting you since that night. Hell, the truth is, I've desired you since the first moment we met."

Speechless, she stared at him, her heart racing while a slow heat built inside her.

"But," he continued, "I want to do things right with you. Get to know you without all this evil hanging over our heads. Hunt with you, run with you, have a picnic in the park in the spring, go on a real date, all the things a man should do to court a woman."

"Court?" She liked the old-fashioned word.

"Yes." He came closer, his gaze intense. For a second, she could have sworn she saw a hint of his bear self in his eyes.

When he stopped less than six inches from her, she swallowed hard. Her entire body tingled with anticipation. "I could tell you everything I want to do to you, starting with my mouth on your lips, but I won't. My bear is already agitated. But I can promise you this—once all the danger is past and those crazies are safely locked up, if you're game, we'll begin our courtship."

Courtship. She liked that. The way he said it sounded as if he meant for them to have a real shot at a future together. "I'm game," she told him, smiling. "Now go and let your bear out to play. I'll be here once you get back."

He did kiss her then, a light, lingering kiss that he broke off too soon. "I won't be gone long," he promised. "I'll go right after I put Garth down for the night."

Though her wolf stirred at the thought of hunting, she knew she could wait a few more days before she'd need to change. The idea of shape-shifting with Eric, hunting and running as they'd done once before, filled her entire being with longing.

Someday, she told herself. Someday.

Finally, after bathing and feeding Garth, Eric had him settled in his crib. The baby fussed for a moment or two, but eventually drifted off to sleep.

Though Eric practically vibrated with impatience, still he hovered. "Are you sure about this?"

"Yes." She gave him a small shove. "Just go. Run. Hunt. Let your beast out to play."

Finally, he nodded. "All right. But JJ, stay vigilant, just in case."

"I will."

He kissed her on the cheek, a chaste kiss that plainly showed his worry. Once she heard the front door close, she went to the bedroom window and watched as he hurried across the frozen field toward the woods.

Before she settled down with her book, she went from room to room, checking every window and door, making sure no lock had been left unfastened. Once she was satisfied, she settled in the rocking chair next to Garth's crib to read.

A loud roar startled her from a restless doze. She picked up her book from the floor where it had fallen and listened. Nothing.

Had she dreamed it? First she checked on the baby, relieved to see his chest rising and falling with deep, even breaths as he slept. Padding to the window, she looked out, barely able to make out the dark outline of a man crossing the field toward the house. Eric! On his way back.

Her soft smile became a frown as she saw him stop. He turned back to look at the woods. Or something at the edge of the trees. As she tried to make out what it might be, the thing moved into the clearing and roared again.

Now she saw it. A giant bear lumbered a few steps toward Eric and stopped, eyeing him. Her heart skipped a beat. She remembered what Eric had called Rhonda, and whispered it to herself, hoping against hope that he'd been wrong.

Berserker.

If Eric's suspicions were reality, then he was in great danger.

Indecision froze her. She should call someone, except 911 was clearly out and she didn't have Felts's or DeLeon's number. JJ knew objectively that Eric was capable of defending himself, though she wanted to help him if at all possible. But how?

As she watched, the giant beast circled around Eric, as if sizing him up. His best chance would be to change into his own bear self. Except she knew he had already done that earlier, and like all shifters, he'd have little energy to do so again. Shifting a second time so soon after the first wasn't always possible. There were only a few rare individuals strong enough.

Her heart pounded as she watched. She couldn't just stand here and let him be cut down. Which meant she would have to save him.

After another quick glance at the sleeping infant, JJ decided. Garth would be fine left alone, as long as she made sure the place was locked up. For his sake—and hers—she couldn't let Eric be killed. Garth needed his father. And she needed Eric, too.

Shedding clothes as she went, she ran out through the door and locked it. When the outside air hit her skin with a blast of icy cold, she began the change, faster than she'd ever done before. She was wolf before her paws even left the cement.

And she ran. Blasting through the snow, past a startled Eric, who had turned to face the charging bear. He'd crouched low and had his arms up, as if he thought his human strength would be enough to deflect the blow.

JJ snarled, drawing the huge beast's attention. The bear skidded to a stop and swung its huge, shaggy head from her to Eric and back again. As wolf, JJ knew she wasn't huge, but she still made a threatening figure. She'd become a skilled hunter and would fight to the death to defend someone she loved.

Like Eric.

Of course she loved him. She filed this bit of astounding information away. Now was not the time to philosophize. She had to either frighten the bear away or fight it. Right now, she thought savagely, she was good with either choice.

Planting herself in front of Eric, JJ bared her teeth and made it clear she would defend him. The bear tossed its head and grunted. It was either Yolanda or Rhonda, but JJ couldn't tell which one.

"Rhonda, please stop," Eric said, speaking directly to the beast. "You don't have to do this."

Rhonda. Okay. JJ cut her gaze from Eric to the bear. So Rhonda had returned and taken the shape of her beast. Did that mean Yolanda and Shawn were somewhere nearby?

While she struggled to assimilate this information, the bear—Rhonda—roared again. Another roar came from deeper in the trees, and then a second bear emerged. JJ's heart sank. As wolf, she had strength and skill, but against two bears?

"Yolanda," Eric said, his voice resigned. "I'd recognize her anywhere. Damn."

In response, JJ crouched low, preparing to spring at her, and snarled, letting him know she'd fight with him.

"Where's Garth?" Eric asked her, low-voiced.

Since she couldn't answer in words, she cut her eyes back toward the house, where she'd left the baby asleep in his crib. And then she realized what she'd done in her mad rush to help Eric. She'd left his son unprotected. The doors were locked, but with Rhonda and Yolanda this close, surely Shawn wasn't far behind.

"Go. Now." Eric kept his voice calm. "I can deal with the two of them."

Since she could run much faster as a wolf, JJ kept her shape and spun around. The instant she did, the wild-eyed first bear charged, heading directly for her.

Bracing herself, JJ readied for the moment of impact. Crouching low, she'd slash up with her teeth, going for the vulnerable belly and throat.

Just before the beast was upon her, a shot rang out. The bear fell backward, almost in slow motion, clawing at the air and then at its bloody throat.

Disbelieving, but aware Garth had to be her first priority, JJ jumped up and raced off again. She took a final glance back. Eric stood frozen, one arm extended, his hand holding a pistol. He stared in sorrow and shock at the downed bear, which didn't move. As they watched, the bear began to shimmer. Slowly, it turned back to its human form. Rhonda.

Though the shot had given the second bear pause, after watching Rhonda fall, it resumed racing toward them.

Eric shook his head, his anguish plain to see even from this distance.

JJ swallowed, her heart pumping. She hated that Rhonda had died, and she definitely didn't like leaving Eric alone to face Yolanda in her possibly Berserker form. But Garth needed her now, especially since the third member of the trio—Shawn—hadn't shown up. For all she knew, he could be in the house right now, snatching Garth from his crib.

In the end, she did the only thing she could. She tucked her body as low as possible and sprinted for the house. She would change back to human once she got there, and then she'd make sure the baby was safe.

Facing Yolanda as bear, Eric kept his pistol up, finger near the trigger. Both he and Yolanda watched as the wolf took off, running low to the ground, across the field toward the house, as fast as the snow would let her.

JJ. His heart swelled. He'd recognized her immediately. She'd come out here to try and save him. He knew she wouldn't have left Garth if she had thought there was any alternative. Now, he could only pray she got back in time. Once he dealt with Yolanda, he hoped he'd be able to help JJ against Shawn, who probably wasn't far behind.

Yolanda growled, her eyes glinting red. Berserker? Most likely. If so, once she launched an attack, nothing would stop her but death. He had loaded silver bullets and he'd already killed Rhonda. He hoped like hell he wasn't forced to shoot his ex-wife, as well.

Across the clearing, Yolanda paced, sizing him up, her massive body vibrating with rage. She seethed with hatred, yet something held her back. He suspected she understood what his pistol would do. Either that, or she was waiting for Shawn to appear with Garth.

Luckily, Eric considered himself an excellent shot. While he couldn't and wouldn't kill her outright, in cold blood, self-defense was a different matter entirely.

In his pants pocket, his phone vibrated, indicating a text. DeLeon had called right after Eric had changed, and left a voice mail warning him that the trio was on the move, most likely in his direction. He'd been glad then that he'd packed his pistol and the silver bullets. Better safe than sorry.

Across the clearing, the massive bear continued to pace at the edge of the trees. The third time she swung her head toward the house, he knew.

Furious, he raised his weapon. While he was an excellent marksman, hitting her from such a distance would be a stretch. But since he had no other choice, he squeezed off a shot.

Yolanda jerked back and he knew he'd hit her. She roared, this time the sound more of a cry of pain than a belligerent threat. Dropping to all fours, she disappeared into the woods. He knew if he wanted to track her, a trail of blood would lead him right to her.

Instead, he turned away and holstered his pistol. As he passed the dead woman lying naked in the snow, he reached for her shredded and tattered clothes and covered her the best he could. His bullet had hit her right between her eyes.

Then he headed off at a jog for what truly mattered

now—his son and the woman he loved. Though he wanted to run, the best Eric could manage was a series of short sprints. The earlier change and subsequent hunt had zapped his energy.

On the way, he dug his cell from his pocket and jabbed the call back button for DeLeon. The call went straight to voice mail.

Running as if the devil nipped at her heels, JJ didn't slow down until she reached her house. Since without opposable thumbs she couldn't open her front door, she'd need to change back to human.

So she did, right there on her back doorstep, under her porch light, praying no one saw her. As soon as she'd become human again, she fumbled with the doorknob and let herself in. Moving quickly, she yanked her previously discarded clothes on piece by piece, following the trail she'd left earlier, all the way to Garth's room.

Taking a deep breath, she stepped inside. To her infinite relief, the baby still slept in his crib. Unbothered and safe. Thank goodness for locked doors and windows.

Exhausted, she wished she could drop into the rocking chair next to the crib and exhale in relief. Instead, she crossed over to the window to see how Eric was faring with the other bear.

As she squinted to see what was going on out in the field, she saw Eric and his ex-wife had apparently reached a standoff. The massive bear circled at the edge of the field, keeping her distance. Eric still had his gun at the ready, careful not to let down his guard. She watched him bring his pistol up and fire off a shot.

Clearly, he'd hit his target. While his bullet didn't take Yolanda out, the huge bear went to all fours before disappearing into the trees.

Hand to her throat, JJ watched as Eric holstered his gun and began running for the house.

"There you are."

A shudder went through her and she froze, her heart stuttering in her chest. It was a voice she knew intimately, and one she'd hoped never to hear again. Shawn. How long had he been there? Had he seen her shape-shift from wolf to human? And if needed, did she have enough strength to change again? Her life might depend on her being able to do it.

Of course, Eric would be here in a few minutes. Clearly, he was armed and wasn't afraid to use his pistol. Even Shawn would have to respect that.

Until Eric arrived, she'd have to try and stall Shawn. And keep him the hell away from baby Garth.

Turning slowly, despite her racing heart, she managed a completely fake smile. "Hey, there," she said calmly, as if terror hadn't immediately turned her blood to ice. "Shawn. What are you doing here?"

Casual, casual. Even though they'd already faced each other down, in his arrogance and narcissistic pride, Shawn wouldn't have considered her lost to him. In the time they'd spent together, she'd come to know him well. He considered himself a shark of a man, an alpha male hunter, even though he was only human and she the true huntress. The bitter irony in that had never been lost on her. At least right now, she had a small advantage. A larger one, once Eric reached them.

Except as she stared at Shawn, she noticed he, too, had a gun. A black, dangerous-looking pistol, pointed at her. She wondered if he knew how to use it, but figured he'd probably taken the time to learn. She prayed the baby wouldn't wake, wouldn't make a sound. Shawn knew her well enough to know if he threatened an innocent infant, she'd do whatever he wanted.

"I've been looking for you," he said, the grimness in his voice matching his expression. "You really didn't think I'd let you go so easily, did you?"

"Why?" Though she already knew. He'd never actually understood that she was a person with real hopes and needs and desires. To him, she'd been his possession. Something to do with as he pleased. And when she'd fled, he'd been infuriated, as if she'd tried to steal herself away from him.

"Because you're mine. And you're coming with me," he declared. "Right this instant."

"No." Lifting her chin, she met his gaze to let him know even though her response had been quiet, she meant it. "I'm not. This is my home now."

He hadn't been expecting this; she could tell from the way he cocked his head and narrowed his eyes. "You're different," he finally said, his tone hard with fury. "Impertinent. I don't like it."

"I really don't care what you like."

"Bitch." He hit her. Hard, an uppercut fist under the chin. She went down like a rock, fighting to stay conscious, swallowing back the nausea and pain. She'd bitten her tongue, she figured, tasting blood. And maybe lost a tooth or two. The coppery taste woke her wolf. Inside, the beast rose, less exhausted now, alert once again. And dangerous. After all, she hadn't let her beast hunt.

"Get up."

Blinking up at him, she tried to focus, but everything had gone blurry. Still, she could make out the black outline of his weapon. *Garth*, she thought. She had to keep Garth safe.

"Get up," he repeated, spraying her with spittle.

Moving carefully, she somehow managed to push herself to her feet. She had to get him outside, away from the house and the baby. She couldn't risk anything happening to Garth. Though Eric had been heading this way, he'd been moving relatively slowly, attesting to his fatigue. She figured there was a fifty-fifty chance he'd show up in time to save her. Therefore, she'd need to save herself. She'd come a long way in the months since she'd freed herself from Shawn. She could do this.

Chapter 26

Once she'd made it to her feet, using one hand to hold on to the wall, she eyed him. If she appeared overeager to get outside, he'd suspect something might be up. Instead, she had to appear to *not* want to leave the house.

"I refuse to go anywhere with you," she declared, her voice shaky and breathless. "If you're going to kill me, you might as well do it here and now." He had no way of knowing a bullet wouldn't kill her. Not unless it was made of silver. Her kind could die only from a silver bullet or fire. But she'd keep that information under wraps for now.

Her statement had the desired effect. "Outside," he growled, prodding her with the gun. "Now."

Since outside was exactly where she wanted to go, she didn't put up too much of a struggle. She wouldn't have been able to resist too much, anyway, with her head throbbing from the blow she'd taken. Dragging her hand across her mouth, she found her fingers came back smeared with blood. Again, just the taste of it infuriated her inner beast.

Pacing, her inner wolf snarled. She pushed it back, drawing strength from the sure knowledge that she—with her razor-sharp teeth and massive wolf claws—could take him down and rip out his throat easily, even after being shot.

Pack law declared she'd have to be careful. While wolf, she could attack a human only in self-defense, and then only if her life was seriously threatened. She couldn't do such a thing lightly, and she'd prefer not to have to do it at all. She'd rather have him arrested and sent to jail.

For now, Shawn appeared to have forgotten about the baby. Good. The longer she could keep his focus on her, the better.

"Yolanda is taking care of your new boyfriend, you whore," Shawn spat. "After she's done with him, I'm going to let her work you over, too. We'll see how defiant you are after that."

Now he had her wondering how much he really knew. "Umm, Shawn? Do you have any idea what Yolanda can become?"

"Of course I do. Why do you think I'm helping her?" Eyes wild, he gestured widely. "She has a special gift—a superpower. And if I continue to help her, eventually she'll let me have it, too. Once she does, I'll be unstoppable. Just wait, you'll see."

Oh, brother. JJ knew better than to roll her eyes, but she really wanted to. With each second that ticked past, she felt herself grow stronger.

Downstairs, she heard the sound of the front door crashing open. Though Eric knew better than to call her name, he made a lot of noise as he rushed up the steps.

Shawn swung his pistol from left to right, covering her and then the doorway, making her wonder if he actually knew how to use it. If he accidentally squeezed the trigger while aiming at the crib, Garth could get shot. This helped her make her decision.

The next time Shawn had his gun pointed at the doorway, she sprang up, launching herself at him. A second after she did, Eric came rushing in the front door.

The gun went off. No silver bullet, but Eric jerked back and fell. He'd been hit. The echo of the gunshot woke Garth, who let out a frightened cry.

Outside, sirens sounded in the distance. The Pack Protectors to the rescue, she supposed. It appeared they would arrive too late.

Somehow, Eric struggled to his feet. Grinning, Shawn grabbed JJ and held the gun to her throat. "First her, and then the kid," he gloated. "You might as well watch."

Garth had been through so much already with his pneumonia. Babies' bodies hadn't yet built up the strength adult shifters had. In his weakened state, it was entirely possible a gunshot wound might kill him. If not, he'd surely suffer.

JJ could see that Eric was fading fast. While she knew he wouldn't die, seeing him in such a state terrified her. Blood seeped from the new wound in his leg and he swayed as he tried to reach them.

With his arm around her throat, Shawn could see it, too. Tightening his hold, he dragged JJ over to the crib. "Such a cute little baby," he mocked. "Wonder how adorable he'll look with a big ole bullet hole right through his forehead."

"No," JJ protested, struggling to get the words out while choking. Her vision went gray and she nearly fell, causing Shawn to loosen his grip so that she could breathe. "Leave the baby alone!"

Shawn only laughed in response.

Eric roared. The inhuman sound alerted JJ to the unbelievable. He had changed. Somehow, Eric had shapeshifted back to bear in a furious instant, tearing his clothes.

He attacked Shawn, saving his son, saving her. As Eric slammed into Shawn, he pushed her aside hard enough that she hit the side of the crib, jostling Garth.

This, as well as Shawn's pain-filled screams, frightened the baby, who began to wail. One swipe of Eric's powerful claws and Shawn went down. JJ grabbed Garth, startled to see the baby appeared to be shimmering in between a human and a bear. No way. Shifters couldn't actually shape-shift until they were in their teens.

Trying to process this, she ran for the door. Behind her, the two wrestled—man and bear—in a fight most certainly to the death.

She heard the report of the gunshot at the exact same instant she felt the flash of pain in her back. Somehow, she kept going, aware she couldn't fall while carrying the baby. Once she reached the living room, she managed to place Garth carefully on the sofa before her legs gave out and she crumpled to the floor.

When Shawn shot JJ in the back, Eric relinquished his tenuous grip on restraint and let himself go. With one hard swipe of his mighty paw, he whacked at Shawn. He meant to only knock the other man unconscious, but he must have hit him in such a way as to break his neck. He knew instantly, looking at the awful angle Shawn lay, that he was dead.

Full of worry and remorse, he eased himself to the floor, light-headed from the loss of blood. He'd need to shape-shift back to human so he could call 911. To do that, he'd have to find the strength from somewhere.

Initiating the change, he couldn't keep from crying out as the pain sliced through him. Once he was man, he wrapped a baby blanket around his wound in an attempt to stop the bleeding, and crawled into the living room, to find JJ unconscious and Garth unharmed.

He checked her pulse, relieved to find her heart still beating. And then, because he had no strength for anything else, he picked up the phone and dialed 911, just as DeLeon and his crew burst through the door.

They came for him at sunset. Three men, grim-faced and silent. They put the steel handcuffs on without a word and led him to their car. Eric didn't resist. They didn't bother reading him his rights. Because of his crime, he had none.

He went willingly, glad JJ didn't have to witness this. His heart ached, already missing her and Garth. He'd saved her, protected her and himself both, and for what? The crime of killing a human in his bear form was punishable by death. Unless he could prove it wasn't him or that it had been self-defense. Unfortunately, he had no proof. Only his and JJ's word. Once again, he wished he'd had a camera.

"Get in the car," the tallest man ordered.

Unable to help himself, he glanced back once at JJ's house, foolishly hoping for a final glimpse of her before the Protectors took him away. He imagined there'd be a trial, a mock hearing at best, giving him a chance to explain himself before they killed him. Meanwhile, people would be working behind the scenes to mess up the forensic reports, to make sure nothing showed the dead man had been attacked and killed by a large bear. Among his kind, humans finding out about their existence was considered the worst of all threats.

And for nearly revealing this, someone would have to pay. The Protectors seemed determined to ensure that someone would be him.

Heart racing, Eric opened his eyes, momentarily disoriented. Instead of being cuffed in the back of a government-issue sedan, he lay prone in a hospital bed, hooked up to machines. His heartbeat slowed as he realized his arrest had been only a dream. Hopefully, not a premonition.

Garth. Suddenly, everything came crashing back to him. JJ hit in the back, finding her on the floor, Garth unhurt. Was JJ all right? And where was his son?

He located the call button and pressed it. When no one immediately answered, he pressed it again. And again. Until finally an annoyed feminine voice asked how she could help him.

"My son," he croaked. "I need to know who has my son."

"I do," DeLeon said, as he walked into the room. "And JJ is recovering in the room next door."

Briefly, Eric wondered if he was dreaming again. "What do you mean? Do you really have Garth?"

DeLeon ducked his head as if embarrassed. "Well, actually, my wife is babysitting him while the two of you recover. Seemed like the least I could do after what happened with my brother."

His brother. Shawn. Eric swallowed. "I'm sorry about your loss, Frank. Please know that I never intended to—"

"Stop." Gently, the Protector placed a hand on Eric's shoulder. "It was very clear what occurred. You did what you had to do in order to protect your family. I'm just glad Shawn didn't manage to kill anyone before you took him out."

"Still, I know how difficult it is to lose a family member, especially a brother."

A shadow crossed the other man's face. "My mother is taking it hard. But we'll get through it. Rhonda's and Yolanda's deaths were a bit more difficult to explain. Sadly, we made Shawn the scapegoat there, too, at least publically."

Inwardly wincing, Eric nodded. He couldn't help but

wonder if DeLeon would casually add that, oh, by the way, Eric was under arrest.

Instead, the Protector released him. "Your prognosis is good. They got the bullet out and it doesn't appear to have done any serious nerve or muscle damage. You both were lucky he didn't know to use silver bullets."

"I'll say." Eric thought of his own weapon, and what he'd loaded. He'd known if he was going to shoot, he'd have to shoot to kill. He'd hoped he wouldn't have to, but Garth had to be protected and kept safe. "What about JJ?" he asked. "She was shot in the back."

And while she might not die, she could still end up paralyzed. For a shifter, that would be a special sort of hell. Trapped in a nonworking body, unable to die.

DeLeon looked down. "The good news is that the bullet didn't go anywhere near her spinal cord. The bad news is she hasn't regained consciousness yet. The doctors don't understand why not."

"I want to go see her." Eric pushed himself up, using his elbows. "Please. Can you take me to her?"

"I don't think you can walk." DeLeon appeared uncertain. "Maybe you should wait until you're better."

"What about a wheelchair? Surely you can ask the nurse. Wait, I'll do it." Eric pressed the call button again. This time, the voice said someone would be with him in a moment.

When the nurse arrived, she seemed surprisingly amendable to locating a wheelchair and helping get Eric to the room next door. She paged someone else and a few minutes later an orderly came in with a chair. The nurse and the aide helped Eric out of bed and got him settled, hanging his IV pole on a bar on the wheelchair.

"I'll take him," DeLeon said, stepping forward. "I'll call you when he's ready to get back in his bed."

Once the nurse had gone, Eric drew a deep breath. "Let's go," he said.

Though the Protector placed his hands on the chair handles, he didn't push it forward yet. "I should warn you that she looks pretty bad."

Eric nodded. "And I should tell you that she'll always be beautiful to me, no matter what shape she's in."

His comment made the other man smile. "Let's go," he said, and wheeled him out of the room.

JJ felt light, as if she could float along without the heaviness of her earthly body weighing her down. The sense of calmness and peace felt so profoundly beautiful that she wanted to weep. At first, she'd struggled to remember, to ground herself back where she knew she needed to be, but the effort seemed too much, so she let it go. She knew there had been turmoil and violence. Bloodshed even. But there'd also been love.

She needed to focus on the love. But doing that was so difficult, she didn't. So much easier to simply let herself float.

A familiar voice called her name. Not once, but twice, lingering lovingly over each letter. She wanted to respond, goodness knows she even tried, but she couldn't summon up the necessary strength.

With silence came abject disappointment. Had the voice gone? Suddenly, desperately, she wanted it to stay. Moisture filled her eyes. But then—then—he spoke again, so close to her ear she felt the tickle of his warm breath. Her heart gave a little skip of joy as the voice surrounded her with love, gently and firmly grounding her.

"Come back," he pleaded. "We've got too much of a future for you to go away now. Garth needs you. I need you."

Still, though she understood the sentiment, the context

of the words didn't quite make sense. Who was he, the man behind the love? His name… Still frozen, still trapped in that strange sort of space between asleep and awake, she struggled to remember the name of who the deep, masculine voice belonged to. Somehow she sensed doing so would be vitally important.

Eric. It finally came to her. *Eric Mikkelson.*

And just like that, she remembered everything. Him, his baby Garth and the love that filled her heart. Still.

But with love came fear. Terror. Shawn and his pistol. She remembered nothing after he'd shot her in the back.

She struggled to open her eyes. But the ethereal, unfocused self she'd become had no control over anything. Especially her earthly body. Yet she could feel a tear track moisture down her frozen cheek. And when his calloused finger softly brushed it away, she knew he remained at her side.

"Don't go," she said silently, hoping against hope that Eric somehow heard and understood. "Keep talking to me. Stay."

As if he heard her, he did.

"My brave little wolf," he said, tenderness and love making his voice rough. "You've been through so much. But that's over now. We're safe. You're safe. And the future—our future—looks so bright, you gotta wear shades."

This last comment made her smile. More than smile—laugh. She felt the joyful sound bubble up inside her and was actually able to open her mouth to let the laughter out.

"JJ?" Sounding stunned and joyous, Eric took her hand. "Are you back, sweetheart? Squeeze my fingers if you can hear me."

With her strength returning, JJ did better than that. She opened her eyes.

Later, when the astounded doctors had finished examining her, after all the multiple tests were completed and she'd been brought back to her room, she and Eric were finally alone again.

Exhausted and relieved, JJ smiled at him. "Thanks for sticking with me," she said softly. "Hearing your voice felt like a lifeline, keeping me grounded, keeping me here. I'm not sure what would have happened if you hadn't started talking to me."

He kissed her again, this time on the cheek. "I'm not letting you go anywhere."

Smiling at his comment, she wished she had enough strength to turn her face so his kiss landed on her mouth. "Where's Garth?" she asked. "Since you're not worried, I know he's somewhere safe."

"He's with Frank DeLeon."

Shocked, she could only stare. "The Pack Protector? Shawn's brother?"

"Yes. And he's perfectly safe." Eric pulled out his phone. "Frank's been sending me videos. Apparently, his wife works in a neonatal unit in a hospital and loves taking care of infants. Look."

Rapt, JJ watched as a woman with long, slender fingers dangled a set of bright plastic keys in front of Garth, letting him play with them.

"He looks good," she mused.

"Yes, he does."

Though part of her didn't want to know, she had to ask. "Is Shawn…?"

Eric knew what she was asking without her having to say the words. "Dead? Yes. He is. I killed him."

Considering his words, she realized she felt nothing. Not joy, not sorrow, just a huge blankness. "How?" Selfishly, part of her wanted to know.

"Vedjorn claws and teeth," he whispered. "I was worried the Protectors would arrest me, but since it so clearly was self-defense…"

Closing her eyes as relief flooded her, she nodded. "So it's really over? All of it?"

"Yes."

Her gaze drifted to the window. Outside, she saw it had begun to snow.

"To new beginnings," he said, following her gaze with his own.

She smiled, glad that he'd remembered her words about how snow made her feel. "To new beginnings," she repeated.

Gently, carefully, he gathered her in his arms and held her close. "Now you just need to focus on getting well so we can go home."

Home. The word had never sounded so beautiful.

* * * * *

*Don't miss other great shifter stories
by Karen Whiddon:*

*TEMPTING THE DRAGON
BILLIONAIRE WOLF
SHADES OF THE WOLF
THE WOLF SIREN*

Join Britain's BIGGEST Romance Book Club

50% OFF your first parcel

- **EXCLUSIVE offers** every month

- **FREE delivery direct** to your door

- **NEVER MISS a title**

- **EARN Bonus Book points**

Call Customer Services
0844 844 1358 *

or visit
millsandboon.co.uk/subscription

* This call will cost you 7 pence per minute plus your phone company's price per minute access charge.

BKCB3

MILLS & BOON®

Why shop at millsandboon.co.uk?

Each year, thousands of romance readers find their perfect read at millsandboon.co.uk. That's because we're passionate about bringing you the very best romantic fiction. Here are some of the advantages of shopping at www.millsandboon.co.uk:

* **Get new books first**—you'll be able to buy your favourite books one month before they hit the shops

* **Get exclusive discounts**—you'll also be able to buy our specially created monthly collections, with up to 50% off the RRP

* **Find your favourite authors**—latest news, interviews and new releases for all your favourite authors and series on our website, plus ideas for what to try next

* **Join in**—once you've bought your favourite books, don't forget to register with us to rate, review and join in the discussions

Visit **www.millsandboon.co.uk** for all this and more today!